DATE DUE

AUG 1 3 2013			
OCT 0 1 2013			
OCT 2 6 2013			
NOV 0 4 2013			
NOV 2 6 2013			
JAN 1 7 2014			

BEYOND THE LAW

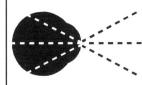

This Large Print Book carries the
Seal of Approval of N.A.V.H.

BEYOND THE LAW

A WESTERN DUO

WAYNE D. OVERHOLSER

THORNDIKE PRESS

A part of Gale, Cengage Learning

GALE
CENGAGE Learning®

Detroit • New York • San Francisco • New Haven, Conn • Waterville, Maine • London

GALE
CENGAGE Learning®

LIBRARY OF CONGRESS CATALOGING-IN-PUBLICATION DATA

Overholser, Wayne D., 1906–1996.
  [Shadow of a lobo]
  Beyond the law : a western duo / by Wayne D. Overholser. — Large Print
edition.
     pages cm. — (Thorndike Press Large Print Western)
  ISBN-13: 978-1-4104-5902-2 (hardcover)
  ISBN-10: 1-4104-5902-0 (hardcover)
  I. Overholser, Wayne D., 1906–1996. Beyond the law. II. Title.
PS3529.V33S525 2013
813'.54—dc23   2013008689

Published in 2013 by arrangement with Golden West Literary Agency

Printed in the United States of America
1 2 3 4 5 6 7 17 16 15 14 13

PERMISSIONS

"Shadow of a Lobo" first appeared in *Action Stories* (Summer, 47). Copyright © 1947 by Fiction House, Inc. Copyright © renewed 1975 by Wayne D. Overholser. Copyright © 2011 for restored material.

TABLE OF CONTENTS

SHADOW OF A LOBO

I

It was not yet noon, but Cliff Jenson had worn a path behind the counter to the front of his store looking for Shortcake Hogan's freight outfit. Hogan should have been on his way hours ago. Cliff finished with a customer, looked at the barren shelves, and returned again to his street door, eyes on the gray lane that ran northward. There was only dusty emptiness, bright now in the midday sun.

Bill Trent came along the boardwalk from the bank, his thin face holding a quiet malice. He owned the Mercantile, the only other store in Palisade, and he had never forgiven Cliff for starting a rival business. He drawled a lazy — "Howdy." — and stopped in front of Cliff, the thumb of his left hand hooked into the arm hole of his vest within inches of his star. He was Palisade's marshal for no better reason than that he was the only man in town who would take the job for the small salary that it paid.

"Howdy, Bill," Cliff said, his eyes on the street.

"Shortcake ain't started yet, has he?" Trent asked, grinning.

"No."

"Shortcake ain't one to start at noon, now, is he?" Trent's voice was filled with mock solicitude.

Trent's words fanned the long smoldering rage in Cliff close to flames. He pinned his gray eyes on Trent. "Bill, one of these days you're gonna talk me into beating hell out of you."

"And I'll have you eating county grub in jail." Trent tapped his star. "I'd be plumb happy to lock you up for a spell. If you hadn't started a price war, my business would have stood up fine. I ain't sold nothing but a pair of shoestrings for a month."

"I didn't start a price war," Cliff said sharply.

Trent's face was ugly. "The hell you didn't." He waggled a bony finger at Cliff. "But you ain't staying in business long. Meldrum wants to see you."

Cliff knew what Meldrum wanted, and, judging by the pleased look on Trent's face, he knew, too.

"So you're running errands for the banker, are you?" Cliff asked contemptuously.

"It's a chore I'm happy to do." Trent was grinning again. "Wouldn't surprise me none if my competition just died a natural death."

It was then that Cliff heard the jingle of bells, the signal that Shortcake Hogan's outfit was approaching. Cliff pushed past Trent and started up the boardwalk as Hogan's six-horse team made the turn at the end of the block and straightened out into Main Street. The wagon stopped in front of the store.

"What's wrong with you that you've got to stay in bed till noon?" Cliff bellowed.

Then Cliff had a look at Hogan's red face, and he knew he shouldn't have said it. Hogan, mounted on the near wheel horse, cuffed back his hat, his sun-puckered eyes filled with more anger than Cliff had ever seen in them. He yelled: "I ain't been in bed. I've been chasing these ornery devils!"

"Why didn't you put 'em up last night?"

"I did, damn it!" Hogan howled. "Somebody let 'em out!"

Cliff, thinking about what Bill Trent had said, felt the rising pressure of his anger. He handed the freighter a sheet of paper. "There's the order. Keep 'em rolling."

"You bet."

Cliff, stepping back on the walk as the freight wagon rolled by, saw that Trent was no longer on the street. There was a streak of wildness in Cliff Jenson that made people who knew him wonder why he had taken a prosaic job like running a store. Now that wildness was pressing him. If a man ever deserved a licking, Trent did. He started toward the Mercantile, his hands fisted, when Vance Meldrum called from the bank door: "Cliff, will you step in here a minute?"

Cliff paused, not wanting to talk to Meldrum, but knowing it was foolish to slap him in the face. Now that he took a moment to think, he knew it was foolish to give Trent a licking. He said — "All right, Vance." — and stepped into the bank.

"We'll go on back," Meldrum said, and led the way to his office.

Vance Meldrum had come to Palisade less than six months ago just after the old banker, Abel Smith, had died. He'd bought the bank from Smith's widow, and already the basin was beginning to feel the difference.

Meldrum closed his office door behind Cliff and, motioning to a chair, stepped around his desk and sat down. He gave Cliff a cigar and took one for himself.

"Old Abel ran the bank with his heart and

I'm trying to use my head, Cliff. The way I see it a banker has to look at things from the standpoint of the whole community."

Meldrum touched a match to his cigar and pulled on it for a moment. Cliff, watching him, said nothing. Vance Meldrum was a bigger man than Cliff with cool green eyes and an overlapping lower lip that gave his face a bulldog appearance. He wore an expensive tailored gray suit, and affected a broad-brimmed Stetson and riding boots. Despite his efforts to become a part of this community, he had somehow failed to achieve it. Cliff, measuring him now, felt the cold driving quality of the man, and wondered as he had so many times why Meldrum had come to this isolated cow town.

"This basin will be a great country," Meldrum said as if sensing the question in Cliff. "I'd like to grow up with it, but now we're in chains, held back by Sam Dunning's tollgate in Tentrock Pass and Ben Armfield's gate at the Narrows." He paused, and then added as if suddenly thinking of it: "By the way, Cliff, Armfield is gone. Apparently he's disappeared and his daughter Bonnie is coming to look for him."

"Plenty of folks around who'd like to take a shot at Armfield," Cliff said dryly.

"Including Cliff Jenson?"

Cliff shrugged. "I've got reason enough."

"That's what I've heard." Meldrum nodded soberly. "As I was saying, we're slaves and we'll stay slaves as long as those tollgates guard the only entrances into the basin. But the railroad will end Armfield's and Dunning's domination." Meldrum puffed hard for a moment. "I'm saying this because I want you to stay in this basin. You belong on a ranch and not in a store. We can't afford to lose men like you."

"You're running your rabbit around the bush mighty hard," Cliff said.

"Then I'll run him into the field. Your shelves are practically bare, Cliff. You're a failure as a storekeeper. You don't have the capital to hire enough freighters, your prices are too low, and Hogan can't keep you supplied. Why don't you get out, Cliff?"

"I guess you'd want me to walk out and leave the business to you," Cliff said sourly.

"I'll buy it from you." Meldrum was carefully reluctant. "I'll put somebody to running it who can charge the prices necessary to show a profit."

"Like Bill Trent."

Meldrum shook his head. "Between you and me, Trent is so tight he squeaks every time he sits down. No, my man wouldn't be like Trent, but he wouldn't be a generous open-handed fool like you, either."

"You'll have to take the store if you want it."

"But you're a good buckaroo," Meldrum pressed.

"I'll hang on and rattle."

"Then I'll have to call in your loan the first of the month." The banker's face was grimly sober. "You're a fool, Cliff. I'm showing you the way out, but you're too . . . well, let's say proud to take it."

Cliff rose. "I'll try to raise the money."

"Think this over. I've been in business since I was a kid, and the principles are the same whether it's here in southeastern Oregon or San Francisco."

"Ben Armfield's principles," Cliff said bitterly.

"No. There is such a thing as having a sense of human values." Meldrum got to his feet, a genial mask on his face. "Anything that's good for the community is good for us."

Vance Meldrum didn't mean what he was saying. Cliff was sure of that, but he didn't know what the man was after. He said —
"So long." — and went out of the bank.

Cliff found a rancher waiting to buy barbed wire. After he had supplied the man, he stepped into the Bon Ton Café for his dinner. If Shortcake Hogan had good luck, he could make two trips to Winnemucca by the first of the month, but even with good luck Cliff's chance of meeting the bank's note was next to nothing. The shoestring he'd started with was still a shoestring.

Cliff could lay most of the Jenson bad luck to Ben Armfield. He was not one to hate another man, but it was hard not to hate Armfield. A dozen years before when there had been no bank in Palisade, Armfield had gone through the country offering loans to cattlemen who wanted to expand. And, as if Nature had been allied with Armfield, drought years had followed. A dozen ranches had fallen into Armfield's hands including Cliff's father's J Bar. With it had gone the Narrows, a short swift stream carrying the overflow of Blue Lake into Palisade Lake.

Armfield had rocked a few miles of the road and set up a tollgate. It had been a gold mine to him because eighty percent of the travel into the basin came through it, and Ben Armfield became the most hated man in that section of Oregon. He was, Cliff thought, cut from the came cloth as Bill Trent, but the bolt was longer.

His meal done, Cliff idled for a time under

the wooden awning of the hotel, keeping an eye on the store and wondering how much difference the half day Shortcake Hogan had lost would make. He was still standing there when the stage from The Dalles made the turn at the north end of Main Street and rolled to a dust-billowing stop in front of the hotel.

More often than not the southbound stage was empty, but today there were three passengers. The first to get down was a girl, fashionably attired in a dark blue dress, a bright parasol in her hand. The other two were men, one tall, skinny, and bucktoothed, the other short, freckled, and clad in black range garb that was expensive and new. Both wore two guns, something Cliff had never seen in Palisade. It took one glance for Cliff to read their brands. They were hardcases, their guns for hire.

The girl waited patiently for her luggage, the early afternoon sun hard upon her, bringing out the gray coating of dust that the hours of travel had given her. The short gunman said something to her and anger stirred in Cliff. She was pretty and fine and decent. It was as plain to read that in her as the evil in the other.

"No," the girl said, and drew back.

"You don't need to be so damned uppity,"

the gunman snarled. "Why, for all your fine duds, you ain't no better'n the girls. . . ."

Cliff took two long steps, grabbed the short man by the shoulder, and whirled him around. His right came through in a short explosive punch that snapped the gunman's head back on his shoulders and took the starch out of his knees. He fell loosely against a wheel and slid off into the dust.

"You don't do that to Dan Harl, mister," the skinny one squalled, and grabbed for his gun.

Cliff, straightening up, felt panic crawl through him. His gun was in his desk at the store.

After his father had died, Cliff Jenson had drifted south. He'd tarried in Arizona border towns, then worked eastward into New Mexico and Texas. He had been thrown against gunmen like these, and in self-defense had developed his own gun speed. But the lake basin had always been a peaceful land where men were willing to live and let live, and there had been no need of guns.

Both Dan Harl and his skinny mate, typical of their breed, had arrogantly assumed that a man's limitations were decreed by his gun skill. Well aware of this, Cliff knew he had never been closer to death than he was now. He tensed his muscles to spring, fully conscious of the futility of it.

He heard the girl scream. Then the gun, coming up smoothly and swiftly, stopped, and the skinny man swung around. Vance Meldrum, running along the walk, called shrilly: "Don't, Connors! Put that gun away."

Cliff didn't know why Meldrum's voice had stopped the gunman, but his own reaction had gone too far. He dived at Connors, a shoulder point smashing into the man's middle and doubling him over. The gun went off and the wild shot splintered the boards of the walk. Then Cliff caught Connors on the jaw with the impact of an upswinging sledge. The gunman came up on his toes, straightened out by the force of the blow, and went down like a tall thin aspen before an axe.

Cliff scooped up Connors's gun and stepped back. He heard the girl's long drawn sigh, saw relief break across Meldrum's face. Other men crowded around them, wanting to know what had happened. By the time Cliff told them, Harl was on his feet, a long-fingered hand feeling gingerly of his jaw, muddy eyes mirroring the fury that was in him.

"Get into the stage," Meldrum commanded sourly. "We don't need men of your caliber in this town."

"You're damned right we don't," Bill Trent echoed, a fingertip caressing his star. "You show up here again and I'll lock you up."

Men grabbed the still unconscious Connors and heaved him into the coach. Harl paused, eyes on Cliff. He said thickly: "I'll see you again, mister." Then he stepped up, the door was slammed shut, and a moment later the stage clattered out of town southbound to Winnemucca.

Not until the crowd had drifted away did Meldrum come up to the girl. He said softly: "I'm sorry you had to be subjected to this indignity and I'm equally sorry I wasn't here to take the brunt of it for you." He motioned to Cliff. "Miss Armfield, meet Cliff Jenson. He's one of our store men."

This, then, was Bonnie Armfield. Cliff, taking her outstretched hand, had his first good look at the girl. She was not at all the sort of person he had pictured Ben Armfield's daughter to be. Her eyes were deep brown, friendly eyes reflecting the smile that her scarlet lips held. She murmured: "I could have managed, Mister Jenson, but thank you."

She did not know how close to death he

had been, but Vance Meldrum did. Cliff saw that, sensed the edgy temper that was in the banker, and he wondered at it. He said thoughtfully: "Gunslicks like those two are always dangerous, ma'am. We've never had men like them in Palisade, and I'm wondering why they came."

"I don't know anything about them," the girl said, "except that they got on at The Dalles."

Meldrum picked up her bags. "Thanks, Cliff, for doing a job that should have been mine."

"I guess the thanks are going the other way," Cliff said.

II

Bonnie crossed the lobby to the desk, but Meldrum paused at the door, looking at Cliff, indecision on his wide face as if there was something he wanted to say and wasn't sure he should. Then, making up his mind, he said softly: "Bonnie and I are engaged, Cliff. I hope you'll remember that."

Turning, Meldrum walked swiftly across the lobby to where Bonnie was signing the register. Cliff watched them until they disappeared up the stairs, a small grin on his lips. So Meldrum thought Cliff Jenson might be interested in Ben Armfield's daughter. Then Mr. Meldrum had another guess coming.

But later, when he was back in the cool gloom of his store, Cliff found himself picturing Bonnie — her black hair that ran richly away from her temples, her dark friendly eyes that held none of her father's cold arrogance. Then the jangle of bells broke into his reverie and brought him out of the store on the run. Shortcake Hogan's outfit was back.

A sense of failure beat at Cliff. Hogan had been half a day late getting started. Now, in the middle of the afternoon, he was in Palisade again, empty. Cliff could not doubt Hogan's loyalty. So he stood waiting, a sense of final disaster washing through him.

Other men had come to stand along the street, staring at Hogan and not understanding his being here any better than Cliff. One yelled: "Quick trip to Winnemucca, wasn't it, Shortcake?"

Hogan didn't answer. He stared straight ahead at Cliff, his mouth a thin line across his broad Irish face. Bill Trent, watching from his store, suddenly darted into the street. He called: "What's wrong, Cliff?"

"Maybe you scattered his horses again," Cliff said sourly.

Trent drew in a sucking breath. "No."

Hogan stopped in front of Cliff, climbed down, and slowly walked around the wagon. He stopped before Cliff, his feet still in the dust. "All right, son. Give me hell. I should have been 'way past the Narrows."

"Let's have it," Cliff said.

"It's Ben Armfield. He's raised the ante. They put up a new sign at the tollgate. Fifty dollars a horse when they're hitched to a vehicle." Hogan shook his fist at his string. "Think of it. Three hundred dollars to get through and another three hundred to get back. It's hell, boy."

Cliff wheeled on Trent, grabbing the man by the shirt front and shaking him the way a terrier shakes a rat. "How'd you fix it with Armfield?"

"So help me, Cliff, I didn't," Trent spluttered. "This hurts me just like it does you. I've got a ten-horse wagon trailer outfit coming north."

"He ain't lying," Hogan said dourly. "His outfit's on the other side of the Narrows and Job White is cussing to beat hell."

"I told Job to hurry," Trent said eagerly, " 'cause I figgered Meldrum would be taking over your place and I wanted a good stock of merchandise to grab the trade back before he got started. Now I'm into the same trouble you are, Cliff. If I can't get my goods, I'm busted."

Cliff, looking at Trent, was forced to believe him. He said thoughtfully: "Maybe Meldrum fixed this to bust both of us."

"It's Armfield," a rancher said. "Ain't he done everything he can to milk the basin dry?"

"That's right," Trent agreed. "Armfield runs the gate. Nobody else does."

"Galtry was there," Hogan growled. "Said he'd just got his orders from Armfield."

"Fifty dollars a horse," Cliff murmured. "It ain't legal."

"You think the county court is gonna worry," the rancher demanded, "when they're plumb on the other side of the Palisades? We're just country cousins, Cliff."

Cliff nodded. "Sure, but Armfield can't make it stick. Besides, he won't have any business. No sense to it."

"He'll tie us up and starve us out," the rancher said with deep rancor. "He knows we can't bring in enough stuff over Tentrock Pass before snow flies to last us till spring."

"Maybe Dunning's got the same notion," Cliff said.

Trent shook his head. "Dunning will take what he can get."

"Shortcake, put your outfit up and saddle

a bronc'," Cliff said in sudden decision. "Buzz, throw a saddle on my paint. I'll be over in a minute."

"You ain't going out there alone," the rancher said. "This is everybody's business. We'll throw Galtry into the Narrows."

"That ain't the way," Cliff said quickly. "It'd put us outside the law which maybe is what Armfield's after. I just want to palaver with Galtry. I've got a hunch there's a rat in the woodpile, and I aim to smoke him out."

Cliff, wheeling into the store, strode along the counter to his desk. He was taking his gun and belt out of a drawer when he felt Bill Trent's presence. He asked sharply: "What's biting you, Bill?"

"I've got some turkey to eat," Trent said humbly. "I've pulled off some dirty tricks, Cliff. I've kept my prices too high, but I never let a man go hungry."

Cliff buckled the belt around him, eyes pinned on the store man. This wasn't like Trent. He said bluntly: "I don't trust you, Bill. You've done everything you could to fry my hide since I started this store. What's got into you now?"

Trent ran his tongue over dry lips. "I'm scared," he blurted. "This Armfield business don't smell good."

"You know more than you're letting on,"

Cliff said.

Trent looked away. "I'm guessing like I reckon you are. Maybe it is Armfield, I don't know, but I know one thing. If you and me work together, we can keep our noses above water. If we don't, there'll be hell to pay."

"It would be kind of hard for us to work together," Cliff said dryly. "There's a little thing called a dollar you and me don't see alike."

"I know, but I'm a piker alongside a pirate like Ben Armfield." Trent came close to the desk, his black eyes brightly eager. "Look, Cliff. I've got a lot of grub in my store . . . sugar, flour, molasses. Stuff like that. You got some odds and ends that'll add up." He ran a quick eye over the shelves. "And you've got good-will. Let's throw in together. We'll call it Jenson and Trent. You can figure the prices yourself."

There was a tight grin on Cliff's face as he reached for his hat. "I guess I've seen all there is to see except a horse with wings, and I wouldn't be more surprised if one flew by." He went out. Scowling, Trent followed.

Cliff locked the store and slanted across the street to the stable. His paint was saddled. Stepping up, he swung north to Hogan's place. The Irishman was throwing gear on his roan as Cliff reined into the

28

yard. He called: "All ready, son!"

Neither spoke until the town was behind them. Then Hogan said: "What's in your head, Cliff? You ain't packed an iron for a 'coon's age."

Motioning westward to where the rimrock made a long line against the sky, Cliff said: "You couldn't get a wagon down there with a rope, could you?"

"Hell, no," Hogan said.

Cliff pointed north to where Tentrock Cañon ran like a giant knife slash through the rugged Palisades. "And you'd have quite a time getting a road through the mountains anywhere except by way of the pass."

"I ain't augering."

"And we're blocked the same way east of here with the lakes running plumb to the rimrock. It gives anybody owning the Narrows a pat hand."

"Sure, but this here geography ain't changed since you and me was born. Why would Armfield come up with a big boost now?"

"That's what I'm aiming to find out, and I've got a hunch. There's a lot of land here open for homesteading, Shortcake. When the sodbusters hear about it, they'll come in like locusts."

"This is range country," Hogan said irritably. "Ain't fit for farming."

"Ever know that to keep 'em from trying?"

"No," Hogan admitted, "but this basin is a long ways from anywhere. What would bring 'em in?"

"A railroad."

Hogan let out a gusty sigh. "Now who's gonna build a railroad?"

"Meldrum allows it's the reason for him coming here. If it is, a man who had the only store in Palisade would have a fortune. And something scared Trent so bad he wants to throw in with me."

"Bill scares easy," Hogan grunted, and spat into the sagebrush.

They rode in silence for a time, and presently came to the ridge that formed a peninsula between the lakes. Blue Lake lay eastward, stretching to the barren hills that formed a distant brown horizon, the wind raising white caps that caught the sun and sparkled in eye-blinding brilliance. Palisade Lake was on the west. Having no outlet, it held the mineral residue the Narrows had poured into it for centuries. It lay a barren gray, without life.

The road followed the ridge top, tulles high along the marshy shore. Ahead of them a rickety bridge that Cliff's father had built fifteen years ago spanned the Narrows. As

Cliff and Hogan rode up, Ron Galtry stepped from a log tollhouse that stood snugly against the north end of the bridge.

"You've got a name for being a tough hand," Galtry called in a belligerent tone, "but don't try shoving me around, Jenson. See?"

There was no reason for Galtry taking that attitude unless he expected trouble and wanted to beat Cliff to it. Galtry was big of body and long of tongue with meaty lips, a bulbous nose, and colorless eyes set so close that folks in Palisade said a cigarette paper wouldn't slide between them edgewise. Cliff had never liked the man, and now, with Galtry standing on the bridge, thumbs hooked in gun belt, big head rolled forward on his shoulders, Cliff liked him less.

Stepping down, Cliff handed the reins to Hogan. He asked mildly: "What makes you think I'm aiming to shove you around?"

"Armfield raised the ante. See?"

Galtry jerked a hand at the newly painted sign. "Said he was tired of getting peanuts from this gate. Quoted me the toll I had to charge. Just got the letter yesterday. See?" Cliff glanced at the frame structure set on the south shore of Blue Lake that had once been his home. He asked: "Where is Armfield?"

Galtry jumped as if he'd been prodded by a knife blade. "How the hell would I know?"

"Meldrum said he's disappeared." Cliff paused, closely watching the big man. "I was wondering if he was in that house."

"Hell, no. Now get out of here if you ain't going through. Go on now. I said you couldn't bulldoze me about those rates. See?"

"You're right proddy today," Cliff murmured.

Galtry waved a hand at the tollhouse. "Let him see your arguments, Dan."

Then Cliff understood why Ron Galtry had acted so tough. Dan Harl stepped out of the tollhouse, both guns fisted, his freckled face split by a wide grin. "I said we'd meet again, mister. Now you can go for that smoke pole you're packing."

Ben Armfield was being held in the house on the south shore. That thought ran through Cliff's mind with the explosive force of lightning.

"You look a mite peaked," Harl sneered. "Maybe you're a little sick, mister."

It went against Cliff's grain to back up in front of a man like Dan Harl, but he hadn't expected to find Harl here with a brace of guns in his hands. He shot a glance at the tollhouse. He couldn't be sure, but he thought Connors was standing behind the sun-brightened glass of the window. Even if by some miracle of speed he got his gun clear of leather before Harl cut him down, Connors would shoot him down from the protection of the tollhouse.

"You ain't tough at all now, are you, Jenson?" Galtry was grinning. "You'd better mount up and git. See?"

"Funny you need a hardcase like Harl to back up your sign," Cliff said as he stepped into the saddle.

"Armfield sent him along," Galtry said quickly.

"You're smart, mister," Harl jeered. "Smart men live a long time. You'd be real smart if you got out of the basin 'cause I'm fixing to stay."

"It takes a bigger man than you to make me run," Cliff said contemptuously. "Next time we meet maybe you won't have a pair of irons in your fists."

Swinging their horses, Cliff and Hogan set a fast pace toward Palisade, but not until they were out of gun range did the freighter take a deep breath. "You know, Cliff, that freckled-faced runt was a trigger-happy slug slammer if I ever saw one."

"Did you notice how proddy Galtry got when I asked him if Armfield was in the house?" Cliff asked.

Hogan nodded. "Don't make no sense, though."

"It would if Armfield was in the house. Looks to me like we've got our noses into a bigger game than we guessed. Want to play it out?"

"Sure, I'll play it out, but it ain't no big game. Armfield just decided to make a lot of *dinero* fast."

"More than that," Cliff said grimly, and nodded at a juniper-clad ridge running parallel to the north shore of Palisade Lake. "They can't see us from the tollhouse now. You belly down on top. I'll be back after dark."

Hogan swore sadly. "Gonna be damned lonesome, but I'll do it. Can't do no freighting now. That's sure."

III

The sun was low over the western rim when Cliff rode into town. He had supper in the Bon Ton. Bonnie Armfield was in the back booth with Vance Meldrum and Sam Dunning. He caught Bonnie's quick smile before he turned to give the order to the waitress. Then a new thought raced through his mind. *Sam Dunning might well be the man who was behind this pattern of high prices and starvation that was being woven for the people of the basin.*

As Cliff ate, he turned this thought over in his mind. Sam Dunning had come to the basin before Cliff's father had. He'd taken land along the north shore of Blue Lake and was making a good start when Ben Armfield had come with his offer of a big loan and low interest. Dunning, like so many more, had taken the offer and lost his ranch. Dunning had disappeared for several years. Then he'd come back, filed on a quarter section atop Tentrock Pass, and had approached the county court with a proposition of building a toll road down the cañon. The court, realizing the basin's need for more than one outlet, had consented. Now that the fantastic rates that Galtry had posted would practically close the Narrows, the travel down Tentrock Cañon would increase four or five times, and Dunning's tolls would mount correspondingly.

Cliff paid for his meal and, returning to his store, began to pace along the counter, thinking about this and how it would affect him. Shortcake Hogan might be able to make one trip to The Dalles before snow blocked the pass, but no more, and in one trip he couldn't bring more than a fraction of what Cliff would need for his winter stock.

"You busy, Jenson?"

Sam Dunning was standing in the doorway, tall bony frame almost filling it. A wariness came into Cliff. He had never liked or trusted Dunning, nor had his father when they were ranching. He said: "Come in, Sam."

Dunning strode along the counter, reached the cracker barrel, and dipped into it. He filled his mouth and began to chomp noisily, dark eyes fixed on Cliff. He was a sullen, barren-faced man who had, so rumor ran, a couple of killings to his credit in the mines around Baker City. Cliff, waiting for Dunning to speak, remembered he had never seen the man smile.

"You and me have got no reason to love Ben Armfield." Dunning reached for another handful of crackers. "He fixed your dad same as he did me."

Cliff nodded, filled his pipe, and held a match flame to it.

Dunning opened his mouth and shoved the crackers in. He swallowed with effort. "Your dad wasn't tough. I'm remembering he lived along the lake shore in a covered wagon watching Armfield run his old J Bar. Reckon he died of a broken heart. Now I'm wondering if you're as tough as some folks claim, or whether you're soft like your dad was."

Anger stirred in Cliff. He asked: "What are you driving at, Sam?"

"When Hogan got back from the Narrows with news about Armfield's new rates, you said maybe I had the same idea." The tall man paused, eyes slitted. "I ain't raising a nickel, just because Armfield aims to skim the milk off with the cream, and I don't like that talk. Savvy?"

"That's good, Sam. It'd be tough on the basin if you raised."

"Then see you don't get off no more gab like that." Dunning rocked back on his heels. "Reckon you'll be pulling out soon as you lose your store."

There could be no doubt about the veiled threat in Dunning's words. Cliff bit hard against his pipe stem, holding his temper back, letting Dunning talk himself out. He said: "Didn't figure on it."

Dunning swung a bony hand toward the shelves. "Hell, man, you'll be busted flat before Hogan gets to The Dalles and back. Tell you what I'll do, Jenson. I'll buy you out. I always wanted to run a store."

"I ain't selling."

"I'll give you a job running my gate. Name

your own figger."

It was crazy. Not many hours before, Meldrum had wanted to buy the store. Then Trent had asked to come in as a partner. Now Sam Dunning, who had about as much business with a store as a hungry cow would have with a manger full of moonbeams, wanted to buy.

"No thanks, Sam."

Dunning cursed fiercely. "Jenson, you're a damned fool bent on buying yourself a chunk of ground six feet deep if. . . ." He checked himself and, wheeling, stalked out.

Cliff watched Dunning disappear into the Silver Dollar. Smiling grimly, he thought that one thing was becoming clear. Cliff Jenson and his store were slated to play a major rôle in this mysterious drama. Twilight had come, the last scarlet streamers flaming above the western rim. The gloom deepened in the store to near darkness. Cliff picked up a flour sack and began filling it with supplies. He had finished dumping coffee into the grinder when a slim figure slipped through the door. Bonnie Armfield called: "Mister Jenson?"

"Here," he said, and turned the crank. He was both surprised and puzzled at her coming, and he didn't want to talk to her. Bonnie came along the counter and stood beside him until he was done. Then she said: "Please don't light a lamp."

He finished with the supplies, knotted the sack, and laid it on the counter. "What can I do for you?"

"Can you close the store for a few days? Or get someone to tend it?"

"Reckon so, but I don't figure on doing it."

He heard her catch her breath. "Mister Jenson, I know my father's been kidnapped. Or killed. I've got to have somebody's help, and I'm hoping it will be yours. Would you consider one hundred dollars a day fighting wages?"

"Ben Armfield's daughter can buy almost anything she wants," he said bitterly. "Only I'm the gent who keeps the *almost* in there."

"Ben Armfield is rich because he's squeezed blood out of every pound of flesh he could get his hands on," the girl cried, "but that doesn't make his daughter rich enough to buy the things she wants!" There had been as much bitterness in her tone as his.

He said slowly: "I never thought I'd hear that from you."

"I know. Most people don't know how I feel."

"What do you want to buy?"

"Happiness and good-will and all the fine things that can't be bought. I know what money can buy. So does Dad. It doesn't include happiness." She laid a hand on his arm. "But I'm going to try to find Ben Armfield because he is my father. Will you help me?"

There was nothing Cliff Jenson could say in the face of this girl's confession. "What do you want me to do?"

"My father may be dead, but, if he is being held prisoner in the basin, I want you to help find him."

"Why pick on me?"

She stepped back, withdrawing her hand. "Because of what happened this afternoon, and because Vance recommended you for the job."

"I didn't know Meldrum thought that much of me," Cliff murmured.

"He says you're a poor businessman, but you'd be perfect for this job."

"Does he know what you're planning?"

"Yes."

Cliff resumed his pipe, amused by the irony of Ben Armfield's daughter coming to him for help. He asked: "How do we start?"

"Get two horses and bring them to the alley behind the store. I have my riding clothes here in a bundle. I'll change into them."

He moved toward the door, thinking that this girl was nothing like he had imagined Bonnie Armfield. Turning back, he asked: "Why do you want this to be kept a secret?"

"I don't know who our enemies are."

"Nobody knows but Meldrum?"

"That's right."

He went out then, locking the door behind him, and stood in front of it long enough to relight his pipe, his eyes sweeping the street. Buzz, the stableman, coming out of the Silver Dollar, saw him and paused. "What happened up at the Narrows?"

Cliff told him, inwardly restless at the delay but not wanting to appear hurried. Buzz listened, and, when Cliff was done, he said: "There's talk going around that Armfield raised them rates just to bust you so he can get the store for a song, and you're gonna kill him if he does."

"Who says?"

"Nobody knows where the talk started. Sam Dunning says he heard it, but he can't remember where."

"I didn't put out any such talk," Cliff said angrily, and pushed past Buzz. "I want a couple of horses. I'll take my paint and that bay mare of yours."

"What do you want two horses for?"

"I might be gone a long time."

When the horses were saddled and Cliff had stepped up, Buzz asked: "I don't figger you'd quit. You ain't, are you?"

"No," Cliff said and, leading the bay mare, headed south.

As soon as he was out of sight from the town, Cliff circled and rode back into Palisade from the east. Reining up in the alley behind his store, he dismounted, and tapped on the back door. Bonnie opened it. She asked: "Aren't you taking the grub?"

"You bet. I forgot all about it."

Cliff threaded his way through the crates and boxes, found the sack, and returned to the back door.

Bonnie whispered: "Somebody's out there."

Hand on gun butt, Cliff stepped into the alley and saw Bill Trent standing beside the paint. Trent asked: "That you, Cliff?"

"Sure is." Cliff tied the sack behind his saddle. "Making your nightly prowl, Bill?"

"That's right." Trent came closer. "You changed your mind about taking me in?"

"No."

Trent sighed. "I wish you would. I tell you I'm scared, Cliff. Reckon I'll turn my star in. I just ain't man enough to rod this town if she gets hot."

"You know something you ain't telling me," Cliff said angrily.

"No, I don't." He motioned to the bay. "Cliff, what are you taking two horses for? You ain't forked anything but that paint for a year."

"Figure I might be gone a spell."

Trent turned away, but before he'd gone ten feet, Bonnie sneezed. Trent whirled and came back, his gun in his hand. "Somebody's in there," he said hoarsely.

Trent lunged toward the door, showing more courage than Cliff thought he had. For an instant Cliff wavered in indecision, then he brought his gun barrel down across Trent's head, sending him into a loose-jointed fall.

"Let's ride!" Cliff called, and pulled the door open. He closed it behind Bonnie, and a moment later they were riding south, the lights of Palisade fading into pinpoints in the sage.

It was a still and far-reaching land, the distant rimrock losing itself against a nearly black sky. The sea of sage stretched to the horizon on both sides of them, and somewhere it had rained, the wind bringing the clean smell of it across the great emptiness. A coyote called from some nearby butte, weird and spine-chilling.

Bonnie, riding close to Cliff, shivered. She said: "It's too big a country to find a man who's hidden."

"Not if you know where to look. What makes you think your father was kidnapped?"

"He only intended to be gone a couple of days. He's the kind of a man who keeps a schedule, Cliff."

"Who knew he was coming to the basin?"

"Galtry."

"That all?"

She hesitated. Then she said: "Vance knew. And, Cliff, those new rates aren't Dad's."

"How do you know?"

"Would a smart businessman try to get more milk from a cow by drying her up?"

"I guess not," Cliff agreed. "Who do you think is holding your dad and what's the reason. Ransom?"

"I don't think so," she said thoughtfully. "I'd have heard from them by now, wouldn't I?"

Cliff groaned. "It strikes me we travel a long way to get nowhere."

They fell into silence again, and presently the lights of Palisade were gone and ahead of them the windows of the big house at the

Narrows made a bright shine on the water. They reached the butte where Cliff had left Hogan and turned from the road toward it. Hogan appeared out of the darkness, calling cautiously: "That you, Cliff?"

"It's me and Miss Armfield."

Hogan reined in close and leaned forward in his saddle, trying to see the girl. "What in blazes is she doing here?" he demanded.

"Looking for her dad," Cliff said. "See anything?"

"I sure did. Galtry and that freckle-faced trigger tripper and a tall skinny gent augered quite a spell after you left. Stood out there on the bridge and swung their arms. Galtry and Freckles went back into the tollhouse still augering. 'Bout dusk Galtry, Skinny, and another jasper rode out. Galtry went into town. The other two swung left."

"You know Armfield, don't you?"

"Yeah, I've seen him. The light was getting too thin to see right good, but I figgered it was him with Skinny."

"What does it mean?" Bonnie cried.

Cliff told her what had happened at the gate that afternoon, and added: "My guess is that Galtry got scared enough to want your dad moved. Chances are he's gone to town to talk it over with whoever else is in the deal with him."

"Another thing happened that's plumb interesting," Hogan said. "Just after you left, a wagon train rolled in from the south. Biggest outfit I ever seen. Two hundred wagons or more. Sodbusters, I reckon."

"They want across?"

"They sure did. Shook their fists at Galtry, but he just stood there pointing to the sign. Purty soon they went back to camp."

"You go back to town, Shortcake," Cliff said. "Keep your eyes peeled. Me and Miss Armfield are gonna look for her dad."

"You can't find a man in the dark," Hogan remonstrated.

"We'll find him, Shortcake, unless I've forgotten how to add."

Hogan took the road to town. Cliff and Bonnie, swinging left, followed a trail through the sagebrush. A mile from where they left Hogan they reined up. Cliff dismounted and held a match to the ground in front of the horses. Stepping back into the saddle, hc said with satisfaction: "They're ahead of us all right."

It was after midnight when they reached the foothills of the Palisades. An hour later they were in the pines, climbing steadily, and the air grew thinner and colder and the mountain wildness pressed in around them.

"Is this Dunning's toll road?" Bonnie asked.

"No. It's an old Indian trail. Dunning ran his road up the other side of the cañon. Easier grade."

"What are you going to do, Cliff?"

"I think Dunning is into this up to his neck," Cliff answered. "Chances are Galtry sent your dad to Dunning, but, if I was Dunning, I wouldn't want to keep him in the tollhouse. I'd keep him around close, though, maybe in a miner's shack a mile or so away. If I'm guessing right, we'll get your dad about dawn."

An hour later they swung away from the trail, circling upgrade into the timber. Presently Cliff said: "Hungry?"

"A little."

"We'll stop and risk a fire."

Cliff picketed the horses, found pieces of deadfall pine, and made a fire. He brought water from a spring, fried bacon and boiled coffee, and, when they had eaten, he leaned on an elbow, smoking, his eyes on the girl. If anyone had told him a dozen hours ago that he'd be here in the Palisades with Bonnie Armfield hunting her father, he'd have said that person was completely crazy. Yet here he was, confident that Armfield was not far away, and he wasn't sorry he had come.

Bonnie, meeting his eyes, smiled as if guessing what was in his mind. "I'm thankful for a moment like this," she said. "The present is enough." She sobered, the low flame throwing a bright shine on her black hair. "But the present always points to a future. I hope you'll never regret this, Cliff."

"I won't."

"I'm hoping this experience will change Dad," she said thoughtfully. "Whether it does or not, I'm trying to make my life into something worthwhile. People have told me I'm like my mother. She always wanted to live differently than Dad would let her, and she died unhappy. I'm not going to die that way. Dad can keep me from getting his money, but he can't take away my hands."

Again the thought came to Cliff Jenson: *This can't be Ben Armfield's girl.*

She was studying him now, smiling again. She asked: "Why are you running a store?"

"Abel Smith wished it on me. He was an old friend of Dad's. Had the bank until he died. I got tired of drifting and wanted him to set me up ranching. He staked me to a store instead. Said folks in the basin had a right to buy things at a fair price instead of having Bill Trent rob them."

She lay back, her head on her saddle, and presently dropped off to sleep. Cliff covered her with a blanket and let the fire die down until there was only the dull glow of the coals. An hour passed, and then another and the chill of the high altitude crept into him. Suddenly he sat up, ears keening the wind. The run of a horse had come to him, downgrade on the trail he and Bonnie had followed. He woke the girl, cautioned her to silence, and drew her back into the shadows. Then he threw more wood on the fire, and waited there.

The horse had stopped. Not far away. Cliff knew he was being watched. He filled his pipe and began to smoke. Another five minutes passed. Presently he heard the horse passing along the trail below him. When the sound had died, Bonnie whispered: "What did it mean?"

"I don't know, but I'm guessing he'll be back. With help."

"You think it was Dunning?"

"Dunning would have stayed on the toll road. It was someone who didn't want to be seen."

Cliff let the fire die down again. There was silence except for the wind that made a high howl in the pines. Yonder a tree creaked dismally. It seemed hours later that a limb snapped under foot. Somewhere above them.

"Get around to the other side of the fire and stay back," Cliff breathed. "Don't make any noise or you'll get a slug."

She slipped into the darkness. He heard her once, a brushing sound as if she'd rubbed against a pine trunk. Instantly a gun roared not more than ten feet from Cliff, its tongue of flame rushing into the blackness. Cliff pulled trigger, raking the man's position with his fire, laying his bullets a foot apart. He heard a shrill cry, high and thin, heard a moment of hard breathing, and then nothing.

Cliff rolled away. There would be two of them, the man who had come up the trail and Connors. He reloaded his gun and waited. A gray light filtered through the timber. Tension built in Cliff. He had heard nothing of Bonnie since the man had first fired. The need to end this grew in him. He tossed a rock against the dead fire, heard it hit a tree trunk and bounce off into the brush. Hard on that sound came the quick sharp breath of a man.

IV

Morning came slowly, each minute drawing out far beyond its sixty seconds. Silently it spread a thin light across the land. The quiet lay all about, unbroken and heavy, and death waited.

"It's Dunning!" Bonnie screamed, and began firing a small pistol, the reports coming closely together like dry twigs being sharply snapped.

Dunning, flushed out of his hiding place by Bonnie's fire, reared up into Cliff's view, a shadowy figure in the dawn light, and began to curse as he fired at Bonnie. Fury and greed and lust were embodied there in Sam Dunning. Cliff, lying belly flat, fired upward, his bullet catching Dunning in the chest and slamming him back against a pine. He propped his weakening body there as he tried to lift his gun to fire at Cliff.

"Who came up the trail tonight?" Cliff called.

"I'm damned to hell," Dunning flung back, "and you'll be there with me as soon as you get to Palisade. Meldrum knows you've got the girl with you." Then breath stopped in Sam Dunning, and he crashed earthward.

"Bonnie, you all right?"

"All right, Cliff." She came around the ashes of the fire, pale and shaky, and clung to him for a moment.

"We can go looking for your dad now." Cliff motioned to the first man who had died. "That's Connors. Chances are your dad ain't guarded."

It was full daylight when they topped a ridge that broke steeply off into Tentrock Cañon and looked down upon a log cabin, a faint pencil of smoke rising upward from its chimney.

"Looks safe enough," Cliff murmured, "but the gent who came up the trail last night might still be there." He fell silent a moment, studying the cabin. "Can you use a Winchester?"

"Yes."

He pulled his rifle from the boot and handed it to her. "Give me fifteen minutes. Then cut loose. Shoot high. Into the roof or the upper part of the window."

Cliff rode around the edge of the cup-like depression in which the cabin was set, reaching the other side in the fifteen minutes he had given the girl. He dismounted, and, when he heard her first shot, slid down the slope, bringing a small avalanche of rocks and earth with him. Reaching the door, he flung it open, gun palmed.

Ben Armfield was there, crouched against the wall at the head of the bed. His shoulders stooped, a week's white stubble on his face, he resembled but little the arrogant millionaire Cliff had seen on Palisade's streets.

For a moment Armfield stared at Cliff. Then recognition came to him. "You're Cliff Jenson, aren't you? You've been trying to kill me." Armfield gripped the head of the bed and, pulling himself upright, leveled a long-barreled Colt at Cliff. "But you aren't going to kill me, Jenson, because I'm going to kill you first."

Cliff had time to shoot Armfield, but he couldn't do it. Not now that he knew Bonnie. He leaped sideways as Armfield's gun thundered, the bullet screaming through the doorway. He slammed the door shut and, moving to the corner of the cabin, waved his hat.

"Come on down!" he called, and waited until Bonnie reached the bottom. Then he opened the door a crack. "Your daughter's here, Armfield. You understand, your girl Bonnie?"

Cliff had a bad moment, not knowing what Armfield would do. Then the old man croaked: "Bonnie? What's Bonnie doing here?"

"Trying to save your life if you had sense enough to see it. Throw your gun away. You won't need it now."

Armfield ran into the clearing, gun still clutched at his side. "Bonnie! Bonnie girl." She came to him, and the old man put his arms around her, the gun dropping from his hand. He was crying then, his gaunt body shaking. He repeated over and over: "Bonnie. Bonnie girl, how did you find me?"

She led her father back to the cabin, Cliff keeping behind them. When they were inside, Bonnie said: "Cliff Jenson found you, Dad. He saved your life."

"Jenson?" He saw Cliff standing in the doorway and pointed a trembling finger at him. "That man wouldn't save my life, Bonnie. He's the one who wants to kill me."

"Who told you that?" Cliff asked, coming into the cabin.

"All of them. Galtry and Dunning and all of them. Galtry's been keeping mc at the Narrows ever since you tried to kill me the day I came in."

"I didn't try to kill you, Armfield."

"Lying won't do you any good," Armfield said heatedly. "Galtry ran you and your killers off. He told me all about it, how you'd been making a lot of threats. Said you'd get me because I took your father's ranch. That wasn't my fault, Jenson. Just business. That's all. Just business."

"Why did they fetch you here?"

"Galtry said you knew I was at the Narrows. He said you'd bring all the men who lost their ranches and murder me."

"Has Vance Meldrum been to see you?"

Armfield was silent for a moment, a sly cunning creeping into his eyes. Then he said: "No. Meldrum hasn't been here."

Bonnie, standing at her father's side and a little behind him, caught Cliff's eyes and nodded at the door. "Will you get us some wood, Cliff. We'll all feel better if we have breakfast."

"Sure," Cliff said, and left the cabin.

Bonnie cooked breakfast, but there was little appetite in either her or Cliff. For a time they sat watching Armfield eat hungrily. Then Cliff rose and kicked back his chair. "Guess I'll slope along to town."

Armfield raised his eyes. "You won't get another chance to kill me!" he said shrilly. "As soon as I can get to the sheriff, you'll be in the jug."

Bonnie followed Cliff outside. She said bitterly: "He believes all they've told him. He thinks Galtry has been protecting him."

"I've got a pretty good idea what happened. Galtry would know just about when

55

your father was coming in, wouldn't he?" When she nodded, he went on. "I'd say Galtry and some of the rest cornered him and did a lot of shooting. They scared him so bad he's probably been a little loco."

"Then Galtry rode up, said he'd chased you off, and promised to hide Dad out." She shook her head. "I never trusted Ron Galtry, but I didn't think he'd do a thing like that."

Cliff stepped into the saddle. "If you start telling the truth now to your dad, he might believe it by night."

"He'll believe me. It's a funny thing about Dad, Cliff. He hasn't been any happier than he's made the rest of us. Maybe it's his conscience, or maybe he's physically afraid of men he's hurt." Her eyes locked with Cliff's gray ones. "What are you going to do?"

He made no answer for a time, remembering that Vance Meldrum had said he and Bonnie were engaged. Agony was in Cliff then. He knew what he had to do, and he knew how Bonnie would feel when the truth about Meldrum came out. At this moment she thought well of Cliff Jenson, but before this was finished she would hate him.

"I don't know till the time comes," he said evasively. "Get your dad to town as soon as you can. You'll be safer there." Turning his horse toward the east side of the cañon, Cliff angled up the steep slope until he reached the toll road, and then set a fast pace to town. There was much he didn't know and couldn't guess, but he was convinced of one thing. Vance Meldrum's shrewd brain was behind the scheming that had brought this trouble to the basin. Cliff aimed to face him the instant he reached Palisade, yet with this slow burning rage was the tempering knowledge that he had little real evidence against the banker.

When Cliff reached Palisade, he found the biggest crowd he had ever seen in it jamming the short main street. Puzzling about it, he turned into the stable. Buzz came out of the gloom, swearing fiercely when he saw who it was.

"I thought you'd keep on riding," the stableman said. "You're a bigger damned fool than I thought you were. Where's that mare you took?"

"She'll be along." Cliff stepped down, seeing something on the other's face he could not read. "I don't take to being called a damned fool without some reason."

"You'll be called worse than that before this is over," Buzz said darkly. "Threatening to kill Armfield is one thing. Stealing a girl is something else."

Cliff grabbed a handful of the man's shirt. "Who says I stole the girl?"

"Everybody," Buzz snarled, and tried to jerk free.

Cliff hit him then, a quick-swinging blow to the side of the head that knocked the stable man flat into the barn litter. "Who says?" Cliff demanded.

Buzz lay staring up at Cliff, one hand gingerly rubbing the side of his face. "Bill Trent says so," he muttered. "Says he heard a girl sneeze last night. When he headed for your back room, you slugged him. This morning the hotel people said she was gone. Meldrum saw her go into your store last night." Buzz pulled himself up and stood against the wall, eyes narrowed and ugly. "You're in a hell of a fix, mister. They found her clothes in your back room. How do you aim to get out of that?"

Without answering, Cliff pulled his gun, checked the loads, and wheeled into the street. Buzz had called it right when he'd said Cliff was in a hell of a fix. A combination of half truths and Meldrum's lies were forming a noose that would fit Cliff Jenson's neck perfectly.

The walks were crowded. Then a strange fact broke through Cliff's thoughts. These men were not basin ranchers. They were farmers. Strangers. Men he had never seen before. There were, he guessed, more than one hundred along the street, gathered in tight little knots here and there, and the snatches of talk that came to him were about Armfield and how he had a hanging coming.

Then a ringing voice broke along the street. "I'm coming after you, Jenson. I'm gonna kill you, slow-like, so you can tell what you did with Bonnie Armfield."

Dan Harl stood in front of the Silver Dollar, short legs spread apart, his face evil and without mercy. Within a matter of seconds the crowd cleared away, the scuff of shoes on boards as men dived for shelter coming clearly to Cliff. Harl stepped into the dust and angled toward Cliff, his face a cold killer's mask. Cliff knew his breed — gunmen who earned their pay with as little distress to their consciences as an ordinary butcher would have in slaughtering a beef.

Cliff moved into the street and paced slowly toward Harl. They were in the middle of the dust strip, facing each other, both watchful and neither walking fast. Thoughts ran in a swift stream through Cliff's mind, a multitude of them in these seconds into which was telescoped a lifetime of living.

One thought towered giant-like over the others: he had to kill this man before he could get at Vance Meldrum.

They were close enough now for Cliff to see Harl's freckles, his yellow teeth as his lips pulled away from them, the narrowed muddy eyes. Cliff said: "You're going to hell with Connors and Dunning, Harl."

The words hurried Harl, pressed him into action before his mind was ready, and the mental confusion slowed his draw. His hand whipped downward, fingers closed over gun butt, and came up swiftly — a draw faster than most men's, but not faster than Cliff Jenson's. The roar of the guns beat into the street's quiet, struck the false fronts, and was flung back in a rolling wave of echoes. There was the familiar kick of the walnut butt against Cliff's palm, the burst of powder flame, the spread of smoke. Then Harl was on his face in the dust, dropped gun within inches of outstretched fingers.

Cliff stood motionlessly, Colt held in his hand, a trickle of smoke lifting from its barrel as his eyes scanned the street. Men rushed out of doorways, and stopped when they saw him standing there. Blurred talk came to him, sound without meaning.

Bill Trent stood in front of his store, uncertainty stamped upon his knife-thin face. Galtry was there under the wooden awning of the Silver Dollar. Shortcake Hogan came into the street, and hesitated when he saw Cliff holster his gun and stride past Harl's body toward the bank. It was then that Meldrum came to stand on the boardwalk. He was in his shirt sleeves, his bulldog face set and wicked.

"Take off your gun belt, Jenson," Meldrum said coldly. "I make no pretense of being good with a gun, but I'm going to kill you with my hands. I told you Bonnie and I were engaged, but you couldn't let her alone."

Vance Meldrum knew that Bonnie was going to ask Cliff to work for her, but the men along the street didn't. Not knowing it, they couldn't understand how Meldrum was cunningly manipulating the facts to make a pariah out of Cliff. It was a bold public challenge that Cliff could not escape, nor did he want to. Yet there was little he would gain. He could batter Meldrum into the dust, but public sentiment would still back the banker.

Cliff stripped off his belt and handed it to Hogan. He stood there, a slim raging figure, and waited while Meldrum swung around the tie rail and advanced upon him.

Meldrum had asked for trouble. He was

braced for it, but he didn't expect the kind of trouble that exploded before him. There was no more waiting in Cliff Jenson. He drove at Meldrum, fury incarnate. He parried Meldrum's first looping blow, and then he was on the banker, swinging hard with both fists and paying no attention to his own defense. He cracked Meldrum on the cheek, rocked his head with a savage right, closed an eye, and knocked loose a mouthful of teeth. Then he caught the banker in the belly, and wind rushed out of him.

Half blinded and sucking painfully for air, Meldrum retreated. Cliff was after him, cruelly stalking him, battering down his defense. He slashed Meldrum fully on the nose and felt it flatten under his knuckles. He hooked a left to the pit of Meldrum's stomach, sledged him on the cheek. Rubberlike, Meldrum's joints gave away, and he went down, belly flat.

Meldrum pulled himself up to his hands and knees. The power to rise farther was not in him. He held that position for a moment, dust and blood on his face, head bowed. He raised it as he strained to gain his feet, his one good eye staring at Cliff. Then he dropped down.

Cliff stepped back as Hogan jeered: "Thought you was gonna kill him with your hands, Meldrum."

"What are you aiming to do, Marshal?" Galtry called to Trent. "You can't let a man go who's kidnapped a girl."

Cliff, eyes sweeping the crowd, saw the farmers nod their agreement. He wondered why these strangers who had only come to the basin the day before would be completely behind Vance Meldrum.

Trent, needled into action, pulled his gun and lined it on Cliff. He said: "I'm arresting you for kidnapping Bonnie Armfield. Got anything to say?"

"Go on," Hogan called. "Tell 'em what's going on."

Cliff shook his head. Without Bonnie here to back his talk, his defense would be a waste of words. He said: "Not now."

"All right, mister," Trent said coldly. "Head for the jug."

Jangled nerves and the crack Cliff had given Trent on the head the night before had brought the marshal to the place where any quick action on Cliff's part would bring a bullet. Cliff shook his head when Hogan called: "That hairpin ain't man enough for this job, son!"

"We'll show him that later when the sign's right," Cliff said, and turned toward the jail.

The crowd fell back. As Cliff moved along

the street, he met Ron Galtry's eyes. There was no weakness in them. Only a feral hatred. Now, even with Dan Harl dead, Galtry was not quitting.

Trent gave a relieved sigh when the cell door clanged shut behind Cliff. "Want to tell me about this girl stealing?" he asked. Bill Trent was still scared. Cliff, watching him now in the thin light of the jail's interior, was as uncertain of him as he had been the day before. He said: "You know what's going on, Bill, and you know I'm not the kind of a polecat who'd steal a girl. I'm sorry I slugged you, but I didn't have a choice. Now you'll have to decide which way you're going. If you play on Meldrum's side, you'll wind up with a stretched neck just like he will."

Trent sucked at his lower lip, eyes suddenly thoughtful. "I ain't sure about that. He's smart, Meldrum is, and right now you're playing a lone hand except for Hogan. I've got a notion you'll be dead before your friends in the basin hear about this and get to town. Either way, I've got to keep you here till I know the girl's all right."

Trent walked away, his steps echoing hollowly along the corridor.

V

Trent brought Cliff's supper at 6:00. The worry lines in his forehead had deepened. He said: "The sodbusters are getting liquored up and they're laying all their troubles on Armfield. He won't last long if he shows up."

"What have they got against Armfield?"

"They're sore because they can't get their outfits into the basin. They ain't got the *dinero* it takes to pay Armfield's toll at the Narrows."

"How'd they get into town?"

"Horseback. Galtry didn't charge 'em no more than the old toll. Fifty cents, wasn't it?"

Cliff nodded. "Seems to me the new sign had raised all the tolls."

"It did. Five dollars for a horsebacker."

"Then Galtry wanted these men in town. He figures Armfield will show up."

Trent shifted uneasily. "I'm sizing it up the same way. Galtry and Harl and even Meldrum have done a lot of talking about how the basin is paradise for the farmers, but Armfield is gonna raise hell to keep 'em out. They say that's why he raised the ante."

"Where did the sodbusters come from?"

"It's a colony from Iowa."

"How'd they hear about the basin?"

Trent scowled. "I couldn't prove it, but Meldrum wrote to 'em that they'd find what they wanted here. About the time he got the bank they wrote a lot of letters to bankers all over the country."

"Are you going to protect Armfield if he gets to town?"

"Hell, I can't protect him," Trent groaned. "How can I?"

Cliff told him what had happened on the old Indian trail. He gripped the bars then, his eyes locking with Trent's. "Let me out of here, Bill. I'll meet them before they get to town."

"Can't do it," Trent muttered. "Mebbe you're lying."

"You're thinking maybe Meldrum'll come out on top, and you want to be in good with the winner. That it, Bill?" Cliff asked contemptuously.

Trent didn't answer. He walked back along the corridor and slammed the door to his office.

Sitting there in the evening gloom, Cliff pulled on his pipe and thought sourly that even now there was no proof against Vance Meldrum. Nobody could say he'd broken a law in encouraging the farmers to come to the basin, nor could he have been jailed if

Connors had brought Armfield to town and turned him loose while the colonists were at the peak of their drinking. Now the plan might work exactly as Meldrum had schemed it. If Bonnie followed Cliff's advice, she'd bring her father to town.

Dusk came and full darkness and the threatening rumble of the crowd rode the air to Cliff. Meldrum, not knowing that Connors was dead, would be expecting the gunman to bring Armfield to town and would be carefully staying out of sight. And all the time Cliff Jenson was penned up like a chicken in a hen coop.

Then it happened, and Cliff froze. The crowd rumble became a bloodthirsty roar. Through it a dozen voices cried for Ben Armfield's life.

"Trent!" Cliff yelled, and rattled the cell door. "Trent!"

But when Trent came along the corridor, it was not in answer to Cliff's call. Short-cake Hogan was behind him, a six-gun prodding him in the back.

"You've got the one huckleberry locked up who can save old Armfield's life," Hogan raged, "and by hell you're gonna let him go. You saw the girl yourself. You know you ain't got nothing to hold Cliff for."

"Who cares anything about Armfield?"

Trent said sourly as he unlocked the cell door.

"Mebbe he ain't worth saving, but it's hell of a thing for a lawman to stand around while they hang a man." He tossed Cliff's gun belt to him. "Strap her on, boy. I'm with you."

"All right, Bill." Cliff buckled on the belt. "Make up your mind. If you decide wrong, I'm coming after you soon as this is over."

For a moment the mental struggle went on in Trent's mind. "All right, Cliff. I'm on your side."

"What's the game they're playing?" Cliff asked as he strode into the corridor.

"I overheard Dunning and Meldrum talking about it yesterday," Trent told him hurriedly. "Meldrum figgered on promoting the valley so a lot of farmers would come. Him and Dunning and Galtry had fixed it so they'd have a syndicate controlling both tollgates. They aimed to get our stores. Then with the bank, they'd be in shape to milk the basin dry."

"The railroad?"

"Honey to get the farmers in."

They were running along the street now, Trent on one side of Cliff, Hogan on the other. Ahead of them the crowd was milling in front of the Silver Dollar, the smoky

68

flames from their torches throwing a lurid light across the street. Someone had tossed a rope over the big sign in front of the saloon. Two men held Armfield while a third dropped a loop over the old man's neck and tightened it.

Then the earth seemed to rise up and explode behind Cliff in a wind-whipping roar and a burst of flames. Splintered boards and stones and twisted metal rained into the street.

The blast knocked Cliff off his feet. He lay there, half stunned. Hogan and Trent were on the ground beside him, and for a moment the crowd had scattered. Cliff, coming to his feet, fought off a wave of nausea and saw what had happened. The jail had been dynamited.

Hogan and Trent were standing now, staring at what was left of the jail, Hogan cursing and Trent shouting in a high terrible rage: "The dirty son-of-a-bitch! The dirty damned son-of-a-bitch! He aimed to get both of us, Cliff!"

Cliff wheeled and ran on toward the Silver Dollar. Ben Armfield was still in front of it, the rope around his neck. Bonnie was beside him, trying to free him from the loop. Then the crowd rolled back around them. A man pinned Bonnie's hands and dragged her away.

Cliff hit the edge of the crowd, a charging bolt of fury, gun barrel swinging like a war club in his hand. Hogan and Trent were behind him, Trent still muttering: "The dirty murdering son-of-a-bitch."

Cliff reached Armfield, tore the rope from his neck as a man yelled: "Stay out of this, Jenson! We've got nothing against you!"

"I've got something against you!" Cliff yelled back. "You've been guzzling Meldrum's and Galtry's whiskey till you're ready to swing a man they want killed. Tomorrow you'll wake up with a headache and a conscience that'll give you hell."

"You'll be in hell mighty quick if you don't clear out!" the farmer bellowed. The crowd rolled in again. Cliff, Hogan, and Trent pressed in close around Armfield, guns in their hands. "Stand pat!" Cliff yelled, and, when they didn't stop, he squeezed the trigger. A man screamed and grabbed his arm. Again Cliff's gun thundered, a red flash dancing from its muzzle. A hat flew from a baldhead and the man dropped with a bloody furrow along his skull.

They stopped then and stared in sullen silence. They'd seen Dan Harl die. Drunk as they were, those shots reminded them what this man could do.

"Why do you want to hang Armfield?" Cliff shouted.

"He's keeping us out of the basin," a man answered. "We've got a right to settle here. It's government land."

"Same old story of cattlemen hanging together!" a second shouted. "We aim to hang 'em separately."

"Then you'd murder a man who had nothing to do with your troubles!" Cliff thundered. "The high tolls are Meldrum's and Galtry's doings!"

"You're lying!" a farmer shrilled. "Meldrum's our friend!"

"The hell he is!" Trent cried. "He's pretending to be now, but, when the sign's right, he'll take everything you have!"

Cliff held up his hand. "Listen! Armfield has owned the Narrows for years and he never raised the toll before. Legally he couldn't charge the rates Galtry has posted, but the county seat is a long ways from here. Might be weeks before the county court acted, but he'd wind up by losing his franchise. It's Meldrum's and Galtry's doings, I tell you. They've got their own crooked axe to grind."

"Tomorrow morning," Armfield said, his voice even and distinct, "I'll post a new sign at the gate quoting the same tolls I've always charged."

"Go back to camp and sleep on it," Cliff urged. "In the morning you can bring your wagons across the bridge and pick out the quarter section you want." He swung his gun to cover the man who held Bonnie. "Let her go."

The man released his grip and Bonnie came quickly to them.

"We're leaving," Cliff said. "I'll gut-shoot the first man who tries to stop us."

Lynch lust had gone out of these men. They stood in silence while Cliff, still holding his gun, walked quickly along the street behind Bonnie and her father.

At the end of the block Cliff said: "Short-cake, you and Bill stay here and watch that bunch."

"Where are you taking us?" Armfield demanded as they moved away.

"Do you want to go back there?" Cliff asked.

"No. I'm beholden to you," Armfield said grudgingly. "I've tried to understand why you've done what you have, but I can't. I don't even know why you're blackening Vance Meldrum's name. It's hard to believe Galtry has had a hand in this, but I have no choice after what you did tonight. You would not have risked your life if you had really wanted to kill me like Galtry said."

"You've pulled off some raw deals, Armfield," Cliff said. "I have no reason to risk my life for you. I've done what I have for one reason . . . because your daughter asked me to."

"Then you must be in love with her," Armfield said arrogantly. "I'm telling you now to forget any ideas you've got. She's engaged to Vance."

"You made the engagement," Bonnie said. "From now on I'm living my life the way I see it. Your threats about leaving your money to Vance won't make me marry him." Bonnie whirled and walked rapidly away toward the hotel.

"Bonnie!" Armfield cried after her. "Bonnie girl!"

Armfield would have followed if Cliff hadn't caught him by the arm. He called after her: "Send Trent to Meldrum's house!" Then he propelled Armfield along the walk beside him. "You're going to learn something now whether you want to or not. Did you stake Meldrum to the bank?"

"Yes. He wouldn't double-cross me. He had a good business and he knew I was behind him."

"He double-crossed you all right," Cliff

said grimly, "so he must have had a reason. Was there a will?"

"Of course there was a will. All of my money goes to Bonnie except. . . ." Armfield's voice trailed off as if a new thought had struck him.

"Except what?" Cliff prodded.

"Vance has been like a son to me," Armfield said defensively. "There was plenty for Bonnie."

"What did you leave him?"

Armfield cleared his throat. "Your father's old J Bar. That's all."

"Which included the Narrows. There's your answer. You've always been money crazy, Armfield, but this man you say was like a son to you was a damned sight crazier."

"I don't believe it."

"You'll believe it all right if you'll listen. This is Meldrum's place. All I want you to do is to stay outside and keep your ears open. Don't let him know that you're here."

They turned up the path that led to Meldrum's house and moved across the porch. When they reached the door, Cliff whispered: "You stay here." He twisted the knob, shoved the door open, and went in fast. Meldrum and Ron Galtry were both there in the big living room. Galtry had his back to the door. Meldrum was seated, facing Cliff, one hand on a carved oak table, a short-barreled gun lying on the table top within a scant foot of his fingers.

Galtry came up out of his chair and, whirling, saw Cliff and began to curse. Meldrum rose slowly, his bruiscd face paling.

"You missed by a few feet, Meldrum," Cliff said. "Disappointed?"

"What are you talking about?" the banker snapped.

"You couldn't even guess, could you?" Cliff laughed softly. He motioned to the gun on the table. "Trent talked, Meldrum. Want to wind this up permanent?"

"I told you I was no hand with a gun," Meldrum snarled.

Trent had come in behind Cliff. "Don't believe him, Cliff. Maybe he ain't much on the draw, but he's the best damned shot in the basin."

Meldrum's lower lip was pulled hard against his upper one, his good eye glittering like green ice.

"I told you what I'd do to you if you talked, Trent. Remember?"

"Yeah, I remember," Trent snarled, "but you made a mistake when you tried to get me with that dynamite. I've taken the last one of your kicks I'm gonna take. I scattered Hogan's horses like you told me. I prodded Cliff and tried to scare him and tried to get him to take me into his store so I could bust him. What did I get? A ticket to hell that damned near took me there."

"You sure worked hard on getting me out of the way, Meldrum," Cliff said coldly. "You didn't want Connors shooting an unarmed man yesterday when the stage pulled in because that would have put a stop to his usefulness, but you recommended me to Bonnie so Connors would have a chance of beefing me from the brush. Then last night you went up the trail to see if everything was fixed so Dunning would turn Armfield loose for the mob. You watched us a while, and decided you'd send Dunning and Connors back to get us."

Meldrum laughed, self-assurance pouring back into him. "That's about it, Jenson."

"You had it working both ways," Cliff went on. "You started the lie about me threatening Armfield. If the mob didn't get him, you'd have shot him and framed me."

"I knew you were smart," Meldrum taunted. "That's one reason I wanted you out of the way. Now what's it got you, Jenson? You can't take a bunch of guesses into court."

"But you'd be doing fine with the J Bar

and the Narrows."

"I'll still do fine, my smart friend." Meldrum grinned.

"I don't think so, Meldrum. The mob didn't do the job you talked and whiskied them up to. You can come in now, Armfield."

Meldrum's gaze whipped to the door, glimpsed Armfield, and color washed out of his face. An incoherent cry was jolted out of him. He looked at Galtry, an unspoken message passing between them. Then, driven by his words that had been spoken within Ben Armfield's hearing, Meldrum grabbed the gun from the table and dropped hammer.

Cliff drew his Colt a split second ahead of Galtry and fired, blasting life from the tollkeeper with a single shot. He heard Meldrum's gun thunder, felt Trent wilt beside him. He swung his gun to Meldrum and squeezed the trigger. Two ribbons of flame lashed out at each other across the table, Cliff's shot coming ahead of the banker's and jarring his aim. His bullet caught Meldrum squarely on the second button of his vest.

The banker swayed there a moment, his mouth springing open, then he took a toe-dragging step and spilled forward in a curling drop.

Bill Trent had been shot squarely between the eyes. Shortcake Hogan thundered in, and came to an abrupt stop. "Hell's bells, I got here too late."

Cliff nodded at Trent. "Funny thing how some men live one way and die another. He had guts, Shortcake."

Hogan nodded soberly. "More guts than I figgered he had."

Cliff stepped around Armfield and went out of the house.

"I've been wrong about a lot of things, Jenson!" Armfield called. "Hold on and. . . ."

But Cliff didn't hold on. He ran along the walk and into the hotel. He asked for Bonnie's room number at the desk and raced up the stairs. She opened the door to his knock and for a moment they stood facing each other.

"I guess I'm broke, Bonnie," Cliff blurted. "Your dad'll take the bank and he'll call in the loan, but . . . but . . . I love you. Is that enough?"

"I'll have my two hands and my heart, Cliff. Is that enough?"

"It's all I'd want from you," he said, and kissed her.

"Jenson, I said if you'd wait I'd tell you. . . ." Armfield coming along the hall stopped, panting. Then, after a moment, he tried again. "I'm obliged for what you've done. If you and Bonnie want . . . Jenson, are you listening?"

Cliff lifted his head and looked at Armfield. "No, I'm not listening. If you ain't blind, you can see I'm busy." And turning back to Bonnie, he became busy once again.

■ ■ ■ ■

BEYOND THE LAW

■ ■ ■ ■

I

Sherman Rawls said: "Tie his hands, Fred." He stepped back and studied the big cottonwood limb over his head. He nodded and turned to Joe Miles. "It'll do. Toss the rope over it."

Fred Ashton's bearded face had turned gray. "We're not sure he was stealing the horses, Sherm. Anyhow, they're my horses. I don't think. . . ."

"Sure you don't think," Rawls said. "Well, I've got some horses on this mesa, too. I did have more'n I've got now, but I never caught anybody stealing 'em. We caught Billy Combs stealing yours and we'll hang him. If he wasn't stealing 'em, why was he headed south with 'em toward his hangout on Disappointment Creek?"

"I don't know, but. . . ."

"Of course you don't know." Rawls motioned toward Joe Miles. "He's got horses, too, and he's lost some, same as me. We're not going over this again. Now do as I tell you."

"You want me dead, don't you, Rawls?" Billy Combs said. "It don't make no difference whether I was stealing them horses or not. Nothing's important to you except seeing me dead."

Billy Combs was twenty-one, but he appeared younger. Rawls looked at him, hating him and hoping he'd break, but knowing he wouldn't. Combs's face had turned pale, but he showed no other signs of fear. Rawls wanted him to get down on his knees and beg for his life, but Combs was going to die like a man, and Rawls hated him all the more because he was.

Rawls motioned to Fred Ashton. "We're wasting time. Tie his hands and get him up on his saddle."

Ashton obeyed because he was in the habit of obeying. Joe Miles, a weaker man than Ashton and less inclined to argue, had already tossed the rope over the limb. Miles led Combs's horse forward, and, with Ashton's help, lifted Combs into the saddle, with the noose around his neck.

"Stand up," Rawls ordered.

"Go to hell," Combs said. "Why should I co-operate at my own hanging?"

Rawls shrugged. "It's up to you. This way

you'll choke to death."

Ashton tried again. He said: "Look, Sherm. This is wrong. We ain't the law."

"We are the law," Rawls said. "All the law there is on Red Rock Mesa . . . and you know it. If we let this go, every cow and horse on this range will be over the Utah line in a year. Now shut up." He looked at Combs and shook his head. "He ain't gonna drop this way. We've got to stand him on his saddle."

Rawls rubbed the left side of his face as he always did when he was thinking hard. He had fallen into an open fire when he was a boy and the left half of his face had been terribly burned, leaving a mottled scar that disfigured the entire side so that people seeing him for the first time turned their eyes away, shuddering. Although he was fifty years old, this was something he had never got used to. He was still bitter when it happened, and it steadily added to the smoldering hatred he had for all mankind.

He walked to the tree where he had tied the end of the rope, and loosened it. "Fred, you and Joe bring up your horses and stand on your saddles. You'll have to hoist him up. We want a good, clean drop that'll break his neck."

Combs laughed, an unpleasant sound.

"Filled with mercy, ain't you, Rawls? You've got a rock for a heart. I sure feel sorry for Nancy. She gets sick every time she looks at you. Why you ever married a young, purty girl like Nancy I'll never know."

Combs was using his tongue like a knife. He aimed to hurt Rawls with it, but Rawls refused to let him see that he was succeeding. He said: "Damn it, Fred, what are you waiting for?"

Joe Miles was standing on his saddle beside Combs, but Ashton hadn't moved. He did now. He often argued with Rawls, but in the end he always bowed to him. Together Ashton and Miles lifted Combs until he stood erect on his saddle, with the rope, slung over the limb and around the trunk of the next cottonwood, held taut in Rawls's hands. Now Rawls tied it again and motioned for Miles and Ashton to ride away.

"Got anything to say before you meet your Maker?" Rawls asked.

Combs stared down at him, breathing hard. He was handsome, his features as near perfect as Rawls had ever seen. Combs had ridden for Rawls two years ago when Rawls brought Nancy home. He'd made a mistake by marrying her when she was only sixteen. He knew it, now that it was too late. He didn't know how far the affair had gone between her and Combs, but he believed it had gone as far as it could. He should have killed Combs then. He wasn't sure why he hadn't. Instead, he'd sent him away and told him never to come back to the mesa. But Combs was a fool. He'd married and returned last spring, and now he was going to die.

Combs didn't answer Rawls's question until Rawls said: "We ain't standing here all day waiting for you to speak your piece. It might be easier on you in the hereafter if you admit you was stealing them horses of Fred's."

"You'd like that, all right," Combs said. "Well, I wasn't stealing 'em. As long as you live it'll be on your conscience, if you've got one. Why don't you tell Ashton and Miles why you're swinging me from this limb?"

Rawls lifted a big hand. "Our Father who art in Heaven, receive this miserable soul into Your gracious presence. . . ."

"Don't pray to your God for me!" Combs yelled. "I don't want no part of Him! Tell 'em about your wife and how you found us kissing that time and how. . . ."

Rawls raised his voice to drown Combs out: "And forgive him of his sins of the flesh."

Combs was still yelling: "Tell 'em, Rawls,

about the girl you abuse every night . . . !"

Rawls swung his quirt across the rump of Combs's horse. The animal went out from under him in a great, sudden jump, the limb groaning under the weight that suddenly dropped against it. Combs's body swung like a giant pendulum, his words stopped suddenly as the noose closed against his throat. His head twisted grotesquely on his shoulders and his lips sprang apart, his tongue protruding between them.

Ashton stood on the ground. He started to lead his horse away, then stopped and was sick. Miles mounted and, turning his gaze from Combs's swaying body, rode down the cañon. Presently Ashton mounted and, without a word, rode after Miles, driving in front of him the two horses that Combs had stolen.

Rawls remained where he was, staring at Combs's body, then at his face. Nothing handsome about it now, for it was as ugly and terrifying as the left side of Sherman Rawls's own face. For a moment Rawls was at peace with himself and God, a peace that his tortured mind seldom found. A satisfaction filled him, a strange, sweet sense that relaxed his entire body — an experience he had not had for many years.

So intent was he upon draining this moment of every bit of pleasure it held that he did not hear Combs's wife riding down the steep slope to the south, until she was within fifty yards of him. He wheeled toward her, startled and angry at the interruption.

He recognized Bess Combs at once. She was wearing man's clothes, as she often did, and was riding like a man, her hat dangling down her back from a chin strap, her black hair flying behind her. She was a big woman, but a good-looking one with a perfectly proportioned body. Rawls had often admired her wide hips and soft thighs, and had envied Combs for having her as his wife. There would be in her none of the weak, skim-milked passiveness that characterized Nancy and Rawls's two wives that had preceded her.

Bess Combs thundered down the ridge and across the flat, riding recklessly, then yanked hard on the reins and pulled her lathered horse up beside Rawls. She stared at her husband's body, still swaying a little below the big limb, her face blank with shock. An expression of horror replaced the one of shock, but still she sat her saddle as if paralyzed. She must have known what Combs was and expected this, Rawls thought, but apparently she hadn't. She acted as if she couldn't fully grasp what had happened. Then the paralysis left her and her face turned fiery red with fury.

"You killed him, didn't you?" she demanded.

"I helped hang a horse thief," Rawls said. "That never has been and never will be a crime in the cattle country."

She looked around, saw that other horses had been there, and screamed her question. "Who else did it?"

"If you think I'd answer that, you're crazy," he said. "Your man's horse is yonder. Take it with you. It's worth something. So's the saddle." He motioned toward the dead man. "But let that carrion hang there. We've lost too much stock since you came here with him. It's my guess there's more to your outfit. I want him to be a warning to all of 'em."

She cursed Rawls until she was out of breath. Then she stopped and stared at him, unable to hold back the tears that suddenly came in a great flood. When she regained control of herself, she said in a low voice: "I'll see you dead, Rawls. I'm leaving here, but I'll find a man who'll kill you and hunt down the bastards who helped you do this. Billy was the only man I ever loved. You took him away from me, and, by God, I'll see you dead."

She raised her quirt to slash him across the face, but he grabbed her arm in time to stop her. He twisted the quirt out of her hand and threw it aside. "Your husband would be alive if he'd stayed away, like I told him to. Now you'd better take some advice. Get off this mesa and stay off, or you'll hang from the same limb. And don't think I'd balk at hanging a woman, neither."

"I know you wouldn't. You know what you are, Rawls? You're not a man. You're an animal with a face that would give a woman nightmares. Billy told me about you and your wife. . . ."

"Get out of here." He slashed her horse across the rump with his quirt. "You're talking too much."

Her horse reared, but she held a tight rein on him. Whirling the animal, she rode back the way she had come. Rawls yelled after her: "Take your man's horse!" She kept on, not looking back.

He turned to stare at the dead man, but the pleasure had gone out of it. Mounting, he rode away, following the narrow valley for half a mile before he climbed the north slope and struck off across the mesa toward his Rocking R. He remembered how it had been when he'd come here, driving in a shirt tail full of cows and starting the Rocking R the year the Utes had been moved off the reservation and taken to Utah. Twenty years ago it had been, come fall. Now he was a wealthy man, by local standards; he had the biggest outfit on the mesa and the most money in the bank. He'd had the bad luck to marry weak women who couldn't do the work he demanded of them. He doubted that Nancy would do any better.

He needed a woman like Bess Combs, but he'd never found one like that who would marry him. Even Nancy had dallied with him for a time, and that showed how stupid she was, coming from a shiftless family that had a greasy-sack spread in the rough country west of the mesa. She might even have turned him down if her father hadn't told her she'd better marry a wealthy man when she had a chance.

Riding in now, he looked at his sprawling stone house and the big barns and maze of corrals, and tried to find the pleasure in the sight of them that he usually did. But today there wasn't any satisfaction in anything. Not after Bess had called him an animal, and had tried to quirt him.

He stripped gear from his horse, turned him into the pasture, and went to the house. It was late afternoon and he was hungry, but he found Nancy in the parlor reading a novel. He grabbed the book from her hands and threw it across the room.

"You got dinner ready?" he demanded.

She shrank back against the leather couch, her dark blue eyes refusing to meet his. She hadn't put on a pound of weight since he'd married her, he thought. She was eighteen, but she looked like a child, and a scrawny one at that. She had the yellow-gold hair that he liked. She had good features. She'd be good enough looking, if she'd just fill out where a woman's body ought to be round instead of straight.

"No, I didn't start dinner, because I didn't know when you'd be home," she mumbled.

She was looking past him, not at him. The right side of his face was toward her, but it didn't make any difference which side she looked at, he thought. She didn't like either one. She didn't like anything about him, he guessed. She hadn't grown up, and maybe she never would. She'd be a child all her life, sitting around reading novels.

He'd been taken in. Suddenly he was possessed by a crazy rage. He caught her by a shoulder, hauled her to her feet, and slapped her on the cheek. "I want dinner ready when I get home. You've been here long enough to savvy that."

She staggered and almost fell before she

regained her balance, a thin hand coming to her face that was bright red where he had struck her. "I'm sorry, Sherman." She swallowed, her gaze on the wall behind him. "If you'd just tell me when you'd be home. . . ."

"I don't always know. It's your job to have dinner ready when I ride in."

"Yes, Sherman," she said, and fled into the kitchen.

He walked into his office and, sitting down at his desk, opened a ledger. He toyed with a pencil for a while, unable to concentrate on his bookwork. He put a hand to his forehead, but it did not ease the ache that was never entirely absent from his head. Presently Nancy called dinner and he went into the kitchen and sat down at the end of the long table.

He waited until Nancy took the chair to his right, then he bowed his head and, folding his big hands, said: "We thank Thee, Lord, for this food, and ask Thy blessing upon this home. We thank Thee, too, for the peace that Thou has bestowed upon us, which passeth all human understanding. Amen."

Then he began to eat.

II

Dane Devlin glanced at the face of the big pendulum clock on the wall of the Layton City marshal's office. 11:55 A.M. Five minutes until death. Or, at most, six or seven minutes. It would take a minute, perhaps two, for him to move from the marshal's office into the street and walk east along it. Curly Heston would leave the Belle Union Saloon at the other end of the block and walk west toward him at the same time. But it wouldn't take long. Two minutes. No more. And that was a liberal guess.

The death would be Curly Heston's, not Dane Devlin's. A man had to figure that way when he got sucked into a gunfight. Dane wanted to live as well as the next man, but, if he ever once let himself start thinking he was the one to die, he would be. So he refused to consider the possibility. But Kansas O'Malley, the marshal, figured Dane Devlin was the one destined to go down. O'Malley was a logical man, and any logical man would put his money on Curly Heston because the odds favored him. Heston was a gambler and a cheat, and therefore a killer because he had to be.

Dane wasn't the first to accuse Heston of being crooked. Heston had run the others out of whatever town he happened to be in, or killed the ones who, like Dane, wouldn't run. He'd probably forgotten how many there had been.

Dane checked his revolver for the fifth time and glanced at the clock. Four minutes. He eased his gun into the holster, lifted it to be sure it wouldn't bind at the vital moment, and eased it back again.

"I tell you you're a fool," the marshal said. It was the fifth time for that, too. "You can still leave town. Go out through the back door and light a shuck for the livery stable. Get on your horse and drift. I'll tell Heston you pulled out."

Dane looked at the lawman and shook his head. "I'm twenty-three years old. I've been on my own for thirteen of those years. I don't figure it's unlucky unless I start crawling, and, if I do, I'll have nothing but bad luck. You know that as well as I do, Kansas."

Dane looked at the clock again. Three minutes. He wondered if Heston's watch agreed with the marshal's clock.

"It ain't just that," the marshal said. "You're bucking a stacked deck, and you know that as well as I do. Heston is Keno King's man, and King protects his men. Everybody in Wyoming knows that. King's said it often enough. If you're lucky and

96

knock Heston kicking, some of the rest of King's bunch will gun you down."

"The stage leaves at one," Dane said. "I aim to be on it. Look after my horse. I'll send for him later, or come back after King leaves."

"They'll get you while you're going from the hotel to the stage," the marshal argued. "Or they'll stop the stage on the other side of the Colorado line and take you off. I tell you that you'll lose any way you make your bet."

Dane glanced at the clock again. Two minutes. He looked at the marshal — Kansas O'Malley, famous law officer who had been hired by Layton City because of his reputation. But O'Malley was a failure, and no one knew it better than he did. It took more than a reputation to buck a man like Keno King, who came here each year after fall roundup, when the pockets of every cowman and cowpuncher along the Little Snake River were heavy. Their pockets weren't heavy long. King and his gamblers saw to that.

Dane had worked all summer for the M Bar, and had saved his money. When he rode into Layton City, he'd had no intention of gambling. He aimed to have a drink, tell Kansas O'Malley good bye, then ride south through Craig and Meeker and on down to the Río Grande, where the winters were warmer than they were here. He'd hole up somewhere, maybe get a job if he could find one.

But the temptation was too great. He'd started playing last night, and he'd played right through the night into the morning. He'd hit a streak of luck that added to Keno King's ulcer pains, and he'd parlayed his $200 in savings into better than $1,000. That was when Heston took a hand and Dane hit the skids. Knowing that Heston was crooked wasn't enough. The man was too slick to catch.

When his last gold eagle went across the green-topped table to add to Curly Heston's pile, Dane accused the gambler of cheating. They'd have swapped lead then if Keno King hadn't stopped it. He had several good days left in Layton City, and a barroom killing over a poker game might hurt the take. So Heston told Dane to be out of town by noon.

Once more Dane's gaze lifted to the clock. One minute. He said: "Kansas, this is your town. Why don't you run King out?"

It was a cruel thing to say, and Dane was sorry the moment the words were out. There had been a time when O'Malley would have done exactly that, but now he had nothing left except a gold-plated star, two pearl-handled guns, and a reputation.

"You know why," O'Malley said bitterly. "Counting King, there are nine of 'em in town. Too many for me to handle. Too many for you, too, but you're so stubborn you've just got to die of bravery. Besides that, we're damned close to Brown's Hole, and King has a hook-up with the Wild Bunch. If I got lucky and ran him out, he'd be back with Butch Cassidy or Harry Longbaugh or maybe Kid Curry, and they'd tree the town."

"I reckon," Dane said, and knew the old man was finding excuses.

There was only one reason O'Malley didn't tackle King. He was scared of the gambler and afraid to die, and that seemed strange, as old as he was. He didn't have many years left, but he wanted to buy every extra one he could, by living carefully. On the other hand, Dane, who should have most of an average lifetime ahead of him, was going out to buck a stacked deck, according to O'Malley. The old marshal was probably right, too.

"Heston's fast," O'Malley was saying. "He'll hold his fire till he's close, then he'll put a slug within a quarter of an inch of where he wants it."

Dane grinned at him. "I'm not one to get killed because I'm polite. I'll cut the bastard down any way I can and as soon as I can. If you're in the street when I do it, maybe I'll have a chance to make it into the hotel."

"I'll be there," O'Malley promised.

Straight up twelve. It was suicide to wait. Play it out too long and your enemy thinks he's got you running. Dane moved to the door.

O'Malley called: "Do you have any relatives, if your luck turns sour?"

"None," Dane said, and went into the street with long, easy strides.

He glanced up at the ugly November sky. A chill wind raced along the street in hard blasts, picking up the dust so it formed a gray haze that at times was a screen hiding the street from the watchers at the windows along it. There would be snow soon — maybe by night.

For a moment Dane stood motionlessly, the wind at his back, an advantage that might save his life. He couldn't see Heston for a moment, so thick was the dust, and he waited, not wanting to move until he was sure Heston was in the street. The wind made a faint hissing sound, and in a hard gust pelted the buildings on both sides of the street with fine gravel. Somewhere the wind picked up a bucket and rolled it along the boardwalk and into the street until it slammed against the end of a water trough and lodged there.

For one brief moment the dust cleared enough for Dane to see Heston standing in front of the Belle Union. Dane drew his gun and ran toward the gambler. He had meant exactly what he'd said to the marshal, that he didn't intend to get killed by being polite. There was only one way to take a man like Heston — throw him off his guard by rushing him, and hope to confuse him.

Heston saw the gun and let out a yell. This wasn't Heston's way of playing the game. Now he had to play it Dane's way, and that was exactly the way Dane meant for it to be. Heston made his draw and started toward Dane, his gun held in front of him.

Again the dust closed in. Dane, grimly intent on forcing the pattern to his mold, kept running. He didn't know how close he was to Heston, or whether Heston had remained where he was. The instant the gust died and the dust began rolling away, he saw Heston and fired. He kept running and firing; it was his purpose to keep the pressure on Heston and not let him off the hook for an instant. He saw the fingers of powder flame dart from the muzzle of Heston's gun again and again, and heard the snap of bullets past his head.

Maybe Heston had dust in his eyes, or it may have been that Dane's plan worked and Heston was unnerved by Dane's act of drawing his gun when he was too far away for accurate shooting. But whatever the reason, Heston didn't score once. Dane did. His third bullet rocked Heston back on his heels, his fourth put the gambler on his knees, and the fifth, fired when Dane was close, drove through his head above his right eye. He was flat in the dust when Dane reached him.

Dane wheeled toward the hotel. O'Malley was running along the walk. Dane expected to be cut down by a hail of bullets fired by King's men, who must have been posted along the street, but none came. He called to O'Malley, loud enough for anyone in the hotel bar or lobby to hear: "You holding me, Marshal?"

"Is Heston dead?"

"He's dead."

"Hell, no, I ain't holding you. I oughtta give you a medal."

Dane plunged through the hotel door into the lobby. Neither King nor any of his men was in sight. Dane went up the stairs, taking two at a time, and ran into his room. He shut the door and, locking it, leaned against it.

For the first time he admitted to himself that he had not expected to live this long. Now he had nearly an hour of life until the stage left. He didn't have the slightest chance of reaching the livery stable alive, but he thought he had a chance of getting on the stage, which stopped in front of the hotel. It seemed unlikely he would be bothered as long as he stayed in his room, but Kansas O'Malley was right. King's bunch might try to get him before he reached the stage. Or maybe they'd take him off later, probably after the stage had crossed into Colorado, because it was a long way from there to the sheriff at Craig.

Dane punched the empties out of his gun and crossed to the window. He reloaded, looking down into the street at the dozen or more men who had gathered around Heston's body. King wasn't among them. From this distance Dane couldn't tell whether any of King's men were in the bunch or not. Actually it didn't make any difference. They held O'Malley in high contempt. They made the brag that they took care of their own, and it included Curly Heston, lying out there in the street.

Dane holstered his gun and wiped his sleeve across his face. The room was cold, but he was sweating. Now that he was past the immediate danger of Heston's gun, fear was in him. There would be eight of them waiting for him, and no amount of raw courage or gun skill could get him past so many. They'd take him here, he decided. They wouldn't wait for the stage to cross the state line.

Suddenly he was aware that someone was tapping on his door. He whirled and drew his gun, putting his back to the window. Let them come.

III

The tapping stopped. Dane expected whoever was out there to put a shoulder against the door and smash it open. Instead, there was a moment of silence, and then a woman said urgently: "Let me in, Mister Devlin. Quickly."

He was stunned. He didn't know any women in Layton City, but apparently this one knew him. Probably she had seen him smoke down Curly Heston, and she was in some kind of trouble and thought he'd help her. To hell with that. He had all the trouble he wanted.

"Let me in, Mister Devlin," the woman said again in that same urgent tone. "Don't leave me out here in the hall."

He crossed the room, the gun in his right hand. With his left he turned the lock, fully intending to tell her to go away and let him alone. But the instant he opened the door, she came in. She was as big as many men and as strong, and he could no more have stopped her than he could have stopped a big mare from plunging through an open corral gate.

"Lock the door again, Mister Devlin," she said, and, walking across the room in graceful strides, looked down into the street.

Dane shut the door behind her, but for a moment forgot to lock it — forgot even that in less than an hour he'd be in the fight of his life. Here was a woman, not for the man who liked his girls cuddly and dainty, but for one who wanted a strong and vital woman who enjoyed being a woman. Some men, Dane knew, were excited by the turn of a trim ankle under a long skirt, or the swell of a woman's breast. But with him it had always been the curves of a woman's hips, particularly viewed from the rear.

Now, watching her as she moved from the door to the window, he noticed the flowing, rhythmic sway of her hips, not the exaggerated, put-on wiggle of a whore parading across the parlor of a sporting house, but a motion that was as natural as eating or sleeping.

She studied the street briefly, then turned. "You didn't lock the door, Mister Devlin."

He obeyed mechanically, thinking he had never seen a large woman as attractive as this one. Her features were far from perfect, her red lips a trifle too full, her chin square and strong, but to him perfection was not the factor that made a woman beautiful. Rather, it was the sum total of face and body. He had no fault to find with her complexion, her face, that was darkly tanned, her hair that was so black it held a bluish tinge, or her dark brown eyes. He liked the uptilted, proud shape of her breasts under her white blouse. When she moved to a chair and sat down, he glimpsed her ankles, which were perfectly proportioned for a woman of her size. Now that she was sitting, her soft thighs flowed out on both sides of the chair.

She was giving him the same close study he was giving her, and, when she smiled, her face held the light of pure pleasure. "Well, Mister Devlin, I hope you like what you see, because I have a proposition to offer you. If you take it, we'll be seeing a good deal of each other. If you don't, you'll be a dead man in about forty-five minutes."

"I won't be the only dead man," he said.

"I'm sure of that," she agreed, "but that won't help you. Perhaps you'll be interested in knowing that I admire what I see. You're a strong man, Mister Devlin, with quick hands. I like that very much. I also liked the way you smoked Curly Heston down. You aren't burdened by conscience or morals or whatever you want to call it. I mean, you weren't bound by the so-called code that is supposed to govern gunfights. If you had waited for Heston to make his play, you wouldn't be alive now."

"Who are you?"

"Bess Combs. I'm a widow. My maiden name was Bess Quinn. I served a term in the Colorado pen at Cañon City for horse stealing. I make no pretense of being a good woman, Mister Devlin. I think you should know that before we go any further."

"I've seen some good women who would slit your throat as soon as they'd bat an eye," he said. "It isn't necessarily a recommendation."

Her smile came again. "I love that," she said. "We don't have much time, so we'd better get down to brass tacks. I'm looking for a man, a particular kind of man, and

107

you fill the bill. I've been looking since the middle of the summer. I came here because I knew Keno King showed up every fall and the chances were good that some of the Wild Bunch would drift in. I thought I might find my man in one of those outfits. Then I heard you were in town, and I began listening."

She rose and, taking a handful of gold coins from her handbag, laid them on the bureau. Then she sat down again. "When you're in the pen or riding the Owlhoot, you hear the leaves rustle. I've heard a good deal about you, but I suppose you've never heard of me."

He shook his head. "No, I haven't."

"I'll tell you what I know about you. You killed your first man on the Niobrara six years ago. You weren't more than seventeen or eighteen then. You shot another man in Cheyenne last year, but both cases were justifiable homicide . . . just like killing Heston . . . so you're not wanted by the law. That's one reason you fit the bill for me. If you want the job, that five hundred dollars on the bureau is yours. When you're done, there'll be that much more. In addition, I'll get you out of Layton City alive. How about it?"

"What's the proposition?"

"That'll wait. Time's running out on us. All I want to know is whether you'll work for me."

"I never buy a horse I haven't seen," he said. "It might be a dead one."

"It certainly could be," she admitted, "but you'll have to trust me that this one is very much alive. I saw you come into the lobby yesterday and I watched you register. Then you went into the bar. I sneaked a look at the register and saw your name. That was why I began to listen. I stayed in the lobby, but men kept coming and going, and I heard enough talk to know you were in a big game and winning. You built up to about a thousand dollars, didn't you?"

He nodded. "Then Heston sat in."

"I knew how you'd wind up. Heston's the slickest card shark in the country. I went to bed, not sure whether you'd be alive in the morning or not. But if you were, I knew you'd need me. When I had breakfast, you were still in the game. It wasn't long before you were broke. I waited until after the fight to see you, because I knew you weren't the kind of man who would drag out of town after Heston ordered you to get out. I've been right on every count. Now it's up to you."

He shook his head stubbornly. "I've got to

know the deal."

"You'll leave town on the stage," she went on, ignoring what he'd said. "Do you have a horse?"

He nodded. "A buckskin named Nero. He's a good animal. I don't want to lose him."

"You won't. Ride the stage south to Meeker. Wait for me at the hotel. If you miss me, go on to Grand Junction and get a room at Grandma Farley's boarding house. Wait for me there, if you have to wait all winter. I'll ride your horse and I'll get him to you."

"What's the proposition?"

"I told you it would wait. I'll get you out of town, and, when I see you, either at Meeker or Grand Junction, I'll tell you. Now let's go downstairs. We've got about twenty minutes. Pick up your war sack."

He shook his head stubbornly. "I told you I never bought a horse. . . ."

"I heard you the first time," she said angrily. "Look at your chances, Devlin. Without me, they're zero." She motioned to the window. "See what you can see."

He strode to the window and looked down into the street. The wind had died and he could clearly see two of Keno King's men standing in front of the hotel. One he knew as Bill Jeeter, a pimply-faced hardcase who had five known killings to his credit. The other one Dane had heard called nothing but Bosco, a nervous kid with white eyes who was probably more dangerous than Jeeter.

"Open the door and look down the hall," she said. "Don't go through the door. Just look."

He hesitated, knowing what he'd see before he looked.

"Go on, damn it," she said. "I'm as good as a ticket on that stage, and, by God, you stand here arguing with me."

He stalked across the room, turned the key, opened the door, and glanced along the hall. A man stood at the far end near the head of the back stairs. Dane had heard him called Ed Trask, the night before. He had been in the game with Heston. Trask was a chill-eyed gambler wearing the traditional Prince Albert coat, boiled shirt, and string tie. King had two kinds of men, the plug-uglies like Jeeter and Bosco, and the card manipulators like Heston and Trask. At a time like this, one was as dangerous as the other.

When Dane stepped back into the room, Bess Combs said: "Without looking, you can take my word for it that two other men

111

are in the alley. Trask won't bother you as long as you don't try the back stairs. If you were lucky enough to nail him, you'd never get through the alley door. You're hipped, friend."

He was sweating again. She was right. He had no more than a few minutes. This was worse than standing in the marshal's office and waiting for the big hand on Kansas O'Malley's clock to touch 12:00. Not one man to buck this time, but eight of them. Even Keno King would be in it if necessary. He measured Bess Combs with a long look. She was not only smart and attractive; she was ruthless. Whatever deal she had for him would be rough, but he'd handled plenty of rough deals and he could handle this one, whatever it was.

She was watching him closely. Now she smiled and held up one finger. "I'll give you your life, Mister Devlin." She held up a second finger. "I'll give you a thousand dollars, which is what you would have had if you'd cashed in at the right time last night. Regarding my proposition, I can promise that it won't put you outside the law, because there is no law where you'll go."

"Looks like you're offering a fair deal," he said. Taking the money from the bureau, he dropped it into his pocket. "But it's only fair to warn you that, if I find out I am buying a dead horse, you're out five hundred dollars and I'll keep on riding with it in my pocket."

"You won't," she said. "I'm honest in my own way, and I judge you're honest in just about the same way."

He nodded. "I guess there are several ways of judging honesty," he said, "and you can be sure I've got mine."

"I wouldn't have made the offer if I hadn't been sure," she said. "I can't afford to lose that five hundred dollars. Now one more thing. How can I get your horse?"

"O'Malley's a friend of mine," he said. "I'll write a note for him. He was going to take care of the horse for me."

He found pencil and paper, scrawled a note for O'Malley, and gave it to her, then crossed the room and picked up his war sack as she rose and came to him. She put her hands on his shoulders and, leaning forward, kissed him on the lips. It was a promise, and he thought, with a sudden rush of hunger for her, that working for Bess Combs would be the most exciting thing he had ever done.

"I'll do anything to help you finish the job I want done," she said. "I guess the first thing is to get you out of here alive. Now let's go find Keno King."

He walked with her along the hall to the head of the stairs, watching Trask closely, his war sack in his left hand, his right wrapped around the butt of his gun. Both of Trask's hands were in the pockets of his coat, but when he saw Dane make the turn to go down the front stairs, he withdrew them. Opening the window above the back stairs, he called something to the men who were in the alley.

Bess Combs reached the lobby and walked briskly across it to the dining room. Dane kept a step behind her, his right hand still on the butt of his gun as his gaze probed the corners of the lobby and then the dining room. King was sitting alone, finishing his dinner. Bess pulled a chair back and sat down across from him. Dane stopped beside her, his gun half out of its holster. He watched King closely, not knowing what to expect from the gambler.

"You're a creature of habit, Mister King," Bess said. "I knew I'd find you here." She drew her chair close to the table, put her handbag on her lap, and, smiling amiably, added: "If my time is correct, the stage leaves in ten minutes. My friend Devlin is taking it. If you make the slightest move to stop him, I'll kill you where you sit."

IV

Dane moved so that his back was to the wall, and from there he watched Keno King. He was the most feline-appearing man Dane had ever seen. He was tall, with abnormally long legs and arms, and very slender. His skin was dark, almost swarthy; his hair was as black as Bess Combs's, his eyes as brown as hers. It was the way he moved — quick and graceful and silent — more than any other quality that reminded Dane of a big cat.

He was about thirty, Dane judged. From the gossip Dane had heard, the man had spent the last ten years putting together the outfit he had brought to Layton City. He was more than a gambler; he was an organizer and a careful picker of men, each of whom was skilled at some particular art in the field of gambling or crime. Heston had been his best gambler; Jeeter was an expert at handling a stolen herd of cattle; Doc Darby, who sat at the next table, was a con man who had literally sold more than one sucker a gold brick. But all of King's men had one talent in common — they were killers. Now, as the seconds fled by, Dane wondered if Bess Combs would be able to fulfill her part of the bargain, as she had so confidently promised.

Like any good gambler, King's face showed no expression. He appeared unaware that Dane was standing a few feet from him, one hand gripping his war sack, the other wrapped around the butt of his gun. King took his last bite of pie, raised his napkin to his lips, and wiped them with scrupulous care, then replaced the napkin on his lap.

After a silence that seemed to Dane to last for minutes, King said: "Ma'am, I'd hate to have that happen." His voice was so soft it could have been mistaken for a woman's.

"I'm Bess Combs," she said. "My husband was Billy Combs. Before I was married, I was Bess Quinn."

"I've heard of you," King said. "I knew your husband before you were married. I tried to persuade him to join me."

"I know," Bess said. "Now he's dead. That's why I want Dane Devlin to get out of town alive. I've hired him to do a job for me."

"I see." King raised the coffee cup to his lips, delicately took a sip, and replaced the cup on the saucer. "Ma'am, I said I'd heard of you. You're a smart woman . . . smart enough to realize Devlin is a dead man."

"Then you're dead, too," she told him. "I

116

have a gun in my hand, under the table. You've got less than five minutes to decide whether you want to live or die. If you've heard very much about me, you know I'll do what I say."

The only King man in the room was Doc Darby, the oldest one in the outfit. He was probably close to sixty, and had the appearance of a benevolent grandfather. He was watching the scene closely, not knowing what to do. If a man had been sitting across the table from King and holding a gun on him, Darby would have shot him in cold blood. But shooting a woman, even a woman like Bess Combs, was another matter. King must have been aware that Darby was watching him, waiting for instructions of some kind, but he completely ignored the man. He said, smiling gently: "Yes, I've heard that much about you. You're a woman I could use, Missus Combs. I admire your boldness."

"Maybe you will, someday." Bess showed the strain of passing time; her face was shiny with a film of sweat, her voice a trifle too high. "We can decide that later. But right now I want your word that Devlin will be allowed to get on the stage and leave here alive."

He lifted the coffee cup to his lips again,

took another sip, and replaced it. "I hate cold coffee," he said. "I dawdled with it too long."

"You'll let Devlin get on that stage," she said, raising her voice, "or you'll find yourself dawdling in hell. If I shot you in the chest, you'd have a chance to live. The bullet might slide off a rib and fail to kill you. That could be true even if I shot you in the head, if your skull's hard enough. But no man will live with a bullet in the soft part of his belly. That's where you'll get it, if that stage leaves without Devlin."

Time had run out, and King knew it. Still, he took a moment to fold his napkin carefully beside his plate. It was the most cold-blooded demonstration of courage Dane had ever seen in his life. King slowly turned his head and nodded at Darby.

"Tell Bill that Devlin is taking the stage."

Darby went out of the dining room on the run. Bess said: "Hold it a minute, Devlin. Let's be sure Jeeter gets the word. You're sitting right here, Mister King. If I hear a gunshot before the stage leaves, I'll kill you."

"That would be a mistake," he said. "As far as I'm concerned, Devlin is free to leave town. What happens tonight or tomorrow or a week from today is something else. Curly was my friend. I think you know I never let a friend's killing go unpunished."

She had won her point, but she couldn't sit here indefinitely holding a gun on Keno King, and the gambler could not have made his threat any plainer. From now on it would be up to Devlin to protect himself.

Dane waited until King said: "Better get your man on the stage, Missus Combs. It's time for it to leave."

Without taking her eyes off King, she said: "All right, Devlin. I'll see you in Denver."

He left the dining room, knowing that Bess wouldn't fool King with the reference to Denver. If a man were going in that direction, he would take the stage north to Rawlins and catch an eastbound train for Denver. Beyond any doubt he would be trailed. From now on his back would be a target for the first King man who caught up with him.

Darby, Jeeter, and the kid called Bosco were all standing in front of the hotel. They stared at him, hating him, three wolves hungry for the kill but held back by the strict order of the pack leader. A temporary order, no more.

Dane stopped, letting his gaze range over the King men. A number of townsmen, standing on the boardwalk, was poised to run for cover if the shooting started. Kansas O'Malley was among them, watching Darby and Jeeter. Dane realized belatedly that he had mentally done the marshal an injustice. The old man would have fallen with his pearl-handled guns bucking in his hands if the King men had made a move to cut Dane down.

"Get on!" Jeeter burst out. "Damn it, get on that stage before I give you a dose of hot lead."

"Hot lead, is it?" Dane said. "All right, if you've got some for me, let's have it."

Darby threw his hand out. "No," he said sharply. "Quit pushing, Devlin. Just get on the stage."

"In good time, Darby," Dane said. "In my own good time."

Still he stood there, his hard glance moving from Jeeter to Darby and back to Jeeter, ignoring Bosco just as O'Malley was doing. This was not merely a reckless bit of bravado on Dane's part. He knew that if he dived into the stage like a rabbit, they'd be on his tail immediately. On the other hand, he had a small hope that they might think twice before starting after him, if he refused to panic.

The kid, Bosco, sour-tempered because he was being ignored, burst out: "I'm the one, Devlin. I'm the one with the hot lead, and, by God, I'll give it to you if I have to chase you all the way to Mexico."

"Why wait, sonny?" Dane asked. "This is a good time, because it'll get Keno King out of the way, whichever gun goes off first."

Darby moved behind Bosco and pinned the kid's arms to his sides. "You've had your fun, Devlin. I won't tell you again. Get on the stage."

Dane shrugged. "I'm ready." He turned to O'Malley and held out his hand. "So long, Kansas. Take care of yourself."

"You do the same." The marshal shook his hand and dropped it, staring past Dane at the King men. "Wish I were going with you. The air's gonna smell a lot better when you get out of town."

"I hope so," Dane said. "Sure stinks around here."

Dane turned to the coach and got in. The driver was already in the high seat. The instant Dane was inside, the silk flowed out and snapped with pistol sharpness in the cold air, and the stage rolled south. Dane slumped back in the seat. He had played it tight there that last minute, perhaps a little too tight, and now he doubted that he had accomplished anything. Bosco was the one to watch out for. A kill-crazy kid, he'd do exactly as he had promised. But Dane was still alive. For that he could thank Bess

Combs. Tomorrow he might be dead, but that would not be Bess's fault. The woman had done her part; he owed her his life. If he survived, he would not forget it.

He sat with his eyes closed, swaying as the stage swung back and forth. His clothes were wet with sweat and clung to him with clammy affection, giving him the feeling he'd been out in a heavy fog. He had never been so tired in his life. It was not physical fatigue, but a wrung-out, emotional weariness that resulted from the long night at the poker table without sleep, and the uncertainty that had followed.

Presently he sat up and opened his eyes. The wind was still cold, knifing across the sage and chilling him. It began to snow, fine flakes hurled along by the wind so that they ran horizontally to the earth and failed to pile up on the ground. As cold as it was, it would be strictly hell if Bess decided to get his buckskin and follow tonight. The snow was likely to get worse. But if Bess decided to do it, he thought, she'd make it, if a man could.

He let his mind linger on her, thinking he had never met a woman as capable as she was, as cold-nerved, as sensually attractive. He wondered what her husband, Billy Combs, had been like. It would take a good man to satisfy her, a hell of a good man. She had said he was dead, and that was why she wanted Dane to get out of town alive. Her husband must have been murdered and she had hired Dane to square for his killing. It seemed the only reasonable guess, and it bothered him, because he had never hired out his gun. He had killed three men, but he had no regrets about any of them. The fights had been personal ones he could not avoid, and none had put him outside the law. Bess had promised that the job he was to do for her would not make an outlaw out of him. Still, the proposition was not to his liking, now that he had time to think about it. But he had taken Bess Combs's offer in exchange for his life, so he was left with no choice, and he was not about to go back on his word.

He dozed through most of the afternoon, his right hand always close to the butt of his gun, never allowing himself to drop off into a deep sleep. The slightest change in direction or speed brought him fully awake. He had not forgotten Kansas O'Malley's saying that Keno King would probably try to take him off the stage somewhere south of the Colorado line. But the afternoon dragged on, and nothing happened. The stage followed a twisting road through the low hills, and somewhere crossed into Colorado. It stopped for a change of horses, then went on. Dusk came sooner than usual, because of the low clouds and the snow that had not yet completely covered the ground. Then lights showed ahead, warm and welcoming, and the coach pulled off the road into the yard of a big house that loomed indistinctly in the thin light.

The driver got up, grunting with weariness, and called: "Night stop!"

A man came out of the gloom to take care of the horses. Dane stepped down from the coach and, taking his war sack in his left hand, crossed to the house, right hand on the butt of his gun. His eyes searched the shadows, the thought occurring to him that some of Keno King's men might have passed the stage and be waiting for him here.

Nothing stirred; there was no sound or movement that seemed suspicious. He went on into the house. A barroom was on the left side of the hall, a dining room on the right. The driver was standing at the bar, a whiskey glass in his hand. Dane closed the door quickly, feeling the welcome rush of warm air. He stepped into the barroom and held his hands out over the hot stove. He closed and opened them, and rubbed them together, realizing he could not have drawn a gun in time to save his life if he had run into one of King's killers.

The barkeep was an old man, wearing a dirty shirt with no collar and gold cuff links. He said: "Name your poison, friend."

"Whiskey," Dane said.

He walked to the bar as the old man poured his drink. He laid a coin on the rough pine plank, gulped the whiskey, and stood there feeling its warmth working through him.

"Cold enough to freeze the balls off a brass monkey, now ain't it?" the barman asked.

"Cold enough," the driver agreed. "Hope the snow don't amount to nothing."

A woman came into the room, spoke to the driver, and then turned to Dane. "Want a room?"

"Yes."

"Come along," she said, and walked out, adding: "Dollar a night."

She led him to a room in the back, opened the door, and, going in ahead of him, lighted a lamp. He followed, tossing his war sack into a corner. The room was sparsely furnished and not clean; the wallpaper was peeling in long, ragged strips from the wall. But it would have to do.

The woman stood by the bureau, waiting. She was in her late thirties, and her dark hair was shot with gray. She had run to fat, and the bulge of a second chin loomed behind her first one. Her cow-like eyes held an acceptance of all the dirt and misery of life. She was one of the lost ones, he thought; she would sleep with him for another dollar. The thought was repulsive.

"Anything else?" she asked hopefully.

"No."

"Supper in half an hour," she said, and turned to go.

"Anybody else here?"

She swung back to face him. "No. A couple of cowhands who look after my stock, the bartender, me, you, and the driver. That's all. It's a hell of a lonesome life here, mister. The stage runs empty most of the time in the fall and winter. Now and then some of the Wild Bunch come in for a drink and raise hell. Elza Lay, Butch Cassidy, The Sundance Kid, Blackjack Ketchum . . . I know 'em all. Or a band of Utes get off the reservation and stop here, damn their stealing souls."

"If anybody asks for me before morning, let me know, will you?"

Interest sharpened her eyes. "Expecting somebody?"

"No. Just thought I'd mention it."

"Sure, I'll tell you," she said, and left the room.

He poured water into the basin from the pitcher on the bureau and washed. Then he examined the lock and decided it wouldn't keep anyone out of the room who wanted in. He was probably worried without reason, he thought. King wouldn't send a man after him tonight, with it snowing and as cold as it was. Still, he wasn't sure. The woman, he knew, would sell him out for another dollar and not lose any sleep because of it.

V

Bess Combs gripped the butt of the gun so tightly her hand ached. She pressed against the table, the edge of it cutting into her stomach, her gaze not leaving King's face for an instant. She would have killed him if he hadn't let Devlin go. There wasn't the slightest doubt in her mind about that.

Now Devlin was gone. At least she had heard the crack of the driver's whip, the rattle of trace chains, the clatter of the big coach as it rolled south out of town. Still she had no way of knowing that Devlin was actually on the coach. So she sat motionlessly, infuriated at her helplessness and at the way Keno King sat there, smiling in that superior way of his, as sleek as a well-rubbed cat.

Presently he said: "How long are we going to sit here, Missus Combs? I'm losing money every minute I'm away from the poker table, you know."

"I'm not concerned about your losing money," she said. "I aim to be sure Devlin's out of town."

"You heard the stage leave," he said. "What else do you want?"

"I want to know he was on it."

"Let's go look."

She shook her head. "It wouldn't prove anything. Besides, if he did get away, I'm buying a little time for him by keeping you here."

For the first time a hint of irritation showed in his face. "Now, Missus Combs, you're smart enough to know you aren't buying a thing. I told you I'd let him get on the stage. I have done that. I made you no additional promise, but I will now. I'll have him killed."

"Not until he's done the job I hired him to do," she said. "You can let him live that long."

"Why should I? He killed the best poker player I ever had. If I let this go, I'd lose my outfit in three months. It took me a long time to put the bunch together. The reason we have survived this long is because of the certainty of death to the man who kills one of my boys."

He had the dress and manners of a gentleman, she told herself, and a heart the size of a mustard seed. His reputation was that of a completely ruthless man, and now she was seeing that his reputation was deserved. There was no use to argue or try to change his mind. Suddenly she realized she had accomplished nothing in getting Devlin out of town except to add a few more hours to his life. Keno King wouldn't let him live long enough to reach Red Rock Mesa.

But, having gone this far, she had to try to go a little farther. She asked: "King, have you ever hated anyone so much you couldn't rest until he was punished for what he had done to you?"

"Certainly. That's the way I feel about Devlin."

"No, no. It's different with me. I married Billy nearly two years ago. I never knew what it was to love anyone until I met him. He was three years younger'n me. I guess that was one reason I was able to steady him a little bit. He was inclined to take chances, but together we made a good team.

We were lucky until we held up a bank in Utah. They almost got us. We outran one posse and fought off another one, and finally holed up in western Colorado, south of Red Rock Mesa. We weren't there long until a man named Sherman Rawls hanged him. I'm going to see Rawls dead, King, if it takes me a lifetime."

"Why don't you kill him?"

"I would have, except that Rawls wasn't alone at the hanging. I had no way of finding out who the others were. But a man like Devlin, going in as a stranger, might be able to find out. It isn't just Rawls. It's got to be all of them."

"Of course." He leaned forward, his swarthy face alive with interest. "How much did Billy get out of that bank hold-up?"

The question surprised her as much as King's sudden interest did. She hesitated before she answered, seeking the reason for it. She wasn't long in finding the answer. King would go anywhere and do anything, if it paid him. Then a new thought struck her, one that was breathtaking because of its boldness. If King wouldn't let Devlin live long enough to do the job she had hired him for, why not use King? But she knew she couldn't manage him the way she could Devlin. Still, it was a second string to her bow she might be able to use later, if she were forced to. She had not, she was sure, seen the last of Keno King. Let him have just a faint smell of the honey, enough to make him think it was a big jar full.

"It wouldn't be smart to tell you that," she said, "but it was too much to carry around with me, if that's what's in your head."

"I see. What did they string Billy up for?"

"Rawls hated him, but it might have been more than that. I don't know. I'd guess he was making off with a horse or two, and they caught him. Horses were Billy's weakness. He couldn't let a good animal alone."

"That's one thing I remember about him," King said.

"We didn't intend to stay there long," Bess went on. "We planned to ride back into Utah as soon as things cooled off, and pick up some help, if we could find any in Robber's Roost. That isn't far from where we holed up. Sherman Rawls is a rich man. He has good horses and a big herd of cattle, and the gossip is that he's got buckets of gold buried in his yard. It's a long way from his ranch to a bank, so the gossip might be true. If we'd had a man like Jeeter, we'd have helped ourselves and gotten Rawls to boot."

"I can let you have Jeeter," he said, "if you can prove to me the deal's big enough."

She shook her head. "The deal's big enough, but we're not after the same thing. You want money. I want to get square for Billy's hanging. That's why I hired Devlin. If you're smart, you'll let him live till I'm done with him. Then you can have him."

King laughed softly. "You know better than to warn me, Missus Combs."

She rose, suddenly restless, and slipped her gun into her handbag. She had planted a seed that in time might grow into a crop she could harvest. She said: "Go back to your poker game, King. I guess there isn't anything more I can do for Devlin."

"You've done plenty," he said. "We'll see each other again, Missus Combs."

She left the dining room. King was still at the table, the last she saw of him. She went upstairs and entered her room, deciding she had made a mistake in letting the name Red Rock Mesa slip. She seldom made a mistake of that nature, because she seldom gave away to impulse. Well, if she lost Devlin, the only alternative she had was to try to maneuver King into a position where she could use him. That was a poor second choice, knowing as much about King as she did. Thinking it over, she wished she had boarded the stage with Devlin. She could at least help keep him alive. The best thing she could do now was to catch up with him.

Quickly she changed into the man's clothes she had brought with her. She hated to ride wearing a skirt. Quickly she packed a small bag that she could tie behind a saddle, put on her heavy coat, tied a woolen scarf around her head, and stepped into the hall. A nagging fear was in her mind that King, thinking she was carrying the money Billy had taken from the Utah bank, might try to keep her in town until he could work out a safe way to rob her. Actually the amount was a piddling $2,000, and $500 of that had gone to Devlin. But from what she'd said to King, he'd think it was enough to make a play for.

When she reached the head of the stairs, she looked down and saw that King was talking to Bosco in the lobby and motioning upstairs. She guessed that King was sending the boy to keep an eye on her room to be sure she stayed there. She hurried along the hall to the back of the hotel, and, glancing out, saw that the alley was empty.

She went down the rear stairs and moved swiftly along the alley to the marshal's office, then followed the side of the building to the street, and went in through the front.

Kansas O'Malley was sitting beside the stove, hunched over it as if having trouble keeping warm.

"You're Kansas O'Malley, aren't you?" Bess asked. He nodded, eyeing her intently. She said: "I'm Missus Bess Combs. Dane Devlin told me you were his friend, so I hope you'll help me."

She handed him the note Dane had given her. After he'd read it, she told him how she had helped Dane get on the stage. "I'll be dog-goned," the old man said. "You know, I figgered there'd be a blow-up, with Jeeter and Bosco and Doc Darby all standing there, but nothing happened. You played it smart, Missus Combs. Real smart."

"Will you get Devlin's horse for me?" she asked. "I've got to get out of town."

"In this weather?"

"I know the country," she said. "I'll be all right. I can't stay here, Marshal. You can see that."

He scratched his nose, scowling, obviously caught between two alternatives and finding that neither appealed to him. He was afraid to let her leave in this weather, but he wasn't sure he could protect her if she stayed. He was not even sure he wanted to try.

"You'll be all right if the storm don't get no worse," he said finally, "but this time of year anything can happen. We might get an early blizzard. It's a long way to the roadhouse where the stage stops. You'd freeze to death."

"If it gets worse, I'll stop at a ranch," she said. "I've been through blizzards before. I'm not nearly as afraid of them as I am of staying in the same town with Keno King."

He took a long, sighing breath and nodded. "I reckon you've made up your mind. I'll fetch Devlin's horse. I ain't got a back door to the jail, so you'd best slide around to the alley again, then circle the town before you hit the road to the south."

"In five minutes?"

"That'll be about right. You figger they think you're still in your room?" She nodded, and he said: "If you change your mind, let me know. I could keep you here in the jail if you'd feel any safer."

"I'll chance the blizzard," she said.

She gave him a good five minutes, not wanting to be caught in the alley, then stepped outside and glanced along the street. She couldn't see anyone; a combination of dust and snow cut the visibility.

When she reached the alley, she found the marshal waiting with the buckskin. She tied her bag behind the saddle and stepped up. O'Malley said: "You're sure this is what you want to do, ma'am?"

"It's what I've got to do," she said. "Don't worry about me. I'm a better man than most men."

"I believe you are," he said. "I do believe you are."

"Thank you for fetching the horse," she said, and rode away.

She circled the town as O'Malley had suggested, riding slowly and, reaching the road, swung south along it, the snow stinging her cheeks. Now the doubts were in her. She couldn't reach the roadhouse where the stage stopped before night, and she didn't think she could keep on the road after it got dark. But she couldn't turn back, now that she'd gone this far. Besides, Devlin would need her.

VI

Dane Devlin did not leave his room until he heard the ringing, metallic sound of the dinner triangle. The two cowhands the woman had mentioned came in from the bar — men who were marked by their trade, long-boned, flat-muscled, dried out by the wind and burned by the sun. They were furtive-eyed men, the backwash of their kind, who would ride on when whim or need struck them, regardless of any obligation they might owe the woman who employed them.

The stage driver and the bartender sat down with the cowboys. The woman motioned for Dane to sit at the corner of the table to her right, and the platter of meat and the other dishes began circling the table. The meal wasn't a good one; the roast was tough, the potatoes soggy, the gravy like paste, the biscuits overbaked and hard. But it was what Dane had expected, and he was hungry enough to eat.

All the men except Dane left the table as soon as they finished eating. The woman poured another cup of coffee for Dane and said: "I'll get you a cigar." She disappeared into the bar. She returned a moment later, handed him a cigar, and, striking a match, held it for him. She settled back, smiling at him, her face showing thc raw hunger that was in her.

He should leave the table, he thought, but the cigar was good, and the best thing about the meal had been the coffee. He was tired enough to enjoy sitting here, so he lingered.

"You're going to Craig?" the woman asked.

"That's where the stage goes," he said.

"You're not staying there?"

"Depends on what I see."

"If you haven't got a job," she said eagerly, "stay here. I'll give you one. I could have a good spread if I had a man with any savvy to run it. You saw what those mavericks were like that I've got working for me, but they're the best I can do. Someday a sheriff will ride in here, and they'll take off."

He shook his head. "Sorry, I can't stay."

Disappointment was in her face. "You ain't trying to say you're on the dodge?"

"Call it that if you want to."

"You don't look like the kind who'd run from anything. I don't believe you are."

She picked up her cup, then held it in front of her and looked at Dane over the rim. "My man died last winter. Since then I've got along the best I could, but it's a hell of a life. I ain't the kind who likes it quiet. That's all I've got here . . . quiet."

He pulled on his cigar, sensing that she wanted to talk. She finished her coffee and put down the cup. "It ain't so bad in the summer. Once in a while some town bunch comes down from Rawlins and stays here to go hunting or fishing. More people ride the stage then . . . cattle buyers, ranchers' wives who have been visiting, drummers, or folks who want to buy a business and figure they'll look around in Craig or Meeker. But the winters are hell."

She leaned forward, her low-cut blouse falling away from her tired breasts. He wondered if she had always been this way, or if a hard life had made her what she was. He thought of Bess Combs. What would she be like in another ten years? It was hard to tell. But she would never be brought to the place this woman was; he was sure of that.

"I need a husband," the woman said. "I'm only half alive without one. I need someone to look after, someone to look out for me, too. You wouldn't believe the things that men say and do to me."

It was a pathetic attempt to prove her virtue to him. He rose, finding this painful, and knowing he had to leave before it became worse. He said: "I've got to roll in. I was up all night in a poker game."

He left the dining room, with the woman staring at his back, angry and disappointed. He stepped through the back door for a minute, and found that the snow was still falling, but not piling up any faster than it had been.

Returning to his room, he took off his boots, slipped his revolver under his pillow, and locked the door, then slid the back of the chair under the knob. Anyone wanting to get in could, but the intruder would make enough noise to wake him.

He blew out the lamp and went to bed, but, as tired as he was, he was unable to sleep for a long time. He couldn't keep from thinking of Bess Combs, very feminine, but still strong and capable of holding her own in a man's world. He had never met a woman like her; perhaps that was the reason he found her so attractive.

The walls of the house were very thin. He heard the woman rattling dishes in the kitchen, the rumble of men talking in the bar. Then all sound was blotted out and he slept the hard sleep of utter exhaustion.

Once he was jarred awake by the rattle of the doorknob. He sat up, reaching for the gun, but the sound was not repeated and he dropped back on the pillow. Probably the woman trying to get into his room, he thought. It seemed ridiculous that Keno King would send a man after him in this kind of weather.

The second time he woke, the room was still dark, but it was cold. Then he felt the rush of cold air through the open window. He was fully awake at once, knowing the woman wouldn't want to get into his room enough to crawl through the window. An instant later he caught the raspy sound of a man's breathing.

Prickles made his spine feel like a live, wriggling thing. He was lying on his right arm, his head on the pillow that covered the gun. Any move to free his arm and lift his head so he could get his revolver would make the bed squeak. If the man had a shotgun, he could fire at a sound and have a fair chance of hitting his target.

Devlin remained perfectly still, listening and hoping he could locate the intruder's position. He caught a sliding sound, as if the man was dragging a foot in an effort to move silently. But Dane still couldn't place the man's exact location until he felt the slight give of the edge of the bed where the man's hand had fallen.

There was no time to reach for his gun. Dane's immediate thought was that the intruder had a knife, and the instant he located Dane's position, Dane Devlin would be dead. Dane threw back the covers with his left hand, raised himself, and dived off the bed, his arms closing around the man's body. They hit the floor hard, shaking the house, and rolled over and over, clawing and striking and kicking.

The man had been surprised by Dane's sudden attack and had dropped his knife. Dane heard it clatter on the floor when he grabbed the fellow. They hit the opposite wall and rolled back, Dane momentarily on top. He lowered his head and batted the top of his skull against the intruder's face, catching him on the nose and mouth, and forcing a bellow of pain out of him.

The man succeeded in pushing him off and gaining his feet. Dane was after him at once but, in the darkness, failed to place his position exactly and caught only the skirts of his coat. The man jerked free, cursing, and swung a wild fist that, by accident more than anything else, caught Dane along the side of the head. Off balance, Dane sprawled full length on the floor. The man wheeled and dived for the window. Dane regained his feet and grabbed for his gun under the pillow. He fumbled for a moment before his hand closed over the walnut butt. By the time he had a secure grip, the man had dived through the window with a tremendous crash, taking the glass with him.

Dane ran to the window. He could see nothing in the darkness and the snow, which was still coming down, but he caught the sound of the man's footfalls as he raced away into the darkness. Dane fired at the sound, and knew at once he was wasting good lead, that he was simply venting his anger. There was no sense in that.

He turned back to the bureau and lighted

the lamp. The house had come to life. Someone was pounding on the door. He kicked the chair out from under the knob, turned the lock, and opened the door. The woman and the old bartender were standing in the hall. The stage driver came out of his room wearing nothing but his drawers and undershirt.

"What's going on?" the woman demanded.

"A man tried to kill me," Dane said.

The woman was dressed, and Dane, noticing this, thought it was odd. Then he realized that the intruder would not have been one of the men who had been here in the evening. Being a stranger and arriving in the middle of the night, he wouldn't have known which room Dane had unless he had been told.

"You'll pay for my window . . . ," the woman began.

"I think not," Dane said. Suddenly he was angry. He had left her at the table, sour-tempered and disgruntled, and she would probably have been happy if his assailant had slit his throat. He grabbed her by the shoulders. "Who was it? How much did he pay you to tell him which room I was in?"

She tried to break free, cursing him. The bartender pawed futilely at Dane. He gave the old man the back of his hand and sent him reeling against the wall. The stage driver said something, and Dane, realizing he wouldn't get anything out of the woman, let go.

She stepped back, glaring at him. "How'd you know it wasn't one of my cowboys, after your money?"

Dane shook his head. "This man was trying to kill me. He wouldn't have come after me with a knife if he aimed to rob me."

The woman whirled and stomped back into the kitchen. The stage driver scratched the back of his neck, scowling. "You figure it was one of King's men?"

"That's exactly what I figure."

"Could've been," the driver said. "King's an ornery cuss. Just like a bulldog. Well, if it was him, chances are the feller's gone now. But you'd better sit up and watch for a while."

"I aim to," Dane said.

Breakfast was little better than supper had been. The woman, bad-tempered and scowling, ignored Dane. As soon as the driver and Dane finished eating, they headed south, one of the hands having harnessed the horses. The snow had stopped, after leaving about four inches on the ground, but the clouds still hung low, retarding the dawn, which was little more than a gray promise.

Dane, huddled in the rocking coach, thought about what had happened. King's man had been bent on murder and he had failed, so he would try again. But next time he might not be alone. Then Dane laughed, thinking about the woman. Glass was scarce and expensive, and, if the woman was going to rent the room out again during the winter, she'd have to replace the window. King's killer had undoubtedly paid her for telling him which room Dane had, but she probably hadn't got enough out of the man to pay for the window.

VII

Bess Combs did not reach the roadhouse the day she left Layton City. The wind got worse, the temperature dropped ten degrees or more, and, with the snow beginning to pile up, she knew she couldn't stay on the road after it got dark. Caution finally overcame her desire to catch up with Devlin, so she stopped at the first ranch she found and stayed the night.

She went on as soon as she could the next morning, and stopped at the roadhouse to ask about Devlin. The woman who kept the place stared at her sullenly for a good thirty seconds before she said: "Yeah, he was here last night. Leastwise a gent answering this Devlin's description was here."

"Was he on the stage when it left?"

"How should I know? I wasn't watching." She turned ponderously and shambled back into the kitchen, calling over her shoulder: "He was lucky to be alive this morning!"

Bess followed her. "What are you talking about?"

"Why should I answer your questions? He cost me a window. The two meals he ate here and the dollar I got for the room sure don't pay for the window."

"All right, I'll pay for your window." Bess laid a $5 gold piece on the kitchen table. "What happened?"

The woman looked Bess over critically. "So you're his woman." She sniffed. "You don't look like so much to me."

"No, I'm not his woman. He's working for me and I'm trying to catch up with him."

"Git on your horse then, and mosey. You ain't catching up with him standing there and jawing with me."

Bess tapped the gold coin on the table. "Do you want this or not?"

"Yeah, I want it."

"Then what's this about a window?"

The woman licked her lips, her greedy eyes on the coin. She said: "Your man went to bed early, said he'd been up all night in a poker game. After I cleaned up the kitchen, I went to bed, but I was too tired to sleep. In the middle of the night a fellow rode in and banged on the door. I got up, and he wanted to know what room a man named Dane Devlin was sleeping in. Said he was this Devlin's nephew and he'd sleep in the same room with him. I told him, and went back to bed. I got to sleep this time, then the damnedest racket broke out in Devlin's room. Sounded like a couple of bulls having it out. The one that asked about Devlin got the worst of it, I guess. He'd crawled in through the window, but he didn't take time to crawl out. He jumped, and took glass and sash and everything with him." She picked up the gold coin. "Satisfied?"

"I will be when you tell me who the man was that asked for him."

"Dunno. He never said, and I never asked."

"What'd he look like?"

"Young. Eighteen, nineteen maybe. Only thing I noticed was his eyes. Too much white in 'em."

Bosco! So King had sent him after Devlin. But, having failed this time, would Bosco follow the stage, or return to Layton City for more help? Bess shook her head, unable to guess.

"What did he do after he went out through the window?"

"He never stayed around to tell me. Devlin shot at him, but there was no blood on the snow, so I guess he missed."

Bess turned to go, knowing there was nothing more to be gained by staying. The woman said in a bitter voice: "He won't marry you. He'll get into bed with you, because you're younger'n me, and you'll get knocked up and he'll go off with the next hussy he meets. They're all alike. In another ten years you'll be like me."

Bess guessed what had happened. She saw the misery in the woman's face and felt pity for her. Bess knew what the woman's life story was without having heard a word of it. She had seen too many cases like this. Then the pity left her. The woman had brought her trouble on herself. She was weak, and there was nothing ahead for her except tragedy.

"No," Bess said, "I'll never be like you."

She left the house and rode south, but again she was too far behind Devlin, and did not reach Craig that night. She stayed at a ranch and went on in the morning, but the Meeker stage had left before Bess got to Craig. She inquired at the hotel and found that Devlin had stayed the night there.

She still couldn't decide what Bosco would do. If he had returned to Layton City, and King had sent another man, or maybe two, back with Bosco, it seemed unlikely that, even with hard riding, they could reach Meeker ahead of the stage. She was tired, and so was the buckskin, Nero. She'd stay here tonight and leave early in the morning. With any luck she'd beat the King men to Meeker.

But she hit more snow on the high ridges than she expected, and it was fully dark before she got into Meeker. She rode through the archway of the livery stable and wearily dismounted. Then the weariness was gone and every nerve was alert. Three men were standing in the back door, arguing. One of them had a voice she could not mistake. It was the cracked, old-man tone of Doc Darby, one of his greatest assets when he found a sucker who appeared gullible enough to bite on one of his con games.

Quickly she led Nero into an empty stall and busied herself with the cinch, as the three men walked past her in the runway. It was too dark in the stall for them to recognize her, so she glanced at them as they went by.

In the smoky light from a lantern, hanging overhead, she recognized Bosco and Jeeter with Doc Darby. Bosco's face was slashed by innumerable cuts and scratches, and one eye was almost swollen shut. He'd have done better, she thought, to have crawled out of Devlin's room the way he'd got in.

"I'm tired and I'm cold," Jeeter was saying. "He ain't going nowhere tonight. I aim to get a drink and some supper. Then we'll get him."

"I say get him now," Bosco said angrily. "I ain't gonna sleep till that son-of-a-bitch is filled with lead."

"You won't have to stay awake long," Doc Darby said. "Bill's got the right notion. We know Devlin's traveling on the stage, and the stage don't leave till morning. Until the Combs woman shows up with his horse, he's got to keep on riding the stage."

"He could buy a horse," Bosco argued. "You went to the hotel and found out he's registered, and he was in the dining room, getting supper. So he's still here, but, by God, you don't know he's gonna be here in another hour."

They stopped in the archway, Bosco so

angry he was trembling. Doc Darby and Jeeter faced him, tolerant and amused. Darby said: "Keno told me to run this little party, sonny, and that's what I'm aiming to do. I say we'll go get a drink and supper, and then we'll nab him. I'm tired of arguing about it. You had your chance to nail him, and all you did was to take a dive through a window. Now let a man tell you how to play it."

They went on through the archway into the darkness, Bosco still grumbling. The stableman had been watering their horses at a trough behind the barn. Now he led the horses in and began stripping gear from them. Bess ran to him, saying: "I left my horse in that empty stall. Feed him and water him. Right now." When the man didn't move, she cried: "Right now. *Pronto!*"

He peered at her in the lantern light. "A woman, by grab. Now why ain't you wearing a dress, ma'am?"

She held up a gold piece for him to see. "My husband will be coming for the horse in a few minutes. Get him watered and give him a double bait of oats. Quick, so the horse will have time to eat."

He reached for the money. "Sure, ma'am. Right away."

"You'll get the money when my husband

comes for the horse. Don't let anyone else have him. The name's Devlin. You understand? Dane Devlin."

The stableman cackled. "*Aw,* you're devlin' me."

"Dane Devlin," Bess repeated, irritated by the man's bad joke. "If you let anyone else have that horse, I'll cut your heart out."

She whirled and ran along the runway and into the street, the stableman staring after her. "By grab," he muttered, "I believe she'd do it." Then he walked to the stall that held Nero.

The hotel wasn't far from the stable. Bess ran, hoping she wouldn't meet Doc Darby and the others. She didn't think she would; they were probably in the saloon by now. The greatest danger, she decided, was that Devlin would leave the hotel and take a turn around the block and, feeling the need for a drink, wander into the same saloon the King men were in.

When she reached the hotel, she glanced into the dining room. Devlin wasn't there. She went to the desk, saying: "I'm to meet my husband in his room. He came in on the stage. His name's Dane Devlin. Will you tell me the number of his room?"

The clerk was a goat-bearded man in his sixties, a bachelor who was virtuous because of his inability to be anything else. He stared disapprovingly at her and suspected the worst. "Mister Devlin said nothing about his wife," the clerk intoned in a sanctimonious voice. "And I might add that we do not favor women wearing men's. . . ."

Bess reached across the desk and, grabbing the clerk's nose between her thumb and forefinger, squeezed. "Mister," she said, "I'll wear what I damn' please, and I didn't fetch my marriage license with me. Now which room is he in?"

She released her grip. The clerk bent his head, tears flowing down his cheeks. "Ten," he choked.

"Is he in it?"

"I think so."

She ran up the stairs and along the hall, found the right number, and knocked. Silence. Then she heard a gun being cocked, and Devlin's voice. "Who is it?"

"Bess Combs."

The lock turned and the door swung open. She slipped into the room, motioned for him to close and lock the door. He looked at her, surprised.

"I didn't expect. . . ."

"I'm sure you didn't," she said, "and we haven't got time to discuss the pleasure my presence brings you. Doc Darby, Bill Jeeter, and Bosco are in town."

He backed away from the door, his hand going automatically to the butt of his gun. "Three of 'em this time," he said.

"I stopped at the roadhouse on the other side of Craig," she said, "and talked to that bitchy woman. It was Bosco who took the window out." She smiled. "I had a look at his face just now. He cut it all to hell."

Dane started toward the door.

She caught his arm. "Hold it. You're not going to turn the town upside down hunting them. You're going to keep running, and I'm going to pin 'em down right here."

"The hell you are."

"You bet I am. We've got a little time, so you're going to listen. I rode Nero pretty hard today, but I told the stableman to water him and give him a double bait of oats, so he'll take you some more after he's rested. I'll catch the stage in the morning. I told the stableman and the clerk downstairs you were my husband, so you won't have any trouble getting the horse. The clerk won't fetch the sheriff because we're in the same room, either." She laughed shortly. "But the old booger wasn't sure he believed me."

She walked to the window and looked out. A spindly cottonwood grew alongside the hotel, close enough so a man could grab a branch and safely drop to the ground. She turned.

"This place got a back stairs?"

Dane nodded. "But I'm not aiming to take it."

"You'll take it, if necessary. Or you'll go through this window. You're not going to get yourself shot to pieces fighting three of 'em or maybe more. I don't know how many are in town. I've gotten you this far, and I don't aim to lose you. I'll stay in this room and they'll think they've got you cornered, so you'll have all night to ride."

He stared at her resentfully. "You saved my hide in Layton City and I made a deal with you, but that doesn't mean I'm going to keep running just because. . . ."

"You're working for me, Devlin, and that means you're taking my orders," she cut in. "Now listen carefully. Ride south from here, and don't wait for me at Grand Junction. Go up the Gunnison. At Delta you take up the Uncompahgre. When you get to Montrose, you go over the divide to the San Miguel River, and from there to Red Rock Mesa. Last summer my husband was lynched by a rancher named Sherman Rawls, but Rawls wasn't alone. That's why I hired you. Your job is to find out who helped him. It might have been some of his crew, maybe some of his neighbors. I don't know. But before I'm done, I'll see to it that every one of the sons-of-bitches that strung up Billy Combs cashes in his chips."

He listened, nodding as she talked. He said: "I'm no detective. How do you expect me to find out what you want me to?"

"I can't because I'm too well known," she said. "A woman like me gets a reputation fast in a country like that, where folks visit around and gossip all the time. Billy worked for Rawls a little over two years ago. Rawls caught him talking to his wife, who's just a kid. Rawls is about fifty. He fired Billy and told him never to come back, but Billy got into a jam and we had to hide out. He knew about a shack on Disappointment Creek that was deserted. Nobody ever goes down there but some sheepherders, and we'd have been all right if we'd stayed there. But we ran out of grub and I went to the store. Billy rode toward Rawls's ranch, saying that if he ran into the old booger, he'd kill him. Maybe he found a couple of horses he liked. I'm not sure, but that's how Rawls tells it. He claims he hanged a horse thief. Anyhow, when Billy didn't show up at the store, I took a *pasear* across the mesa and ran into Rawls. Billy was hanging from a limb. I tried to quirt Rawls, but he's big and strong, and he yanked the quirt out of my hand. I told him I'd see him and anybody who helped him dead, so he knows what's coming."

"You still didn't tell me how I'll go about it," Dane said. "A stranger can't just ride. . . ."

"Sure you can," she said. "Rawls is an ornery booger. He's got a big outfit, but he can't keep help. You won't have any trouble catching on with him. He's the pious kind who thinks God is his cousin. He'll talk about Billy's hanging, but it'll take some doing on your part to find out who helped him. I'll buy a horse in Montrose when I get there and ride to Red Rock. I'll go to the cabin me 'n' Billy had. I'll want to see you in a week or two and hear how you made out."

She handed him a folded piece of paper. "I drew a map so you can find the cabin. It's stone, built along the creek, and up against the south wall of the cañon right under the slick rock rim. You won't see it unless you look close, but there's a corral downstream from the cabin. You'll spot that easy enough. Now there's one thing about Rawls. Remember it the first time you see him. One side of his face is scarred from an old burn. Billy says he was touchy as hell about it. Don't let on you notice it, or he'll never hire you. Stay away from his wife, too. And don't let his praying and Bible spouting fool you. He's a genuwine, twelve-carat bastard."

Dane picked up his sheepskin and slipped it on. He grabbed his war sack, put on his hat, and started toward the door. He said: "If I'm riding out of town, it's time I was starting. They'll have me nailed down here, if I don't."

"Wait."

She grabbed an arm and held him, her dark eyes searching his face gravely. She didn't fully understand her own feelings. She had never worried about any man before except Billy, but she was worried about Dane Devlin. She kissed him quickly, then unlocked the door.

"I'll take a look," she said. "Be careful, Devlin. I've got five hundred dollars invested in you, and a dead man is as bad an investment as a dead horse."

She opened the door and looked up and down the hall. If the King men had taken time to eat, Devlin should have another half hour. Once they cornered her in the room, she could play it out all night with them. The danger was that they'd learn Devlin had hightailed out of town on the horse she

158

had ridden. If that happened, they'd be on his trail, and Devlin would be in trouble. Nero was in no shape to make a hard run.

"I don't see anyone," she said. "Good luck."

He nodded, and stepped past her. He had taken three steps when the King men came into view on the stairs, Bosco in the lead, his revolver in his hand. The kid let out a yell as Dane went for his gun. He got in two shots before Dane could squeeze off one, and missed them both.

Dane's bullet caught Bosco in the chest, knocking him off his feet and throwing him back against Jeeter and Darby. He must have been killed instantly, for he flung out his arms and dropped his gun, his knees turning to rubber. He fell like a dropped rag doll, his slack weight going against Jeeter and knocking him against Darby. The three of them sprawled in a crazy tangle of arms and legs halfway down the stairs. Darby rolled to the bottom before he could stop.

Dane could have followed it up and finished it right there, but Bess caught his arm, dragged him back into the room, and turned the lock. "Get out through that window. There's a big limb you can grab. Light out for the stable and ride."

"I'm not going to run and let you fight."

159

"I'm not going to fight, but I want you out of town. I don't know how many of the bunch are here. Go on." He hesitated, and she said angrily: "Damn it, I'm giving the orders. Can't you get it through your head? They won't hurt me, but, if the whole outfit's in town, they'll fry your hide. There are too many of them."

He obeyed then. She watched until he was on the ground and running toward the stable. Then she closed the window and, taking her gun out of her handbag, moved away from the door and waited, smiling in anticipation.

VIII

Dane followed the route Bess had laid out for him — down the Grand to its juncture with the Gunnison, up the Gunnison to Delta where the Uncompahgre emptied into it, then up the Uncompahgre to Montrose, and over the Uncompahgre Plateau to the San Miguel. He forded the latter, found a break in the steep south wall, and climbed to the mesa.

He had not seen or heard anything of the King men from the time he had left Meeker. The weather had remained clear and cold, with no more snow. Now, riding across the rolling plain that was Red Rock Mesa, the thought struck Dane that here was a land where a man could settle down for the rest of his life and never feel the itch in his feet again. At one time or another Dane had seen most of the Rocky Mountain country and a good deal of the plains, but he'd never been in the southwestern corner of Colorado before. Now a strange and exciting sensation took hold of him, a feeling that he had looked at this same scene before, although he knew he had never been here. Perhaps he had dreamed it, a dream so real that he could not distinguish it in his mind from experiences he'd actually had.

Behind him the Uncompahgre Plateau humped up against the sky in a long, almost level line. Eastward the peaks of the San Juan range looked like the uptilted teeth of a giant saw, covered with white frosting. To the west the great clump of mountains on the Utah-Colorado line would be the La Sal range. He had heard enough about the country to recognize these landmarks, but he knew none of the names of the ridges and cañons that lay to the south, or the name of the single, sharp-pointed mountain that rose above the ridges like a tremendous inverted cone. Cedars were scattered over the mesa, with dark patches of piñons on

161

the slopes to the south. The grass was good, the range showing no indication of being overgrazed. There was no sign, either, of the scars of nesters' plows. Scattered across the mesa were ranch buildings, none pretentious, and none set closely together. All of the ranchers, he thought, had elbow room.

He came to an east-west road and turned west along it, his gaze ranging over the open country in front of him. Here was a land of small spreads, with none of the cowmen making fortunes and none living in poverty, either. All were close enough to the mountains to have ample summer range. He had a feeling that here was a country where men lived in peace and harmony, and he found it hard to believe that Sherman Rawls, as Bess described him, would be permitted to stay.

He laughed at himself over that, realizing it was crazy thinking. You couldn't just ride onto a new range and look at the trees and grass and houses, and think that men lived in peace simply because they had elbow room. There would be all kinds of tugging and hauling between the men who lived here, conflicts brought on by jealousy and greed and hate. Blood could be shed over water. Men could fight over a poker game and be killed, just as he had killed Curly

Heston in Layton City. Yes, and men could be hanged for stealing horses here as well as anywhere else.

The thought had nagged at the back of his mind, and it returned now, that Sherman Rawls might well have been within his rights when he'd strung up Billy Combs, that Bess's compulsive desire for revenge had no basis in justice. But it was not a thought he allowed himself to dwell upon. He was committed.

In midafternoon he came to a settlement that must be Red Rock. A store was on the south side of the road, a gnawed and weathered hitch pole in front, a log house, shed, and corral behind it. A church and schoolhouse, with a teacher's house beside it, were on the north side. A long shed filled with the children's ponies stood in the back of the schoolyard. School, then, was still in session.

He dismounted, tied, and went into the store. Again he was made uneasy by the feeling that he had been here before. A potbellied stove in the back glowed cherry red. A pine board set on upended barrels on one side of the room was the bar; the shelves behind it were filled with an assortment of bottles. The store on the other side of the room had a second pine plank for a counter. Barrels and piled-up sacks of food were scattered around the stove and in the back of the room.

This time he was able to identify the reason for feeling he had seen the place. He had been in many cow-country stores and saloons that varied little in appearance from this one. Usually at considerable distance from a railroad, they were stocked largely with staples, and could not afford much variety. Prices were invariably high, to cover costs plus freight charges. Usually there was little cash in the cattle country, so storekeepers took in hides or furs or perhaps a steer calf to pay part of the bill. Probably this storekeeper was no different.

Dane walked to the stove and held his hands out over it, vaguely bothered by this sensation of familiarity. It was almost as if he had come home. But that was impossible for a man who had no home. He hadn't had one for thirteen years. If this were a time when he could settle down, if he had the money to buy a ranch, this would be the place where he'd want to live. But if he succeeded in doing what Bess Combs had hired him to do, he wouldn't be staying long.

A tall, bearded man came out of the back room. He said courteously: "What can I do for you?"

"I need a drink," Dane said. "This stove is getting me warm on the outside, but I'm not warming up on the inside."

"We'll take care of that," the man said. "Whiskey?"

Dane nodded, and the man crossed to the bar, poured a drink, and brought it to Dane. He was about forty, Dane judged, although he looked older and could have been well toward fifty. His brown beard was cut squarely across the bottom, and Dane noted that he was actually taller than he appeared. His shoulders were stooped; he moved slowly and deliberately as if he were unable to gather enough energy to move in any other manner.

Dane held out his hand. "I'm Dane Devlin," he said. "I'm looking for a job."

"Fred Ashton." The man's grip was firm, and his eyes met Dane's squarely. Then he walked past Dane and sat down on a sack of oats. "Ain't any work in this country that I know of. If I were you, I'd keep on moving."

Dane finished his drink, slipped off his sheepskin, and, finding a box, brought it to the stove and sat on it. "Looked like good cow country to me. Ought to be work hereabouts."

"It is good cow country," Ashton said. "The best I ever seen. Winters are purty hard sometimes, and they don't save all their calves, but the ones that live are strong and healthy. But the thing is, the outfits are small. The men do their own work, with the help of their sons . . . which most of 'em have . . . so there ain't much chance for an outsider to find a job."

"My bad luck, I guess," Dane said.

Ashton's eyes were fixed on Dane as if measuring him for some purpose of his own. He seemed to be a kindly man, and Dane thought the storekeeper would help if he could. He was sure of that even before Ashton said: "I raise horses and I've got a few to break. Trouble is, right now I'm short of cash, so I couldn't pay you. All I could do is to give you board and room. But we've got a houseful of kids, and my wife is the worst cook in Colorado. I don't believe you'd like it."

A forthright man, Dane thought. Suppose he had helped hang Billy Combs? In a few weeks Dane might have to tell Bess that Fred Ashton was one of the men she wanted. Dane might have to kill him, just as he was committed to kill Sherman Rawls.

He glanced away, troubled. "Thanks. I'll keep that in mind. It'll be better'n nothing."

He got up, rubbing his hands up and down on his pants legs. "I haven't had anything to eat since morning. Give me a can of sardines, some crackers, a can of peaches. And how about some cheese?"

"I've got some," Ashton said, "but it's getting pretty ripe."

"I like it that way," Dane said.

Ashton brought the food to him. Dane paid him for it and the drink, and, sitting down, began to eat. He said, his mouth full: "I've heard about a Rocking R outfit, owned by a man named Sherman Rawls. Thought I'd try him."

Ashton was sitting on the oat sack again. He was starting to fill his pipe, but now he stopped, his questioning eyes on Dane. Finally he said: "He's got the only big outfit on the mesa. Chances are he'll give you a job, but, if I were you, I wouldn't take it."

"Why not? A job's a job."

"No," Ashton said. "A job ain't a job. Each one's different. I know Sherm well. He's a friend of mine, buys all his supplies from me. He takes three, four of my horses every spring. He's an honest man. I never knew him to fail to pay a debt. He goes to church every Sunday morning and Sunday night. He leads the singing. He's got a good bass voice. Don't misunderstand me now and think I'm talking against Sherm. I just don't think you'd enjoy working for him."

Dane finished his cheese. It had a good bite to it and he liked it. He picked up the can of peaches and opened it with his pocket knife. He said casually: "I don't savvy. Rawls sounds like a good citizen."

"He is," Ashton said quickly, "but he's a mite hard to work for. He's got some old hands who have been with him for years. They're used to him, so they overlook his peculiarities, but every time some young fellow rides into the country and signs on with him, they wind up having a fight."

He packed the tobacco into the bowl of the pipe and fished into his vest for a match. Dane waited until he had struck the match. Then he said: "Like Billy Combs?"

Ashton jumped as sharply as if he'd been burned by the flame. He dropped the match, then stepped on it, his face turning gray. He got up and walked across the room, his shoulders sagging more than ever. Dane, staring at his back, told himself that here was a guilty man if he'd ever seen one.

Ashton fumbled with some cans on a shelf, making a great pretense of being busy. Presently he asked: "How'd you hear about Combs?"

"Stories like that get around," Dane said.

"I worked all summer for the M Bar on the Little Snake River. A woman was telling about it. Combs's widow, I think she was."

"I see." Ashton had regained control of himself and returned to the stove. "There was some talk about Combs's hanging. Personally I don't know anything about it, but, if Sherm did string him up, he had good reason. We're a long way from the county seat, and the sheriff don't pay no attention to us. So if we have any law, it's law that we enforce ourselves."

"Well, I'm a law-abiding man," Dane said. "I ought to get along with Rawls. How do I get to the Rocking R?"

"If you're bound to try, ride west on the road you came in on," Ashton said. "It ain't far from here. It's the last spread on the west end of the mesa."

"Won't hurt to try," Dane said, and rose.

A slatternly-looking woman came in through the back door, leading a child with each hand. They were about two and three years old, Dane judged, both boys. The small one was rubbing his eyes with both hands, the other had his mouth set in a defiant line. Both were dirty and had runny noses.

"You've got to look after these little bastards," the woman said shrilly. She brushed a stray lock of gray hair from her forehead. "I'm going to beat their heads in if they don't quit waking the babies up."

"All right, Martha," Ashton said. "I'll look after them."

The woman left, apparently not even aware that Dane was sitting there. Ashton looked apologetically at Dane as the bigger boy headed for the pickle barrel. "Let 'em alone, Percy!" Ashton bellowed. "The last time you got into the pickles you were sick all night." He looked at Dane again and shook his head. "Hog dang it, Devlin, raising kids is a full-time job. That's why I ain't got them horses broke."

"If I don't catch on with Rawls," Dane said, "I'll be back and give you a hand."

He left the store, untied Nero, and stepped into the saddle. Every man had his problems, Dane thought, but it did seem that Fred Ashton had more than his share.

IX

As Dane turned into the road, the school-house exploded with children, yelling and pushing as they raced toward the shed that held their ponies. A moment later two boys roared past Dane, kicking their horses as hard as they could, yelling insults at each other about forking a slow-footed nag that wasn't fit for wolf bait and couldn't outrun a snail.

A third boy followed, yelling that both of them were riding horses that ought to be pulling a plow. He was younger than the other two, nine or ten, Dane guessed. He passed Dane, then glanced back, and, seeing he was a stranger, pulled up until Dane caught up with him.

"Howdy," the boy said. "I'm Toby Miles."

"I'm Dane Devlin."

Toby reached out and gravely shook hands. "Them's my brothers that went past like they was chasin' jack rabbits. Pod's the oldest one. He's thirteen. Hec's only eleven. I'm ten, and most of the time I can lick Hec, but Pod's too big."

"Give yourself a few years," Dane said.

He liked the boy. He had dark eyes as sharp as a chipmunk's, a nubbin of a nose, and more freckles than three boys should have. His hair was so curly that it was almost kinky, and it looked as if it hadn't felt a comb for months.

Toby's eyes frankly appraised Dane, resting for a moment on the .45 at his hip. Then he looked away. "Yeah, Ma tells me that all the time, but it's sure hell while you're growing up. The only thing wrong with my

171

life is that I'm too damned young."

Dane grinned, his liking for the boy growing. He said: "You can't do much about time. Just wait and it'll take care of itself."

The boy wasn't listening. He was watching his brothers, who had turned off the road to follow twin tracks through the grass. He said: "Pa'll larrup 'em if he catches 'em riding home that way. He gives it to 'em 'bout three times a week, but he can't break 'em. Can't break us kids of nuthin', he says to Ma." He glanced at Dane again, and asked: "New hereabouts, ain't you?"

"Just rode in," Dane said. "I'm looking for a job. Reckon your pa would have anything for me?"

"Hell no," Toby said. "We don't have enough work to keep us kids and Pa busy. Pa rides for Sherman Rawls during roundup, and helps him hay. He makes enough to keep us eatin', and that's about all."

"Doesn't your pa own an outfit?" Dane asked.

"Outfit?" Toby snickered. "Sure, the JM. It's the right size to spit across when the wind ain't blowing."

"I've heard of this Sherman Rawls," Dane said. "I thought I'd ask him for a job."

"Don't you do it!" Toby yelled. "He'll give

you one, and you'll wish you hadn't taken it."

"Why?"

"*Aw*, he's a mean bastard. Ugly as Old Scratch himself, Ma says. Us kids call him Scarface, but not to his face. We don't bother him none. That's one thing Pa did break us of."

"His being ugly hasn't got anything to do with my working for him," Dane said.

"Naw, that ain't it. Old Sherm's good enough most of the time. He goes to church and don't cuss and don't drink and all that, but he gets mad sometimes, and, when he does, he's like as not to pick up a club and beat your head in." He glanced at Dane, suddenly uneasy, as if realizing he had talked too much. "So long," he said, and struck off across the grass before he came to the side road that led to the JM.

Dane reached the Rocking R a few minutes later. No one was in sight, but smoke lifted from the chimney of the stone house. Someone was cutting wood behind the house, but Dane couldn't see who it was. He was not surprised by what he saw — the size of the buildings, the number of corrals, the general appearance the layout had of being well kept.

He thought about it for a minute and

decided this was exactly what he had expected to see, hearing what he had of Sherman Rawls. The man had built with an eye for utility and permanence. Nowhere was there any sign that a woman lived here, unless it was the row of frost-killed hollyhocks along the front of the house.

Dane tied and walked around the house. Then he was surprised. A woman was chopping wood. She didn't see or hear Dane as he walked toward her. When he was close, he saw she was a girl, probably not more than eighteen, so thin she looked frail. She wore a faded gingham dress that was loose and ill-fitting, and a heavy sweater, too big for her, that had gaping holes in both elbows.

A pile of piñon logs lay on the other side of the bucksaw. She was trying to split the only block that had been sawed off, but it was a twisted grain and was tough. She wasn't getting anywhere with the heavy, double-bitted axe, her blows being little more than pecks.

"I'll give you a hand, ma'am," Dane said.

She cried out and jumped, and looked around. She dropped the axe and backed away, as frightened as a surprised doe. She tensed as if about to streak for the house.

Dane said quietly: "I'm sorry, ma'am. I

didn't mean to scare you. I thought you saw me, but I should have known better."

"I'll do it," she said, and stooped to get the axe.

Dane picked it up, saying sharply: "This is no chore for a woman. I'll take care of it."

She shivered, a brightness in her cheeks from the cold. She would have been a good-looking girl with a little more flesh on her bones. Her features were regular, her eyes dark blue, her hair a rich gold that could have been attractive if she had given it some attention.

"No, I've got to do it," she said. "Sherm says this kind of work is good for me."

"Sherm?"

"Sherman Rawls. He's my husband. He owns this ranch. I guess you're a stranger, so you wouldn't know anything about him."

Dane split the block of piñon, cut each half into pieces small enough to fit the firebox of a kitchen range, then picked up the bucksaw. He wasn't just a mean bastard, as Toby Miles had called him. He was also a fool to treat a girl this way, wife or no wife.

"Why does he figure work like this is good for you?" Dane asked. "Looks like a big house. That ought to keep you busy."

"I'm busy, all right," she said. "But Sherm says that all women are evil, like Eve was in the Bible. It's having children and working hard that purifies them. I haven't had children, so I've got to work hard if I'm going to be saved."

Dane sawed another chunk of piñon off the end of the log, wondering if he could stand working for a man like Sherman Rawls. He split the chunk, and the girl said uneasily: "That's enough. I'll take it in."

"I'll help you."

"No. If you're here to see Sherm, go on out to the bunkhouse and wait for him. He'll be home pretty soon."

She filled her arms with wood and rose as he said: "Do you suppose he'll give me a job?"

"A job?" She stared at him, her lips parted, her eyes wide and unblinking. "He'll give you a job, all right, but don't ask him. Please don't ask him."

Whirling, she ran into the house with the wood.

Dane stared after her until she slammed the door. Then he stuck the axe into the chopping block and walked around the house to his horse. This was the damnedest deal he'd ever got into. Maybe Sherman Rawls, too, would say he'd give Dane a job, then advise him not to take it.

Dane watered his horse, stripped gear

from him, and put him into the corral. The sun was down now, burying itself into a nest of wicked-looking clouds above the western mountains. Dane had started for the bunkhouse to get out of the cold, when he heard a rider coming in from the north.

He waited by the corral gate, wondering if this was Sherman Rawls. But it wasn't. He was sure of that even in the thinning dusk light, when the man reined up. This was an old man, and the years had plowed deep furrows into his weathered face. When he stepped down, he moved slowly and carefully, as if rheumatism was a constant pain in his joints.

Dane held out his hand. "I'm Dane Devlin. I'm waiting to see Sherman Rawls."

"Lucky Fargo," the old man said. "Sherm ought to be along purty soon. Him and Banjo Quail was riding the south rim today. It's quite a piece of riding, but, if he didn't hit no trouble, he'll be in come dark."

Dane waited until Fargo took care of his horse, then walked beside him to the bunkhouse, the old cowboy putting a hand to the small of his back and walking bent forward as if he couldn't quite straighten up.

"Hod dang it," Fargo said. "It's sure cold. Gets into a man's bones and eats out the marrow. Got a notion to light out for south Texas, where it don't ever get like this." Then he laughed. "I can fool myself, but I don't take you for a big enough fool to believe what I just said."

He lighted a lamp on the rickety table in the middle of the bunkhouse, then glanced at the wood box beside the potbellied stove. He said: "Just a few splinters there. Ain't enough to keep a fire going. Mind fetching in some wood while I start the fire?"

Dane said — "Sure." — and wondered if supplying the bunkhouse with wood was part of Rawls's wife's duties. He worked fast, splitting some more wood, and leaving a small pile for Mrs. Rawls to use in the morning. He carried an armload into the bunkhouse and found Fargo huddled over the stove, massaging his hands.

"That'll keep us going tonight," Fargo said. "We won't need a fire in the morning. We'll roll out with our teeth clacking, get dressed, have breakfast, and saddle up. The saddle blankets will be cold. That'll make our horses proddy. Chances are I'll get bucked off and break my neck, which same will be a good thing for all concerned."

Dane filled the stove with wood, then said: "Rawls must be a hard customer. His wife tells me she has to cut the wood for the house."

Fargo shot him a quick glance. "You talked to his wife?"

Dane nodded. "She was trying to split a tough chunk of piñon when I rode up. I helped her, but she didn't want no help. Seems that Rawls claims it takes hard work to purify a woman of her evil ways."

"Yeah, that's what he says." Fargo pulled up a rawhide-bottom chair and sat down. "You heading south, cowboy?"

"I was heading right here," Dane said. "I'm going to hit Rawls up for a job."

"By golly, another one," Fargo said in disgust. "I was afraid of that. Bucko, if I were you, I'd just ride on in the morning and say nothing to Rawls about a job."

"What's the matter with Rawls?" Dane asked. "I stopped at the store and a fellow named Ashton, who claimed he was Rawls's friend, told me not to work for him. I rode for a spell with a kid named Toby Miles, who said not to. Rawls's wife said not to even ask him for a job. Now you're saying the same thing."

Fargo took a foul-smelling pipe from his pocket, filled it with tobacco, and lit it, then leaned back, his legs extended toward the fire. "A funny gent, Sherm is. He's a good man in most ways. He's so honest he wouldn't even cheat you in a horse trade. He goes to church, don't cuss or drink. But he's hard-headed as hell on some things. Nobody can change him. If you work for him, you've got to take him the way he is. Sometimes it ain't easy to do that. He does things he's sorry 'bout afterward, but it's too late then." Fargo tamped the tobacco down into the bowl. Then he said: "If you're bound to try it, remember two things. Don't have nothing to do with his wife. The other thing is, don't pay no mind to one side of his face that's all scarred up." He took the pipe out of his mouth and stared at it. "The thing is, he was the first man to run any cattle in this country. Whatever law we ever had was his law. It still is. A man that steals a horse or steer from anybody who lives on the mesa is mighty likely to get his neck stretched. Outlaws know that, so they mostly keep going."

The sound of horses coming in across the grass reached them, and Fargo rose. "That's him. Might as well go see what he says."

X

The darkness was relieved only by the stars and a thin moon in the east. Rawls and the rider with him had reached the corral by the time Dane and Fargo crossed the yard. As Rawls dismounted, Fargo said: "Sherm, here's a cowhand named Devlin who wants a job. Figure you can use him?"

"I can use a good man," Rawls said. "You a good man, Devlin?"

"Sure I am," Dane said. "You don't think I'd say anything else, do you?"

Rawls laughed. "No, can't say I expected you to. We'll go into the house and I'll take a look at you. Banjo, put my horse up. Supper's about ready. Ought to be, anyhow. Lucky, blow the lamp out in the bunkhouse and come in."

Dane walked beside Rawls to the back door of the big house, having to extend himself to keep up with the cowman's leggy stride. Dane couldn't make out anything definite about him in the darkness, but he did get the impression of tremendous size and strength.

He thought about this in the few seconds it took to cross the yard to the kitchen door. Size didn't always mean strength. Dane had met many big men who were weak. On the other hand, he had known a few men who were both big and strong, not simply in physical strength, but something more, an intangible thing that might be called power of will. He had a feeling that Rawls possessed such a quality. This notion might have had its origin in what he had heard about the man, but he thought it was more than that, a force that flowed out of Rawls to touch those around him.

They reached the porch and Rawls opened the back door, calling: "Nancy, put on another plate!" He stood so that Dane could see only the right side of his face. It was a strong face, Dane thought, and a stern one, with thin lips, a sharp-pointed nose, and a powerful jaw.

Rawls was about fifty, Dane judged, but the years had not taken the toll they did from most men his age. He was as big and strong as Dane had sensed as they had walked through the darkness. He'd work a man half his age into the ground and walk off, leaving him to claw his way out.

A small smile curled the right corner of Rawls's mouth as he motioned toward the pump near the west wall of the kitchen. "Wash up, Devlin. Looks like supper's about ready."

His tone was pleasant, even amiable, but Dane had the impression that Rawls was like a huge, silent dog, slipping along behind you. When you were off your guard, he'd take a bite out of the calf of your leg.

Dane nodded and, going to the pump, filled a pan with water and washed his face and hands. He felt for the towel, found it, and dried. When he opened his eyes, Rawls had turned so that Dane was looking at the left side of his face, his eyes on Dane as if waiting for his reaction.

For a horrible moment Dane thought he was looking at a man who had just put on a terrifying Halloween mask, but he remembered what Bess Combs and Lucky Fargo had told him. Quickly Dane turned to a mirror on the wall, found a comb, and ran it through his hair, certain he had not let his face betray the sick horror he had felt when he looked at Rawls's scar. He might have imagined it, but he thought Rawls was disappointed.

Dane turned away from the mirror as Rawls pumped a pan of water and washed. Even when he wasn't looking at the big man, Dane could still see in his mind the left side of Rawls's face. The skin was red, as if it had been literally fried, the scar reaching from his temple down to his chin, covering the entire cheek and extending part of the way around his neck. It curled the left corner of his mouth down into what looked like a permanent grimace, and even the muscles around the end of his left eye were pulled downward.

Dane moved to the table and stood waiting until Rawls finished drying his hands and face. He had a haunting feeling of having seen two men, one pleasant and human, the other a terrifying creature from an unknown world of total darkness. From what he had heard about Sherman Rawls, Dane had a disturbing thought that the rancher in reality was two men — one the good neighbor who went to church and dealt honorably with his friends, the other the jealous and vengeful part-man, part-animal who had a capacity for terrible violence. It was the latter who had hanged Billy Combs.

Rawls motioned to a chair. "Sit down, Devlin. Banjo will be in before long."

Lucky Fargo was washing at the pump and a moment later came to the table. Nancy brought a plate of gold-brown biscuits to the table, then forked steaks from the frying pan onto a platter, and handed the platter to Rawls. She poured coffee, brought a bowl of beans, and then stood between the stove and the table watching the men to see if any of them wanted something that wasn't on the table.

The kitchen was clean, the floor recently scrubbed. The food was perfect, the biscuits light, the steak tender, and Dane could not keep from comparing the meal to the one he had eaten in the roadhouse south of Layton City. Rawls ate with wolfish hunger, helping himself, and then passing the food to Dane. His attention was fixed on his food; he ignored Dane, so Dane had the feeling he had passed his test and Rawls was satisfied with him.

Banjo Quail walked in a few minutes later, washed at the pump, and came to the table, his gaze furtively going to Nancy. After that his eyes were fixed on his plate. Rawls ignored him, Nancy poured his coffee, and Dane and Fargo passed the food to him He was about Nancy's age, Dane thought, or maybe a year older, a slight, good-looking boy who was striving for maturity with a mustache that was little more than a dirty smudge across his upper lip.

Rawls cut the dried apple pie that was on the table, took a quarter and ate it, then sat back in his chair, thumbs poked through the armholes of his vest. He asked: "Where did you work last, Devlin?"

"On the Little Snake," Dane said. "The M Bar."

Rawls nodded. "I know the outfit. Why did you quit?"

"I didn't quit," Dane said. "They didn't

need me after roundup, so they let me go. I saved my money, but, like a fool, I got into a poker game in Layton City. Ever hear of a man named Keno King?" Rawls shook his head. "He's a gambler. He moves into towns like Layton City after roundup and harvests a good crop of suckers, including me. I lost my money, and I've been looking for a job ever since. I heard you might need a man, so I came here."

"How'd you hear?"

"I don't remember." Dane frowned. This was not a question he had expected. "Montrose, I think it was. I hadn't intended to come this far south, but I didn't hit anything around Delta or Montrose, so I kept riding."

Satisfied, Rawls nodded. "I'm a hard man to work for. They say that about me, and I'll admit it's true. But I pay better than average wages, and, if a man ain't lazy, we'll get along. I have men, like Lucky here, who have worked for me for twenty years." He glanced at his wife. "You'd better eat, Nancy." He brought his gaze back to Dane. "I'm a little peculiar in some respects. No cursing if you work for me. I don't mind a hell or a damn, but I forbid any of my men taking the name of our Father or our Savior in vain. No gambling or drinking while you're working on the Rocking R. If you want to spend your Saturday nights or Sundays at Fred Ashton's store, you can do all the gambling and drinking you want to. But don't ride back here while you're drunk." Rawls laughed suddenly. "You admit you were a fool losing your money to Keno King, so I presume you've learned your lesson. Cards are tools of the devil, just as liquor is."

"I learned a lesson, all right," Dane said.

Rawls rose suddenly. "Better roll in. We start work early. Nancy, come to bed. You can do the dishes in the morning."

He turned and, crossing the room, disappeared into a bedroom. Fargo rose, jerked his head at Banjo Quail, and walked to the door. The boy had finished eating, but he hesitated after he stood up, his gaze on Nancy's face, a longing in his eyes that could not be mistaken for anything but what it was, the love of a boy for a girl. Nancy glanced worriedly at the door through which Rawls had gone, and Dane, joining Fargo at the back door, caught the surreptitious gesture she made under the table. With one simple movement of her hand, she told Banjo to go quickly. He obeyed, his bony, adolescent face filled with utter misery.

The three of them crossed to the bunkhouse, the bitter wind that had come up while they were in the kitchen striking them in the face. Banjo said: "Might blow up a snow. Sure been a dry fall."

Fargo was silent until they were in the bunkhouse and he had closed the door and lighted the lamp. He filled the stove, then turned on Banjo, his leathery old face alive with anger. "You fool! You god-damned, chuckle-headed, hair-brained idiot! If I've told you once, I've told you a dozen times, draw your time and go home while you can still ride."

Banjo sat down on his bunk. He glanced at Dane, perhaps wondering if he'd tell Rawls what was said, then looked at Fargo. "I can't do it, Lucky, and you know why."

"I know Rawls will kill you," Fargo said hotly. "You can't do anything for her. Nobody can. She knew what she was doing. She's made her bed, and now she's got to lie in it."

Banjo shook his head. "She didn't know what she was getting into. Neither did her pa, when he made her marry Rawls. All he could think of was that she'd have a big house to live in and enough to eat, and, if Rawls died, she'd inherit the Rocking R. Trouble is, Rawls will live forever. He'll wind up burying Nancy alongside his first two wives."

Fargo jerked a chair up and sat down. "Then, by God, don't even look at her, and don't stop when you're done eating. Sherm was probably watching you through a crack in the door."

Banjo bent forward, his eyes on the floor. He said, after a moment's silence: "I rode over here twice last summer and talked to her. Both times she had big bruises on her face. He'd hit her, Lucky. She wouldn't admit it, but I know that was how she got 'em. I'm going to kill him. I'm going to kill him as sure as he screws her every night."

Fargo threw up his hands in disgust and looked at Dane. "Well, Devlin, you know what you're getting into. Gonna stay?"

"I'm staying."

"Then don't open your mug about what you just heard. Savvy?"

"I'm no gabber," Dane said sharply.

"Good," Fargo said.

Later, lying on his bunk with the lamp out, Dane remembered thinking he would be bothered about coming here and working for a man he was going to kill. But now he wasn't. Even if it hadn't been for the hanging of Billy Combs, Rawls had lived far too long.

XI

They ate breakfast by lamplight, the meal as good as supper had been the night before. Dane knew he wouldn't have a chance to work up any wood today. Nancy would have to wrestle with it herself unless Banjo Quail had a chance to double back to the house and take care of it. If Rawls had any sense, Dane thought, he'd realize he had a jewel in his girl-wife, and would take care of her.

Rawls had had sense — in most things, anyhow. If he hadn't had, he wouldn't have built the Rocking R to the size it was. He wouldn't get along with his neighbors, which apparently he did. Dane pondered this as he ate. Rawls was slowly killing his wife. No woman, not even a strong one, could stand up under the amount of work he was demanding of Nancy. He could afford to hire help for her. Why, then, was he treating her this way? Dane could not find an answer that made sense.

They saddled up in the slowly deepening light. The sky was covered by black clouds, so that full daylight was a long time coming. The wind, whipping in from the west, clawed at them with icy fingers. The La Sal mountains were hidden by low clouds, and

190

even the broken country between them and the mesa.

Rawls glanced at the sky and shook his head. "Ain't had a real storm all fall, but we've got one coming this time."

He gave Dane a leggy sorrel that bucked and let Dane prove he could ride. Rawls's mount was a big gray gelding that was exactly right for him. He gave the other two men orders for the day, Fargo to ride the north rim again, and Banjo Quail to harness up a team and bring in a load of cedar posts from a ridge to the west.

"Soon as I break Devlin in," Rawls said to the boy, "you 'n' me have some fence to build."

He struck off to the south, seeing to it that Dane rode on his right side. He was silent for the good part of an hour, as they angled slightly to the west. They dropped into innumerable arroyos, most of them with small streams in the bottom. A few were dry, but all had rock-and-dirt dams that held back a fair amount of water. Presently Dane figured out what Rawls was doing. He was showing Dane the water holes, but saying nothing about them. Later he would expect Dane to be able to find them.

Presently he reined up and motioned for Dane to stop, the right side of his mouth curving up in one of the few grins he allowed himself. "Can you find them by yourself?"

Dane nodded. "I think so."

"You're a good man," Rawls said. "Too good to ride in here by accident. What are you after, Devlin?"

"Sure, I'm a good man," Dane said. "I ought to have a ranch of my own. I've been kicking around since I was ten years old. I've made a little money now and then, and always wound up blowing it on some damned fool thing. It takes money to get started now. It was different when you came here."

Rawls nodded. "That's right. But you still didn't tell me what you came here for."

"A job," Dane said. "I've scrounged through a few winters when I got mighty hungry. I don't want to have to do it again."

"All right," Rawls said. "I'll take your word, for now. But I'll tell you this. If you're lying, I'll kill you. If you're not, and we get along, there's a future for you here. I need a man like you. My crew is mostly old men like Lucky Fargo, who've been with me for years and are crippled up in one way or another, or they're kids like Quail, who wouldn't know what to do if they found a cow in a bog." Rawls pointed to the west.

"The mesa drops off about two miles from here. That's where our range ends. Beyond that is some broken country that's dry as a bone. A dozen or so families have squatted wherever they could find a little water. It's a mystery to me how they live. Banjo Quail comes from there. He ain't worth much, except for cutting wood or hauling fence posts and such. I keep most of my crew in line cabins along the rim, to see that my cattle don't drift off the mesa. At least that's what we say. Mostly it's to keep people like Quail's folks from stealing me blind, which they'd do if I didn't have riders working the rim all the time." He turned in his saddle and gestured to the south. "Disappointment Creek's off yonder. Nobody lives there except a few sheepmen, who don't bother me. Your job is to check the water and see that it ain't frozen over, which it will be from now on until spring if we don't keep the ice broken. Then circle along the south rim and drive any cows back that you find drifting too near the edge. I'll show you. A day after it turns cold you have to bust the ice."

They rode on, reaching the rim in another half hour. Generally it was a sheer cliff from fifty to more than a hundred feet high, but in a few places it tapered off in a gradual slope. The clouds had broken away to the south, and from the edge of the Rocking R range it seemed that the country stretched on and on forever in a series of cañons and slick rock rims, with now and then a clump of cedars. Off there somewhere was Bess Combs's cabin. She'd be there in a few days and she'd expect to see him, but he wasn't sure he'd be able to find her in a country as rough as this. He had studied the map she'd drawn until he had memorized it, then had destroyed it so there was no possibility Rawls would find it.

The key had been two tall pillars of sandstone. He kept watching, and shortly after noon he saw them, red fingers pointing skyward. They might have been carved out by some prehistoric inhabitants of the country, but he knew of course they weren't. They were the work of the wind, whittling on them from the beginning of time.

Presently Rawls said: "This is the east side of Rocking R range. I claim about a third of the mesa. One way I get along with my neighbors is to keep my cattle off their grass. This is about the only place where they drift enough to worry about. So when you swing north, follow a line from them two tall rocks you see yonder. Mule Ears, we call 'em."

They rode north, now and then throwing

back a few Rocking R steers that had worked too near the line. Once they found two cows carrying the JM brand, and Rawls grunted in anger. "Joe Miles's outfit," said. "He knows better'n that. We'll chase 'em over to him."

It took an hour to deliver the cattle. Miles's buildings consisted of a small log house, a slab shed, a couple of corrals. Dane remembered what the boy Toby had said about the size of his father's ranch. It was strict necessity, Dane thought, that made Joe Miles work for Rawls. He probably jumped every time Rawls whistled. He wasn't in an enviable position at best, located so close to the Rocking R.

Miles was working on some harness as Rawls and Dane rode up with the cows. He hurried toward them, a fat little man who was terrified the instant he recognized the cows.

"Where'd you find 'em, Sherm?" Miles asked, sweat breaking through the pores of his face.

"On Rocking R grass," Rawls said. "If I find 'em there again, we'll be eating JM beef."

"Sure," Miles said. "I don't blame you, Sherm. I don't blame you one bit. I ain't been over there for a couple of days, so I guess they got to traveling."

"I guess they did," Rawls agreed sourly, and tipped his head at Dane. "My new man, Dane Devlin. Devlin, meet Joe Miles. He's our closest neighbor."

Dane reached down and shook hands with Miles, who beamed at him. "Pleased to meet you, Mister Devlin. You signed on with a good outfit. Yes, sir, a good outfit."

Dane wondered if Miles would have warned him against working for Rawls if they were alone. He said: "I rode a piece with your boy Toby yesterday after school."

Miles's face lost its good humor. "He told me he'd met up with a stranger. Toby's a good boy, but them two older ones, they'll kill their ponies someday and then they'll be afoot. Durn their ornery hides, they never seem to learn."

"You're too easy on 'em, Joe," Rawls said. "If they was my kids, I'd learn 'em."

"Sure you would, Sherm," Miles said. "Sure you would."

"We'd best get along," Rawls said.

"Come in and have a cup of coffee," Miles said. "It's a cold day to ride."

"Storm's coming," Rawls said. "We'd best get moving."

They rode off, and Miles hurried back to his harness. Rawls said: "You see how it is,

Devlin. Some get ahead and some don't. Take Joe there. He's honest, sober, and hard working, brings his family to church every Sunday. But he never has two dollars in his pocket to rub together. If I didn't give him work, I don't know how he'd feed his family."

In late afternoon they dropped down into a cañon, and followed it for a mile until they reached a sprawling cottonwood. Rawls pulled up, nodding at the tree. "This is our hanging tree, Devlin. More'n one man's had his neck stretched from its limbs. I reckon there ain't an outlaw who hasn't heard of it. That's why most of 'em circle this mesa, if they come this way."

"Who was the last one?" Dane asked.

"Billy Combs. For horse stealing, last summer."

"Who was with you?"

Rawls didn't answer. He dug his spurs into his horse's sides and took off up the cañon. It wasn't until they were on top again and Dane had caught up with him that Rawls said: "Why'd you ask about the last one?"

"Just wondering if it was Billy Combs," Dane said. "I ran into his wife in Layton City. She was still hot under the collar. I figured that this was the place."

"I see," Rawls said coldly. "She made some threats before she left here. I told her not to come back to this country. I figured there was more of her outfit hanging out on Disappointment Creek, but, after she pulled out, we didn't have no more trouble."

He was silent for a long time. It was nearly dark and the first snowflakes were beginning to sting their faces when the lights in the Rocking R ranch house showed ahead of them. Then Rawls said: "Devlin, when Bess Combs threatened me, she said she would find a man to kill me. If you're that man, or if she went to the sheriff and you're a deputy he sent in here, make your play right now."

Dane sighed. He said: "Rawls, I lost my money to a professional gambler in Layton named Keno King. I rode south looking for a job and I heard you could use a man, so I came here. You hired me, you showed me what I'll be doing, and I'll do it. Why don't you let it stand at that?"

"I will, for the time being," Rawls said. "But you'd better savvy two things. One is that Billy Combs was a horse thief and he got what was coming to him. The other thing is that this is my mesa and I enforce the law. If I didn't, there wouldn't be no law. No one else has the strength to do it. I do. I keep the church going. If folks need money, or work, or have horses to sell, they come to me. I help them out. People like me, because I'm always ready to help. I'm a good Christian, Devlin. I read the Bible every night. It tells me we have a right to take an eye for an eye and a tooth for a tooth. That's the reason we have peace on Red Rock Mesa. Now do you understand how it is?"

"I sure do," Devlin said. "That's just about the way I had it figured."

"Good," Rawls said curtly. "Don't forget it."

That night after supper, when Dane was in the bunkhouse, he waited until Banjo Quail had stepped outside. Then he asked Fargo: "What's the connection between the boy and Missus Rawls?"

Fargo gave him a long, searching look. "What's it to you?"

"Maybe nothing," Dane admitted. "I was just wondering, after the working over you gave him last night."

"I shouldn't have said what I did," Fargo grunted. "It ain't directly none of my business, either, but I like the kid, and Sherm is a good man in most ways. I don't want no trouble. Well, it seems like Banjo was sweet on the girl before she married Sherm.

Nancy didn't have no business getting married yet, but it looked like a good deal to her pa, him being new in the country and half starved. Banjo couldn't get her out of his head, so this fall he hit Sherm up for a job, figuring if he was close, he could help Nancy. But he can't."

"Does Rawls know about her and the boy?"

Fargo shook his head, his expression turning sour. "He'd kill Banjo if he did. That's his trouble. He goes clean out of his head sometimes."

"Who are Rawls's friends? I mean, among the other cowmen, not men like you who work for him. Or doesn't he have any friends?"

"Sure. All his neighbors on the mesa are his friends. I'd say Joe Miles was his best friend. Or maybe Fred Ashton, in the store. Have you met either one of 'em?"

"Both of them," Dane said.

Fargo stared at Dane, suspicion a sharp shine in his eyes. He asked: "Devlin, you're asking a lot of questions for a new man. If you're a range detective or something like that, by God, I'll cut your throat."

This was strange, Dane thought. Lucky Fargo saw the evil that was in Sherman Rawls, and he was doing all he could to prevent trouble between him and Banjo Quail. Yet he had a deep loyalty to this same man.

"Funny thing," Dane said. "You know what Rawls is. . . ."

"But you don't," Fargo snapped. "You never saw him till yesterday. I know his bad side and his good side. He's taken care of me more'n once. Same with all the old hands. That's why we stay. I ain't gonna let no sneak come in here and shoot him in the back."

"The day I shoot him in the back," Dane said, "I'll hold still for you to cut my throat. That fair?"

"Fair enough," Fargo said, "and, by God, I'll do it."

He would, too, Dane thought, as he pulled off his boots. He went to bed, having no regret for the suspicion he had aroused in Rawls. But he did regret making Fargo suspicious. Dane had no intention of shooting Rawls in the back. When the day came, Rawls would have a gun in his hand. But Dane wasn't sure Lucky Fargo would see the difference.

XII

Bess Combs arrived on Red Rock Mesa exactly one week from the day Dane Devlin reached it. She had not hurried, hating the prospect of living alone in the cabin on Disappointment Creek. She knew that Devlin would be unable to spend much time with her, and, being realistic, she knew that he would not be able to get the information she wanted immediately. It might take all winter. The prospect worried her. She couldn't stay alone that long.

She stopped at Fred Ashton's store, not because she needed anything, for she had brought supplies from Montrose, but because Ashton's store was the gathering place for the mesa ranchers and she might be able to pick up something that would help Devlin. The day was clear and very cold, a recent snow reaching down from the foothills to the edge of the mesa, with patches of it lingering here and there in the shade of buildings and trees. Bess had bought a brown saddle horse and a mouse-colored pack animal in Montrose. She tied in front of the store and went in.

Nothing had changed. She remembered the last time she had been here, the day Billy was lynched. She walked to the stove, took off her coat, and held out her hands, thinking that nothing ever changed with Fred Ashton except that he might be a little more stooped, a little grayer, and his wife might have another baby.

He saw Bess come in and immediately recognized her. He stood back of the counter, his hands palm down on the rough pine plank, and it was a full minute before he could bring himself to ask: "What can I do for you, Missus Combs?"

"Nothing," she said. "Absolutely nothing, Ashton. You don't mind my coming in and getting warm, do you?"

"No," he said. "Not at all." He cleared his throat. "You're going to your cabin on Disappointment Creek?"

She studied him a moment, wondering why he asked. Then she said: "Yes. Your friend Rawls told me to stay out of the country. I suppose you'll run to him and tell him where I am, and he'll fetch some of his hardcases and come calling." Ashton didn't say anything. He kept looking at her, scared and worried, and she said harshly: "You are his friend, aren't you?"

"Yes, ma'am," he said.

"I guess you know how I feel about him," she said. "He killed my husband. You knew that?"

"I heard some talk about it," Ashton admitted.

"I'm going to kill him," she said. "He knows that, so maybe he'll try to kill me first. I'd have got him before I left, but there were some others who helped put the rope around Billy's neck and I aim to find out who they were."

Ashton didn't say a word. He bent over the counter, one hand raised to stroke his beard, the other still palm down against the plank. Even at this distance, she could see the throbbing pulse beat in his temples, the slight trembling of his hand that was stroking his beard. He had been upset when she'd first come in. He was more upset now.

Fred Ashton had no part of the hero in him, but Bess had never considered him a timid man, or even a man who could be easily frightened. He was, for instance, a good hand with horses. Some of them that he broke were pretty salty animals. She had seen him work with his horses, one day last summer. He hadn't been afraid of them. She could tell that, she thought, just by watching him. Horses, she knew, sensed fear in a man and were doubly hard to handle. But Ashton was afraid now. *He knows something,* she thought. Rawls had talked to him, maybe told him the whole story. She said:

"Ashton, I think you know who helped Rawls hang Billy."

"No!" he shouted. "I don't know anything."

"A lot of men come here," she pressed. "Do enough drinking to loosen their tongues. Besides, if you're Rawls's friend, he'd talk to you. It was murder, Ashton. You know that. I don't believe Billy stole any horses, but, even if he did, he deserved a trial."

"Sure he did." Ashton bobbed his head. "But nobody ever said anything to me about it."

Bess put on her coat, sour-tempered and disgusted. "Ashton, you're lying. I'll give you a few days to think it over, then I'm coming back and get the truth out of you. I know damned well you can tell me who was in on the hanging with Rawls."

She started toward the door. Before she had gone three steps, a child started screaming in the back room and ran into the store, with another one about a year older in hot pursuit. Ashton picked up the howling youngster, grabbed the bigger boy, and shoved him toward the back room.

"Stay in there, Percy," Ashton said angrily. "Let Stanley alone."

Bess paused, watching Percy trot back into

the other room, smirking as if he had accomplished a major achievement. Ashton comforted the smaller boy, who hid his face against his father's shirt, his crying gradually subsiding.

Bess had seen Ashton's wife a few times, enough to know the woman was lazy and dirty and shrewish. Ashton deserved better. She remembered how much she had wanted a baby, but Billy had always said they were lucky she didn't get pregnant, that their kid wouldn't have a chance. Ashton's children wouldn't, either. He was burdened with too many, and with a wife who was more of a burden than his kids.

"How many have you got?" she asked.

"Eight. Two are babies, twins." He nodded at the schoolhouse across the road. "Four of 'em are over there."

"You ought to find out what causes 'em," she said, and walked out.

She mounted, and, leading the pack horse, angled to the southwest, being careful to skirt Rocking R range. She dropped off the mesa and threaded her way through a maze of red-walled cañons with a variety of strange formations, obelisks and minarets and grinning gargoyles, that might have been carved out of sandstone by a madman having a nightmare.

Reaching the cabin before dark, she found that no one had been here since she'd left. Cans of food were still on the shelves, a lamp on the rickety table was nearly filled with coal oil, and a pile of cedar wood was behind the stove. The interior of the cabin was dusty, but that was to be expected, since she had been gone so long.

Actually it was not as bad as she had expected. She could thank Billy for that. He'd worked on the window, the door, the roof, and the rock walls, making the cabin tight against the weather. Neither he nor Bess had known how long they would be here, so he'd said they might just as well get set for the winter, if they had to stay that long.

The creek was low; it might even stop flowing during the coldest part of the winter. But she refused to worry about that now. Billy had built a crude stone dam below the corral, and it held back a shallow pool of water. It was very cold; ice formed a lacy network along the bank.

She watered and fed the horses, thinking she'd have to find a patch of grass for the animals before long. There wasn't much here beside the creek. She'd have to go to Ashton's store for oats. She hadn't brought enough grain to last long. If a heavy snow pinned her down in the cañon for any great length of time, she'd be in trouble.

She built a fire, took the bucket, and scoured it with sand, and, filling it with water, carried it back to the cabin. She swept the room out the best she could, the broom being little more than a stub, and by that time the water was hot. She scrubbed the table, the shelves, the pans and tin plates and cups, and, unrolling her blankets, made her bed. Then she cooked supper.

She was tired, but she sat on the floor in front of the stove for a long time, unable to force herself to go to bed. She barred the door, and placed the heavy, makeshift shutters that Billy had built over the window. If Ashton ran to Rawls with the information that she was here and he came after her tonight, he couldn't get in without waking her. She had a Winchester and a revolver. She'd take care of Rawls if he came.

She wasn't afraid. No, it wasn't that at all. It was being alone. Devlin wouldn't come until Sunday, maybe not even then. She faced her future honestly, admitting to herself that she was the kind of person who could not stay here alone long or she'd go crazy. She'd tell Devlin when she saw him that he had to do his job quickly. Then she realized that was foolish.

Devlin had told her in Meeker that he was no detective, and had asked her how he was to go about finding out what she wanted to know. She hadn't been able to tell him, of course. Dealing with a man like Rawls was difficult, to say the least. Her mind turned to Ashton. He was the best bet. He'd break under pressure.

XIII

After breakfast Sunday morning Dane told Rawls he was going to ride to Ashton's store, have a drink, and get into a poker game if he could find one. Rawls scowled, disapproving, but he said nothing. Dane saddled Nero and rode off, grinning. He would have made Rawls happier if he had said he was going to church.

No one was in the store except Ashton. After Dane had a drink, he said: "Thought you'd have a big game going today."

"Might have one this afternoon," Ashton said. "Nobody gets here this early Sunday morning. I always close up during Sunday school and church, then open after dinner. Come back this afternoon and maybe you'll find somebody to accommodate you."

Dane paid for the drink. "Guess I'll ride around and look at some country I haven't seen. If I don't find anything that's more fun, I may be back for that game."

Ashton's eyes were pinned on him, and again, as he had the first day he'd been here, Dane had the feeling the store man was measuring him for some private purpose. Dane walked toward the door, and, just as he reached it, Ashton said: "I hear you signed on with Rawls."

Dane stopped, glancing back over his shoulder at Ashton. "That's right."

"You like your job?"

Dane shrugged. "The grub's good. Otherwise it's just another job. Rawls expects a good day's work out of a man. That's for sure." He paused, then asked: "Why?"

"Just curious," Ashton said. "I was wondering if I was wrong when I told you that you wouldn't like working for him." He cleared his throat. "You staying? All winter, I mean?"

"If I don't get fired."

For a moment Ashton's eyes locked with Dane's, his face an expressionless mask. Then he turned his back on Dane and began to rearrange some cans on a shelf. Dane left the store, and, mounting, rode south.

He thought of the four people who had warned him not to take a job with Rawls —

Ashton, the Miles kid, Rawls's wife, and Lucky Fargo. Ashton and Fargo might have good personal reasons for not wanting him to stay in the country, if either had been involved in Billy Combs's hanging. He remembered thinking that Ashton had the look of a guilty man when he'd mentioned Combs. It was not much to go on, he reflected, no more than a hunch. Bess demanded proof.

It took him most of the morning to find Bess's cabin. He wasted time on two occasions by turning up cañons between narrow red rock walls, only to find they led to dead ends. He had to retrace his steps, locate the red spires again, and continue south.

Early in the afternoon he reached a slick rock rim directly above a small stream. Two horses were in a corral just below a rock cabin that stood close to the opposite cliff. He found a break in the north wall and maneuvered Nero to the bottom, confident that he had the right place.

Bess saw him coming before he reached the creek and ran outside, calling: "Devlin, you're a sight for sore eyes! I never thought I'd be so glad to see anyone in my life."

He swung down, and she kissed him. She had kissed him before, apparently thinking no more about it than if it were a handshake, but this time it was more than that. When she drew back, he asked: "How'd you like to marry me, Missus Combs?"

"I'd like it fine, Mister Devlin," she said cheerfully, "if I had a preacher in the house, but I don't. Put Nero up and come in. I'll fix some dinner."

He stripped gear from his horse and led him into the corral. When Dane stepped into the cabin, he found that Bess had started a new pot of coffee and was frying ham. She motioned to a chair at the table.

"Sit down," she said. "I'll eat with you. I was hoping you'd come today, but I wasn't sure you would, so I was cooking my own dinner." She shook her head as he dropped into a chair. "I kind of liked it here when Billy was alive, but I don't now. It's hell to live alone. I don't know how long I can stand it."

He rolled a cigarette, saying nothing. The more he thought about the possibility of Ashton and Miles, or even Lucky Fargo, being the men who had helped hang Billy Combs, the sicker he was of his bargain. But he had given his word, so the only thing he could do was to talk her into changing her mind.

She turned the meat, then glanced at him again. "Have you found out anything?"

"Yeah." He took the cigarette out of his mouth and inspected the ash. "Rawls hanged your husband. He showed me the tree and said Billy was a horse thief."

"That all?" she asked, disappointed.

"Not quite." He looked at her, knowing she was a stubborn woman and not sure she would, or could, change her purpose, once she had committed herself. "I think Fred Ashton and Joe Miles helped him."

"You think!" she snapped. "What kind of proof is that?"

"It's the best I've been able to do," he said angrily. "I told you before I wasn't a detective. All I've got is a hunch. It could be any man on the mesa. Some of the Rocking R hands, for instance. If you think they're going to come to me and tell me they had a hand in it, or that Rawls is going to tell me, you're crazy."

"I'm crazy enough to know I can make Ashton talk," she said. "If he wasn't in it, he knows who was. I'll get it out of him, if you can't."

"So you had the same hunch I did."

"It's no hunch. I figured Ashton's store is the place where all the mesa men come, sooner or later. They're bound to talk when they get liquored up. And from the way he acted when I was there, I think he's heard something."

Dane rose and threw his cigarette stub into the fire. "I'd shoot Sherman Rawls tonight and be as glad I done it as if I'd plugged a coyote. He's two men, just like he's got two sides of his face. From what I've seen and heard, part of the time he's all right. I've got no complaint about the way he's treated me, but it seems like there are times when he goes loco. If he caught me talking to his wife, I, think he'd try to kill me."

She brought the ham and a plate of biscuits to the table, poured the coffee, and took a pot of beans out of the oven. "I know all that," she said. "Billy told me the same thing. I think it was the reason Rawls hanged him. He must have caught Billy talking to his wife."

Her face was hard set. Dane told himself he was whipped before he started, but he had to try to change her mind, because it was the only thing he could do. He said: "You saved my life and I gave my word, but there's more to it than that. In the little while I've been on Red Rock Mesa, I've learned one thing that's important. People do what Sherman Rawls tells 'em to do. He's responsible for Billy's hanging, not the men who were with him."

She shook her head. "They could have stopped him, whoever they were. That's plenty of reason for them to die."

"Oh, hell," he said, exasperated. He chewed his lower lip until he had his temper under control, then asked: "You know how many kids Ashton's got?"

"Eight."

"You going to support them if you're the cause of Ashton's getting beefed?"

"No."

"They'll starve if somebody doesn't," he said. "What's more, Miles is in about the same boat. He's got several kids, a wife, and a two-bit spread that's worth damned little. You going to look after them?"

She slammed a hand against the table, making the dishes rattle. "No. Why should I? If Ashton and Miles are going to help Rawls do his dirty work, they'd better think about what'll happen to their wives and kids."

"They can't, not if they have to live on Red Rock Mesa and get along with Rawls. He's like a rock slide going down a mountain, taking everything with him. Maybe they tried to save Billy, but they couldn't have stopped Rawls no matter what they did."

"Eat your dinner," she said irritably. "Like

you said, you gave me your word, so it's settled."

"But you've got to live with yourself afterward," he said. "So do I. That's why we've got to talk about it." He leaned back in his chair, studying Bess's flushed face. "I'm wondering if you ever really loved Billy Combs."

From the expression on her face, he knew he had struck home. But she would never admit that her feeling for Billy had been anything but love. She said quickly, too quickly: "Of course I loved him . . . enough to get square for his murder."

"Getting square doesn't prove you loved him. It just proves you're stubborn. You think you've got to do what you've told yourself you ought to do. You're a lot of woman, Bess. I guess I'm in love with you myself, but if I thought you'd spend the rest of your life thinking about a dead husband who was a horse thief and a bank robber, I'd put you out of my mind right now."

She bowed her head, her expression softening. "I'll get over him in time. Eat your dinner, Dane. Please."

He obeyed, knowing that they had settled nothing. But she hadn't cut him off. Loyalty was a quality he admired in a woman. If she ever got over this crazy desire for revenge,

216

she was all he would ever expect to find in a wife. But she had lived with the idea of revenge for months; it was what had brought her to him in Layton City. He wasn't sure she would ever get over it.

When he finished eating, he rolled another cigarette, asking: "What happened in Meeker after I left?"

She laughed, her good humor restored. "It was funny. The marshal showed up after you left, and I told him what had happened. The thing that saved us was the bragging Jeeter did in the lobby. They were going to skin you and hang your hide up to dry. They even got a little rough with the clerk before he told 'em I was in the room with you. Several men in the lobby heard the talk. After the marshal got my story, he went back downstairs and arrested Jeeter and Doc Darby for disturbing the peace. They raised a howl, claiming you'd murdered Bosco, but the marshal allowed it was justifiable homicide and said he wasn't going chasing after you."

"I guess that's the last we'll see of Keno King," Dane said, with more hope than conviction.

The good humor that for a moment had softened her face was gone again. "No, he'll show up here. I made a mistake in Layton

City. I guess I've got to tell you about it. I kept King under my gun for a while after the stage left. We talked some, long enough for me to tell him about Billy holding up the bank. I let him think Billy got away with a big chunk of money, and I told him about Sherman Rawls and what he'd done to Billy. I even said Rawls had buckets of gold buried in his yard."

He stared at her, unable to believe this. "You told him where you were going?" She nodded, and he said: "Then King knows I'm here?"

"I mentioned Red Rock Mesa. If he doesn't know where it is, he'll find it." She rose and, coming around the table, laid a hand on his shoulder. "I think we've got plenty of time. King won't go out of his way to nail you as long as the pickings are good in towns like Layton City."

Dane rose, pushing her hand away from him, completely disgusted with her. "I thought you had more sense," he said harshly, and left the cabin.

"Dane!" she called after him, but he went on toward the corral.

He saddled Nero and, mounting, rode across the creek. Bess, watching from the cabin doorway, suddenly began to cry, the first time she could remember when the tears had come this readily. It was the realization of what she had lost that brought them, of what her stubborn perversity had done. Suddenly the fear that she would never see Dane Devlin again overcame her stubbornness and her pride, and she ran out of the cabin and across the creek, the cold water splashing up around her ankles.

She shouted: "Dane, come back tomorrow!"

He shouted curtly: "I won't have time! Rawls gives me a full day of riding!"

He rode on and disappeared over the rim, not looking back again.

XIV

Fred Ashton was a worrying man. He had worried from the moment he had failed to keep Sherman Rawls from hanging Billy Combs. From talk he had heard in the store, he knew that other similar incidents had taken place on the mesa, but he had never been involved in one before. His worries increased after Dane Devlin stopped and asked about the location of the Rocking R, and then worked around to mentioning Billy Combs's name. Then Bess Combs had returned to the mesa and had stopped here, not to buy anything, but to quiz him about Combs's hanging. Bess Combs was a woman who made the blood bubble in a man's veins, even the tired blood of Fred Ashton. But she was a terrible woman, too, a woman of violence and strong passions. Before she'd left the store, she'd promised to come back. She had sensed he was lying. She had said she'd give him a few days to think it over, and then she'd get the truth out of him.

Now Devlin had dropped in, pretending he was looking for a poker game, but he had certainly known that Saturday night was the natural time for a big game, not early Sunday morning. He hadn't mentioned Billy Combs. He hadn't needed to. He had simply intended to remind Ashton that he was still in the country, that there would be a day of reckoning.

After Devlin left the store, Ashton moved to a window and watched him ride south. Bess Combs's cabin was in that direction. Devlin was hand in glove with her. Ashton was as sure of that as he was sure of anything. Devlin didn't even take the trouble to fool him about the direction he was taking. They wanted him to know, he decided, wanted to give him time to think about it, to realize what was ahead for him.

Devlin was a tough one, maybe tough

enough to be a match for Sherman Rawls, Ashton thought, but Devlin wouldn't start with Rawls. Devlin and the Combs woman would come to the store and start with him. Or Joe Miles, if either of them got the notion Miles had had a hand in Combs's hanging. Miles would talk, so in the end they'd still come back here.

Ashton turned from the window and walked to the stove. He held his hands over it, shivering, although the room was warm. Suppose Devlin killed him? What would happen to his wife and children? His horses and store weren't worth much. His wife had no business sense. She'd sell out for a song and move to Montrose, and in six months she'd be destitute.

Sweat began running down his face. He wiped it off with his sleeve. How had he ever got into a position like this? He was married to a woman who pretended she had no part in the act of procreation except to bear the agony of it, that he alone was responsible for every baby she'd had. She was forty. She might go on having babies for the next ten years. It wasn't that he disliked having a family. He loved every child he had, and he'd love every one the future brought, even if it was ten more. What he hated was the position that the dependents forced him into, a position that, to all intents and purposes, was one of slavery to Sherman Rawls.

He looked at his watch. Time to help Martha get the children ready for Sunday school. She was always nervous when she was under any pressure with them, and she'd have a tantrum if he didn't help.

It took a full hour to get the six children ready for Sunday school. Martha always stayed home with the twins, and he would have to take the older ones. He had developed a talent for being deaf to their quarreling and squealing and bawling, and to Martha's screaming at them.

At five minutes to ten Ashton left the house, holding Percy with one hand and Stanley with the other, the four older children walking ahead of them.

Rawls was superintendent of the Sunday school, and he taught the adult class. When church started, he led the singing, and later presided as elder at the communion table and gave a long prayer. There wasn't very much that Rawls didn't do, even down to paying most of the preacher's salary. Whenever he stood up to teach the class or lead the singing or deliver a prayer, he managed to keep a sideways position, so that only the right half of his face was visible to his audience. Ashton thought about that all through the sermon, with Percy sitting on one side of him, Stanley on the other. He didn't pretend to understand Rawls, but he had a notion that the terrible scar on the left side of the man's face had something to do with making him the strange and twisted person that he was.

Then Ashton thought about himself, and how on every occasion, whether it was a church dispute or an argument during a school board meeting, or a matter of real importance like the hanging of Billy Combs, he always knuckled down to Sherman Rawls in the end. Not that he bowed and scraped in front of Rawls the way Joe Miles and the others did, but the final result was the same. And why? He wasn't afraid of Rawls. Miles and the other mesa ranchers were. With Ashton it was a simple matter of economics. Rawls had made the threat more than once. He could start a competitive store. He could buy his supplies in Montrose. He could see to it that Ashton never sold another horse on the mesa. It was another form of fear, Ashton told himself dismally, just as despicable, perhaps, as the physical fear Joe Miles felt.

Ashton heard very little of the sermon. He nudged Percy automatically with his elbow when Percy leaned forward and made faces at Stanley in an effort to start him giggling. When the service was over and Ashton took his brood home, he was still wrestling with his problem. What would he do when Devlin and the Combs woman came, asking again about the hanging of Billy Combs?

He helped Martha get the children back into their everyday clothes, then he peeled potatoes for dinner. She was a poor cook, without imagination, but today she had baked a custard for dessert to go with the usual beans and potatoes and salt pork.

By the time the meal was finished, he had made up his mind on one thing. He would talk to Sherman Rawls. He rose and said: "I'm going to take a look for a couple of horses I haven't seen all week. If anybody wants anything out of the store, you can wait on them."

"You think that's all I've got to do?" she asked peevishly. "You think that running after the kids and picking up and keeping house ain't enough, so I've got to tend to the store, too?"

She had said the same thing many times during the ten years they had been married; he knew he should ignore it, just as he had in the past, but his burden was too great, and he raised his voice.

"By God, it won't hurt you to look after the store. Won't hurt you to do some picking up and keeping house, either."

She stared at him, startled, then began to cry. "What's the matter with you today, Fred? You never talk to me this way. And all through dinner you acted as if you didn't hear a word I said."

He picked his way across the cluttered floor, took his hat off a peg by the door, and went out, not answering her. With the temper he was in now, he might say too much. Besides, he couldn't tell her what was wrong. He saddled his horse and rode across the mesa toward the Rocking R. He knew he was wasting his time, that there was nothing he could say that would influence Sherman Rawls, but it was an effort he had to make.

He found Rawls in the barn, currying his big gray gelding. Rawls called heartily: "Come in, Fred! You haven't been out to see me for a long time. Soon as I get done here, we'll go into the house and get Nancy to put a pot of coffee on the stove."

Ashton stood in the doorway, shivering a little in the cold wind. He said: "I haven't got time to stay, Sherm. I came out to tell you that Bess Combs is in the country."

Rawls didn't miss a stroke with the currycomb. "Well?"

"I thought you told her to stay away."

"I did, but I'm not going looking for her, if that's what you're getting at. On the other hand, I'll hang her just like we done her husband if I catch her on the mesa. That satisfy you?"

"No. Two wrongs don't make a right."

"You claiming we were wrong to hang a horse thief?"

Ashton hadn't mentioned the subject to Rawls since the hanging, but now that the question was asked, he refused to duck it. He said: "Yes, we were wrong, but that's not what I came here for. When Devlin first stopped at the store, he mentioned Billy Combs. When Bess showed up, she claimed I'd heard some talk and could tell her who helped you. Today Devlin came in, had a drink, then rode south. The Combs cabin is in that direction. I figure they're working together."

Rawls backed out of the stall, crossed the runway, and laid the currycomb on a shelf. He said, his voice controlled: "Just what do you think we'd better do?"

"Fire Devlin. Maybe the two of 'em will leave the country. Devlin looks to me like a hardcase."

"He's a tough hand," Rawls said, "but I

can handle him. I'm way ahead of you, Fred. The Combs woman threatened me the day we strung up her husband. I knew she'd be back and that she'd have a man, but I'm not sure Devlin's the one. If he is, I'll take care of him. If he isn't, he's the kind of man I need. Now you go back home and tend your store. If you need any help, I'll give it to you. But don't ever think I'll need any, if that's what's in your mind."

This was exactly what he had expected Rawls to say. He had wasted his time, as he had known he was doing. But now that he had gone this far, he couldn't keep from saying: "Sherman, I told the Combs woman you were my friend. I am, too, and I reckon it's a friend's job to tell you what you don't know. You can't go on running this mesa like you were a king. You're too high and mighty, and you're headed for trouble. Take folks like Banjo Quail's and your wife's people. And the way you treat your wife. . . ."

Rawls muttered something and turned his face so Ashton was staring at the scarred left side. He stopped talking. He had seen Rawls do this same thing many times. It was his way of threatening a man, the same as if he had shaken a fist in Ashton's face.

"Fred," Rawls said, his voice still under

control, "don't ever talk to me about the way I treat people, especially my wife. If I didn't do exactly what I do, we'd have anarchy on this range. That includes hanging horse thieves."

Ashton sighed. "You're a rich man, Sherm. If anything happened to you, Nancy would be taken care of. But if something happened to me, my wife and children would be destitute. I'd like to leave the mesa. I could, if you'd buy my horses and store."

He had said too much, and he knew it the instant he finished. Rawls fought his temper and lost. He jumped at Ashton and, grabbing him by the shoulders, shook him until his teeth rattled and his beard fluttered back and forth.

"You're staying right here on this mesa, and don't you ever forget it." He gave Ashton a final shove that sent him reeling back through the barn door. "Climb on your horse and git. We're in this together, me 'n' you and Joe, and none of us are leaving. They know I was one of 'em that strung Combs up, but I'm not telling who was with me. If you or Joe do, I'll beat you to death. Savvy?"

"I savvy, all right," Ashton said, and, turning, walked to his horse and mounted.

He rode away, not looking back. He had

failed, but at least he had tried, and that did something for his pride. He had done more than anyone else on the mesa would have done.

As he rode, he thought about Rawls, and suddenly, for the first time, the stark and terrifying truth came to him. Sherman Rawls was a sick man; Ashton had more to fear from him, if he openly rebelled, than from either Bess Combs or Dane Devlin. And he knew the day would come when that was exactly what he must do.

XV

Bess Combs was in Dane's mind constantly during the week that followed his visit with her. He knew now without doubt that he loved her. It was a strange thing that had never happened to him before, a stirring he had felt the first time he had seen her in Layton City. Along with the physical attraction had been a great sense of respect. Bess was strong, she was capable, she was resourceful, all characteristics he admired in either men or women. The point was he had never found them before in a woman. Then he had been disillusioned when he learned that Bess had stupidly told Keno King where she was going and where he would find Dane, and his respect for her had plummeted to zero.

This was the problem with which he wrestled all week. If a man loved a woman, he accepted her weaknesses as well as her strengths. At least that was the way it seemed to Dane it should be. But he wasn't sure he could accept Bess's weaknesses, particularly if they included both stupidity and an unbending passion for revenge. He could think of no logical explanation for Bess's behavior, unless she had not trusted him to do what she had hired him to do, and perhaps, to copper her bet, she had thrown out an attractive bait that would bring King to Red Rock Mesa to kill Sherman Rawls. If that was true, it made her all the more stupid. She should have known that King would never bother with finding out who had helped Rawls with the hanging, and that was what she wanted.

What she had done had been on the spur of the moment. She even admitted she had made a mistake. But that wasn't good enough. He was strongly tempted to leave the mesa and forget the whole business. He couldn't. Two ties held him — his word, and his love for Bess, which he did not deny.

He rode all day, taking a wide swing to the west through the hard-scrabble range that belonged to Banjo Quail's and Nancy's people, and a few other poverty-stricken ranchers who obviously made a bare living and no more. He returned to the Rocking R late in the afternoon, turned Nero into the corral, and walked toward the house, castigating himself for lacking the courage to go to Bess today and have it out.

So intent was Dane upon his own problem that he reached the bunkhouse door before he heard Nancy's sobbing, a shrill sound that was hysterical, then Lucky Fargo's passionate cursing, and the old man's accusing, shouted words: "You finally done it, Sherm! You finally went and done it, and you'll hang for it."

They were standing between the house and the woodpile, Rawls staring at something on the ground, Fargo a few feet in front of him, Nancy crouched behind him, her apron over her face.

Dane started toward them on the run, sensing what had happened before he reached them. Rawls was standing over Banjo Quail's limp body. He glanced up when Dane appeared, his face filled with fury.

Banjo lay on his stomach. Dane knelt and turned him over, and had to fight a wave of nausea. The boy's face had been beaten into a bloody, unrecognizable pulp. Dane lifted an arm and felt for a pulse, but there was no flicker of life. Only an insane man would have done this, and Sherman Rawls surely had been carried by his rage into a state of insanity, or he wouldn't have kept beating the boy long after he was dead. From the condition of Banjo's face, Dane was sure that was exactly what Rawls had done.

Dane lifted his gaze to Nancy. She had pulled the apron away from her face and was staring at Dane. She had a black eye, one end of her mouth was bruised, and blood was running down her right cheek from a cut just below her temple.

Dane rose and turned to face Rawls. "You did this?"

"Of course I did it," he said. "I found them together when I got home this afternoon. Devlin, you and Fargo hitch up the team and put this carrion in the wagon."

Dane hit him in the mouth, splitting a lip and bringing a gush of blood. Rawls staggered back a step, taken by surprise. The thought that anyone would strike him had never entered his mind. Dane was on him like a big cat, both fists working in a hammering rhythm, his left to Rawls's hard-muscled belly, his right to the nose. It squashed like an overripe plum, and blood spurted just as it had from his mouth.

Rawls went back one more step before Dane's driving charge, and that was all. He set his massive legs, took another hard blow to his stomach without yielding an inch, and then swung. His huge fist caught Dane on the head and sent him spinning.

If the blow had been lower, it would have knocked Dane cold. He felt as if a club had struck him, and he knew, as he reeled back, that he was fighting for his life, that Rawls would kill him if he could, just as he had killed Banjo Quail. Dane should have pulled his gun as soon as he saw what had happened, and ended the fight at once. But for a moment he had been as crazy as Rawls, wanting to hurt and bruise and crush with his hands, just as Rawls had done to Nancy and the boy. Now it was too late to go for his gun. He had to keep retreating and circling, had to watch Rawls's hands. The rancher was quick with them, quicker than Dane had thought a big man could be.

Twice Dane reversed himself and moved in, striking hard and fast and rocking Rawls's head from one side to the other. He hurt Rawls, but he didn't slow him down. Then Dane, backing up, stumbled on a stick of wood and fell, and Rawls was on him. They rolled over and over in the dust, Rawls trying to get Dane by the throat, and Dane hitting with both fists when they were free.

Rawls was heavier and stronger, but he was never quite able to use his strength and weight to finish Dane. Once he got his fingers on Dane's throat, but both men were turning and threshing, and Dane, momentarily free of Rawls's weight, smashed a knee into Rawls's chest. The pain was so intense that Rawls released his grip.

Dane rolled clear and gained his feet. Rawls came to his knees, and Dane kicked him in the face and knocked him flat on his back. He dived on the man, dropping with his legs doubled up so that his knees came down hard on Rawls's belly, driving wind out of him. But still Rawls had the strength to fling out a great fist in a sideways swipe, striking Dane on the side of the head and tumbling him to the ground.

Rawls was first on his feet. He grabbed a stick of wood and, just as Dane started to get up, hit him on the head. Dane slumped forward, knocked cold, his face in the dust.

Rawls raised the stick and would have clubbed Dane to death, but he had been too busy to watch Nancy. She had run into the house and returned with the shotgun. She rammed the muzzle into Rawls's back, screaming: "You're not going to kill him like

234

you did Banjo! You hit him again and I'll blow you in two!"

Rawls froze, the stick uplifted for another blow. Fargo ran in and twisted it out of Rawls's grip. "She'll do it, Sherm!" Fargo yelled. "You hit Devlin again and she'll kill you!"

Slowly Rawls got to his feet and wheeled ponderously to face Nancy. Blood was dribbling down his chin from his nose and split lip. Dazed, he wiped a sleeve across his mouth and stared at the red smear; he licked his lips and tasted the blood, and spit a mouthful into the dust.

He said, his words made thick by the battered lip: "You're my wife, Nancy, and you threatened to kill me. I won't forget it."

"She kept you from killing another man, Sherm," Fargo said. "You oughtta thank her."

Rawls turned to Fargo. "I thought I heard you cursing, but I was excited and I wasn't sure what I heard, so I'll overlook it. You harness up the team and take Quail's body home. They'll want to give him a Christian burial." He started toward the house, then stopped and looked back at Nancy. "I'm going to wash up and go to church. When I get back, we'll pray. The devil that has taken possession of every woman since the time of Eve is in you. We've got to pray it out and purify you." He motioned to Fargo. "When Devlin comes around, tell him he's fired." He tossed two gold coins into the dust at Fargo's feet. "That's half a month's pay. Give it to him and tell him to take it and get off the mesa. Tell him to be glad he's alive, and never to come back."

Rawls went into the house. Fargo and Nancy remained motionless until the back door slammed. Nancy whispered: "By morning I won't want to be alive."

"We'll do something," Fargo muttered. "We've got to. Help me get Devlin into the bunkhouse. Sherm might go off again if he sees him when he comes out."

Together they half dragged, half carried Dane across the yard and into the bunkhouse, and lifted him onto his bunk. Fargo, so frightened he was trembling, ran to the door and looked out.

"He ain't showed up yet." Fargo sighed in relief. "Stay out of sight till he's gone. I've got to get the team up and harness 'em. I'll piddle around at it and waste time till Sherm's gone, then we'll decide what to do." He wiped his sweaty face. "I told Banjo to go home. I told him over and over. Why didn't he listen?"

"He loved me and thought he could help

me," she whispered. "What about Devlin? Is he dead?"

"No, but he would have been if Sherm had whacked him again." Fargo motioned to the door. "Go on now, hide somewhere. Don't let Sherm find you in here with Devlin."

Fargo walked to the barn, taking his time. Nancy disappeared into one of the outbuildings and remained there until Rawls left the house, dressed in his Sunday suit. His face was bruised, but he'd succeeded in stopping the blood. He saddled his gray and rode off, sitting his saddle in the same easy way he always rode, not giving the slightest indication that killing Banjo Quail was wrong in any way.

Nancy was crying softly. She couldn't stop. Wiping her eyes, she peered through the narrow crack between the nearly closed door and the casing, and watched Rawls. She knew that, when he got back, he would tell her again that all the sin that had been in Eve was in her. She had caused Banjo Quail's death by flipping her skirt and waggling her hips at him. But Sherman Rawls was like Adam. He had done no wrong.

She began to cry again.

XVI

The late afternoon light that flickered through the dirty bunkhouse windows was very thin, so thin that, when Dane came to, he wasn't sure who was sitting beside the bunk. Then Nancy said: "He's coming around."

Lucky Fargo spoke. "Take it easy, Devlin. You got a hell of a wallop."

His head must have been split wide open. He raised a hand and gingerly felt of the lump that was as big as a hen's egg. Then he discovered that a wet cloth lay across his forehead. As his hand dropped back to his side, Nancy removed the cloth, dipped it into a bucket of water on the floor, wrung it out, and put it back on his forehead.

His vision cleared and he discovered that the light was not as thin as he had first thought. His gaze fixed on Nancy's face; he saw the bruises and the brown splotch of blood that had dried on her cheek. Then he slowly and painfully turned his head so he could see Fargo, who was standing near the foot of the bunk, his weather-beaten face filled with anxiety.

The fog began to lift from Dane's mind. He was surprised he was alive. He asked: "Rawls?"

"He's gone to church," Nancy said, "but he'll be back. We've got to get out of here before he does. You've got to take me with you, Mister Devlin."

"Banjo?"

He thought he remembered feeling for Banjo's pulse and not finding any, but his memory was still cloudy. He was not completely sure of anything, not even the details of his fight with Rawls. He should have killed him, and now, with his head aching so much his mind refused to function, he couldn't remember why he hadn't.

"Sherm beat Banjo to death," Fargo said. "I've got to deliver his body to his folks. You'd be dead, too, if Nancy hadn't got a shotgun and rammed it into Sherm's back."

"Thanks," Dane said, and looked at the girl again.

"If it makes you owe me something," she said, "you can pay it back by taking me with you when you leave." She was terrified. He wondered about that, then slowly the details of what had happened came back to him; he remembered Rawls saying that he had found Banjo with Nancy. If he would kill a man for finding him with his wife, what would hc do to another man who ran off with her? Well, it didn't make any difference. Dane was going to kill Rawls anyway.

He tried to decide what to do. Nancy and Fargo were watching him anxiously. He was in no condition to tangle with Rawls again tonight; he needed a little time. Right now he wasn't sure he could ride a horse, or even stand on his feet.

"How did it start?" he asked. "Rawls killing Banjo, I mean."

"I was taking a snooze on my bunk," Fargo said, "so I didn't see the first of it. I might have stopped it if I'd been awake, but then I dunno. Nothing can stop Sherm when he loses his temper like he done with Banjo. When I got there, he was slamming the boy's head against the chopping block. I told him Banjo was dead, and he finally quit."

"Banjo was cutting wood for me," Nancy added. "Sherm had gone to Joe Miles's place for dinner. We didn't know he was back. He was right there with us before we knew he was anywhere around."

"What were you doing?" Dane asked.

The girl looked away, flushing. "Banjo was holding my hand and we were standing close. That's all. We didn't do anything wrong, Mister Devlin. Banjo was trying to get me to run away with him. Sherm might have heard some of the talk. I don't know."

"Were you going with Banjo?"

"No, but I've got to leave now. I can't stand to stay here another minute . . . not after watching him murder Banjo. I tried to stop him, but he hit me. I couldn't do anything."

Fargo shifted uneasily. "I've got to get started, but I'll take time to saddle a couple of horses for you if you think you can ride."

"I've got to," Dane said.

"Sherm, he told me to tell you that you was fired," Fargo said, handing Dane the coins Rawls had given him. "Said for you to take the *dinero* and be thankful you were alive. He said to get off the mesa and never come back."

"I'll be gone when he gets home," Dane said, "but you can tell him I'll be back. Saddle Nero. I've been riding him all day, but I can't leave him."

"Sure," Fargo said. "I'll saddle that little bay for Nancy." He turned to the girl. "Better fill a sack with grub. You may have to hole up somewhere, or ride like hell. The one place you can't go is home, because that's where he'll look first."

Nancy nodded and ran out of the bunkhouse. Fargo hesitated, his eyes pinned on Dane's face as if not quite sure of him.

Dane asked: "What are you going to do after you take Banjo's body home?"

241

Fargo cuffed his hat and scratched his head. "I've been thinking on that. What I oughtta do is to take a saddle horse along and light out and keep going, but I don't reckon I will. I'll come back. You won't believe it, but Sherm's been good to me. Most times, anyhow. After this he's going to need me. I reckon I owe him and Rocking R something."

"Saddle up for us," Dane said, thinking that this kind of unreasoning loyalty was typical of an old-time cowhand like Lucky Fargo.

Fargo walked to the door, then stopped and looked back. "Don't you lay a hand on Nancy. You hear?"

Dane was angry. "What do you think I . . . ?" He stopped. The old man was fond of the girl, and the warning would not have been out of place with most men. He said: "She'll be safe with me."

That satisfied Fargo, and he went out. Dane picked up his hat from the floor and carefully set it on his head. He rose, the floor tipping and whirling in front of him. He put a hand against the wall to steady himself, his head threatening to split open again. Then the worst of the giddiness passed. He packed his war sack with his shaving gear and a few odds and ends he had been using. At the door he had to pause again and cling to the casing.

He stood there, clenching his teeth against the hammering pain that rocked his head. Presently Nancy came out of the house with a flour sack partly filled with food. Fargo led the saddled horses from the corral and tied the sack behind Nancy's saddle. He gave the girl a hand as Dane walked to Nero, staggering like a drunk. He gripped the horn, waited a moment, then pulled himself into the saddle.

"Gonna stay up there?" Fargo asked.

"I'll stay up here, all right," Dane said.

Fargo had harnessed a team and hooked it up to the wagon. A canvas spread across the bed covered Banjo Quail's body. As Fargo walked to the wagon, Dane said: "You don't know what direction we took."

"I left before you did," Fargo said. "I don't even know you two arc together."

"What will Banjo's folks do?"

Fargo stopped and looked back. "Dunno. They've been kicked around some by Sherm. All them folks out there have. If they knew Nancy was gone and out of the way, so she wouldn't get hurt, they might come calling."

"Don't let them," Dane said. "They'd just get hurt. Tell 'em I'll take care of Rawls."

243

"I'll tell 'em," Fargo said, and climbed to the wagon seat.

Dane rode south, with Nancy beside him. He heard the creak of the wagon as it rolled west. He rode with his head down, one hand holding to the saddle horn. The sun was nearly hidden behind the mountains now. It would be dark before long. Nancy, he was sure, didn't know the country. He would have to make the decisions, and he didn't have even a guess what Rawls would do.

Dane's first thought was of Nancy. He had to get her off the Rocking R and out of Rawls's reach. He would take her to Bess's cabin, he decided. She'd be as safe there as anywhere, and maybe he could persuade Bess to take Nancy south into New Mexico. He needed a day, then he would go back to the Rocking R and settle with Rawls. He would not hold back any longer in the hope of finding out who had helped Rawls hang Billy Combs.

Within an hour the twilight had turned to night, and the heavy clouds covered the stars. He learned two things in that hour — he couldn't find Bess's place until daylight, and he couldn't stay in the saddle much longer. He remembered a deserted line cabin that would be tight enough to keep warm in for the night. Apparently it had been used during the summer. He had stopped once and looked inside. There was an armload of wood banked against the wall beside the stove. The cabin was too close to the Rocking R to be safe, but Rawls was unlikely to do anything before morning. By dawn Dane would be on his way again with the girl.

"There's a line cabin a little farther on," he said. "We'll have to stay the night there."

"All right, Mister Devlin," she said, her tone telling him that she trusted him completely.

As cold as it was, and with the clouds piling up, it might snow by morning. If it snowed just enough to hold their tracks, Rawls would catch up with them by noon, providing he guessed the direction that they had taken. But the chances were, it seemed to Dane, that Rawls would try Nancy's home first, and that would give them all the time they needed. In any case, it was a chance they had to take.

Dane swung slightly to the right, not sure he could find the cabin in the darkness, although he knew he was not far from it. This was country through which he had ridden every weekday since he had been here. Half an hour later they dropped down a steep-banked arroyo, splashed across the shallow stream in the bottom, and climbed out again. Now Dane was able to identify exactly where he was. Presently the line cabin loomed ahead of them.

"Here it is," he said, and stepped out of the saddle.

He tried to stand beside his horse until the dizziness passed, tried to hold to the horn until the girl dismounted, but his fingers went slack. He spilled forward, sprawling face down into the grass, and it seemed to him that he kept falling, pinwheeling down over a high cliff that had no bottom, until at last all consciousness left him and the blackness was absolute.

XVII

Bess Combs had never lived a longer week in her life than the one following the Sunday she saw Dane. She hated the inactivity, having nothing to do but rustle wood and cook her meals and take care of the horses. She hated being alone. But most of all, she hated the future if Dane Devlin had left her for good. He would be back, she kept telling herself, even if only for a few minutes, just long enough to reassure her that he wasn't leaving. He was a man whose word was as good as his bond. She had to believe it; it was that important to her.

Yet, as the slow days dragged on to another Sunday, she began to lose her confidence. The simple truth was she could not blame Dane if he pocketed the money she had given him and rode away, now that he knew what she had told Keno King. She had no defense for herself, even in her own mind. She could not remember when she had done anything so foolish and so completely wrong. Her only excuse was that at the time she had been unable to think of anything except getting revenge for Billy's hanging, but now she knew that was no excuse at all.

Because she had little to do, she thought a great deal about Billy Combs and herself. She hadn't really loved him, even though she had been sure she had. She had fought men off as far back as she could remember. The only reason she was still a virgin when Billy married her was that she could use a gun, and she'd always had one when she needed it. That was the side of Billy that had made him important to her. She had never needed a gun when she'd been with him. He respected her as a woman, never thinking of her in the predatory way that the other ridge runners and high rollers with whom she had been forced to spend so much of her time did. He had been harum-scarum and brash and sometimes foolish, but not once during the months they were married did she have occasion to be offended by the things he did or said.

Still, the marriage had not been entirely satisfactory. She'd had her ideal of a husband, a strong, capable man who would look out for her. Billy had remained a boy until the day he had been killed. She had been both a wife and a mother to him because that was what he required, but it was not the way she wanted it. Dane Devlin was as different from Billy as one man could be from another. It was true that he had obeyed her orders on two occasions, in Layton City when he had taken the stage, and in Meeker when he'd gone out through a window. But he had done what he had because he was working for her, not because he had wanted to.

He was not a leaner. He had courage, and he was deadly cold and efficient when the situation demanded it, a quality she had seen in him when he'd cut down Curley Heston on the street in Layton City. Too, he was a man who could not go against his own convictions. To him, killing Sherman Rawls would be an execution; killing Fred Ashton would be murder, even if Ashton had been with Rawls when Billy was lynched.

The end of the week found her coming to a conclusion that was difficult for her to accept, but one she could not avoid. Dane was right when he said that Sherman Rawls alone was responsible for the hanging of Billy Combs. She would forget the threats she had made about punishing the others, whoever they were. She would be satisfied with Rawls's death; she'd leave the country with Dane, if he would forgive her for telling Keno King what she had. Her feeling for Billy Combs had been one of gratitude rather than love. She was certain of that now. Dane had sensed it, and she would admit it when she saw him. She would settle on his terms. That was the hardest decision she'd ever had to make, but she had thrilled to his saying that he loved her, and she wanted to hear those words again.

Once she made up her mind to surrender to Dane, she was impatient to tell him so. When he didn't come by late Sunday afternoon, she knew he wasn't coming. So she would go to him, as dangerous as that was. Rawls, she thought, was a man who never changed. Billy had told her a good deal about him, that he was a man of habit, and one of his habits was to go to church every Sunday evening. The chances were good, she decided, that she could see Dane without running into Rawls.

Once her mind was made up, she couldn't wait. She put on her hat and heavy coat, and ran outside to the corral. She saddled her horse, her fingers all thumbs in her haste. The light was beginning to thin now in the bottom of the cañon. She would have to hurry to reach the Rocking R before dark.

She raised a foot to the stirrup, then froze, one hand on the horn. Four riders were coming down the north wall of the cañon. She had been so intent on her plans that she had not seen or heard them before. Now she lowered her foot to the ground, stepped away from her horse, and glanced across the creek.

The lead man was almost to the bottom. Her first thought was that these were Rocking R hands sent here to kill her, that Fred Ashton had told Rawls she was in the country and he was planning to hang her just as he had hanged Billy. She whirled to the horse, thinking her Winchester was in the boot. Then she remembered that, in her haste, she had left it inside. She started to run toward the cabin, when a shot rang out from the lead man across the creek. The slug screamed as it ricocheted off a rock, the report echoing as if it were flung back from the high wall above her.

"Stand pat, Bess!" the man called. "You won't get hurt if you behave!"

Keno King. She recognized his voice, and now that he was closer she identified his tall figure. Behind him were Trask, Jeeter, and Doc Darby, in that order.

For a moment she was terrified. Then she told herself that she was in no danger; they were here to kill Dane. She couldn't let that happen, but she didn't know what she could do. She wouldn't know until she heard their plans, so, for the moment at least, she would play along.

"You've got no call to shoot at me, King!" she yelled.

"You know I bet on a sure thing," he said as he reined up in front of her, his rifle lined on her breast. "You're the kind who could kick up a lot of trouble if you got your hands on a gun." He nodded at Jeeter, who had reined up beside him. "See if she's got a gun on her."

Jeeter ran his big hands over her, taking time to fondle her breasts. She jerked away from him, slapping him on the side of the face. "Keep your damned hands where they belong," she said. "King, even a pimply-faced idiot like Jeeter knows I wouldn't carry a gun where he was feeling."

Jeeter, his face red, started toward her,

but he stopped when King said: "Hold it. She's right. You're not man enough to take her, and I can't afford to lose you."

Jeeter wheeled to face King, his face almost purple in his fury. "By God, I can take her. . . ."

"All right," King said testily. "Find a gun?"

"Naw, she ain't heeled," Jeeter muttered, "but that ain't. . . ."

"Take the saddle off her horse," King said. "Doc, give him a hand. Take care of ours." He motioned to Trask. "Rustle up some wood, Ed. Come on, Bess. You're cooking us supper. We haven't eaten since morning."

She walked to the cabin, with King a step behind her, his rifle lined on her back. She had been around the worst kind of hard-cases, but she doubted if she had ever been with any who were tougher than these. She had a revolver in her cabin, but her chances of getting her hands on it were slim. Her mistake in Layton City had backfired on her. She had brought these men here, and she would pay for it, not Dane. The time she'd thought she and Dane had was no time at all.

The fire in the stove was still going. "Fill it up and start cooking," King said curtly. "If you make a wrong move, you're dead. You're a tough gal, but you're not tough enough to buck four of us. Don't try it."

She filled the stove, then turned to face him. Even in the gloom of the cabin, she sensed the cat-like quality of this man. He could be as cruel as a panther if he was opposed, and now, far from law and the inhibiting company of decent men, she knew there was no limit to what he would do if the whim struck him. In Layton City he had played the part of a gentleman. Now he didn't even bother to pretend.

"King," Bess said, "I don't know what's in your mind, but let's get one thing straight. I'll cook for you, but you and none of your plug-uglies are going to paw me like Jeeter tried to do."

"That's a deal," he said. "For the time being."

She filled the coffee pot, asking: "What happened to the rest of your outfit?"

"Dead," he said sourly. "My luck turned bad in Layton City when Devlin got Curly Heston. Then he plugged Bosco in Meeker. We tried holding up a train in Wyoming and ran into trouble. Four of us are all that's left."

"A sure thing," she taunted.

"We thought we had one," he said, "but something went wrong. Now we're going to get a new start. We're taking the *dinero* that

Billy got from the hold-up in Utah. We're going to make your friend Rawls dig up the gold you said he's got hidden in buckets, and we'll clean his range of good steers. We've got a connection in the mining camps in the San Juans."

She started to peel potatoes, her mind racing ahead. He hadn't mentioned Dane. She wouldn't, either, but it wouldn't make any difference. King wouldn't forget him. She could be sure of that.

She said without looking around: "Billy didn't get much in that hold-up. I had it on me in Layton City."

"Whatever you've got, we'll take," King said.

"What do you think I'm going to live on?"

"Why," King said, "I'm not interested."

She had hidden the money under the blankets on the bunk. There wasn't anything she could do to keep them from getting it. But at the moment the money didn't seem important. Dane's life was. She had no illusions about her own position, either. They'd use her and then kill her. She'd be helpless against the four of them. She'd never given way to hysteria in her life, but she felt it threaten her now. She wanted to cry, to scream, to grab up her pan of potatoes and throw them into King's face. But if she had any chance to survive the next terrible hours, she had to keep her self-possession.

The only thing she could do was to talk, so she said, her voice controlled: "You're crazy if you tackle Rawls with only four men."

King laughed. "Don't try to run a bluff on me. Doc Darby has been on the mesa and he knows it. He knows Rawls, too. We stopped at the store and asked a few questions. The fellow with the beard wasn't aiming to talk, but one of his brats named Percy stuck his head in the back door, and Jeeter grabbed him. He put a gun to the boy's head and old Beard Face was running off at the mouth right away."

She kept on peeling potatoes, sick with the knowledge that any lies she told would not be believed, and therefore would not help either Dane or herself. She asked: "What did he tell you?"

"That your man Devlin has a one-man route he follows every day to keep Rawls's cattle from drifting. Darby and Jeeter will take care of him in the morning. Ed and me will go to the Rocking R and work on Rawls. Before we're done, he'll be glad to show us where he hid his *dinero.*"

It wouldn't do any good, she thought, to tell him she'd lied, that Rawls had no gold hidden in buckets in his yard. Besides, she didn't care what they did to Rawls. If they killed him, it would save Dane the trouble.

She finished peeling the potatoes and put them on the stove, still unable to think of any way she could save Dane. She began making biscuits, glad to have something to do. She said: "If you want to run your bad luck out some more, keep it up by jumping Rawls. But I'll tell you one thing. It'll take four men to handle him."

King laughed again as he lighted a lamp on the table. "Don't worry about me and Rawls. I'm too old a hand at poker to get fooled by anybody betting high with a pair of deuces like you're holding. The gent in the store was talking straight, Bill's gun being on that little devil's head like it was. Everything he told us agreed with what Doc Darby knew about Rawls. Seems that he keeps most of his men in line cabins several miles west of the house. We might not catch Rawls, but his wife will be there. I guess she'll know where the gold is."

Bess shook her head. "No, Rawls isn't a man to talk to anyone."

King shrugged. "Well, it doesn't make any difference. If she doesn't, we'll wait till he shows up. When he does, he'll tell us."

"But he's got men at the Rocking R."

"An old bird named Lucky Fargo, a kid named Banjo Quail, and Devlin." King grinned at her. "By noon or sooner tomorrow, Devlin will be dead, and, if me and Ed can't handle an old man and a kid along with Rawls, we don't deserve anything better than we get."

The other men came in, Trask with an armload of wood he dumped beside the stove. He looked at his hands in disgust. He said: "Keno, if we don't get back to the poker table pretty soon, we might just as well find something else to do."

"Right after we finish here," King said. "When we can combine profit along with getting square with a bastard like Devlin, we've got a good thing going. Ed, you and Doc look around. Bess has some *dinero* and maybe a gun or two. We don't want her trying anything tonight."

She put her pan of biscuits into the oven and sliced the bacon, taking advantage of a moment of inattention to slip the butcher knife inside her blouse. They found the money in the bunk, and cursed over the small amount of it, but King said: "It's my guess that's the size of it. From what I heard, Billy took a big chance for damned little."

The Winchester and revolver had not been

hidden, and the shells were in boxes on a shelf. After they found them, the men settled down until supper was ready. They ate with wolfish hunger. Bess refused to sit at the table with them.

Later, when the dishes were washed, King said with mocking gallantry: "We'll bunk on the floor and let Bess have her bed."

"You mean we're letting her sleep alone?" Jeeter demanded, as if the prospect was ridiculous.

"That's right," King said blandly. "I made a deal with her. If any of you hairpins try anything tonight, I'll put a window in your skull. She's no lady, but for the time being we'll treat her like one."

She wasn't bothered during the night except by the snores of the men, but she didn't sleep much. In the morning Dane would walk into an ambush, and there just wasn't anything she could do.

Long before daylight, King woke her to get breakfast for them. Then he left with Ed Trask. Dawn came at last, cold and gray, with a few snowflakes in the air. But with Jeeter and Darby still in the cabin, she was as helpless as ever.

She would saddle up and follow Jeeter and Darby when they left, hoping she could get around them and meet Dane before they did. But it wouldn't work, she told herself. She didn't know where to find Dane. If Jeeter and Darby discovered that she was following them, they'd kill her as soon as they'd kill Dane. But she could think of nothing better, so she would have to try.

XVIII

When Dane came to, he found he was inside the cabin, lying on the floor. A good fire was crackling in the stove a few feet from him. He must have been here for some time, because a coffee pot on the stove was beginning to fill the cabin with its pleasant, pungent aroma.

Nancy was not in sight. Dane sat up and carefully felt his head. The lump was still there, but the pain had died down to a steady, dull ache. He remained motionless for a moment, wondering how a slender, apparently frail girl like Nancy had been able to drag him inside the cabin. He'd have frozen if she hadn't, he thought. But Nancy must be far from being the frail girl she appeared, or she would never have survived two years of living with Sherman Rawls.

Nancy came in a moment later, her cheeks bright with the cold. She said: "There's a shed in back. I put the horses in it and took the saddles off." She held her hands out over the stove. "How do you feel?"

"Fine, considering," he said. "I'll be all right in the morning."

"You need something to eat," she said. "I'll get you a cup of coffee."

She poured the coffee into a tin cup and took it to him. He held it in front of him, waiting for it to cool and asking: "How'd you get me inside?"

"I pulled you," she said, smiling. "You're pretty heavy, but living with Sherm taught me that I always have the strength to do anything I have to do. I was sixteen when I married him." She paused, her face bitter with memories. Then she blurted: "If I could have looked ahead and known what the next two years were to be like, I'd have killed myself on my wedding day."

She took a loaf of bread and a piece of roast beef out of the flour sack. Slicing the meat, she put several pieces of it and some bread on a tin plate and gave it to him. He ate ravenously. Then he stretched out on the bunk, deciding that part of his headache had been due to hunger. He asked: "Why didn't you go home? You didn't have to stay on the Rocking R."

"I was afraid of what Sherm would do to my folks," she said. "Most of the time he treated me pretty good, outside of making me work too hard, but when he thought somebody was making fun of his scarred face or that anyone was trying to get me to leave him, he went kind of crazy. I think that's why he killed Banjo. He must have slipped up on us and heard what Banjo said."

"Didn't you ever talk to your folks about him?"

She shook her head. "There were a few times, like at Christmas, when he had me cook a big dinner and invited my folks to the Rocking R, but he didn't give me a chance to talk to them alone. Ma never had a thought in her life, and Pa has always been poor. He brought Ma and me out here three years ago and squatted on a piece of land about a mile from Banjo Quail's people. When Sherm's second wife died, he began looking around for another woman, and saw me. Banjo was in love with me and I liked him, too. I guess I'd have married him if Sherm hadn't kept asking me. Pa said I'd never get another chance to marry a rich man, and I had to take Sherm. I had always done what Pa wanted me to, so I finally said I'd marry Sherm."

"Did your pa know what Rawls is?"

"No," she said. "Nobody could ever tell

Pa anything. That's why he's always been poor. Banjo tried to tell him, and said he wanted to marry me, but Pa said Banjo was just a kid and didn't have anything. Fiddleback Quail, that's Banjo's father, tried to tell him, too, but Pa said Fiddleback wanted me for Banjo, so he wouldn't pay no heed." She sighed, glancing at Dane. "Sherm said my folks and everybody else who lives out there west of the mesa are trash. I guess they are, but they're better'n he is."

Dane had never felt as sorry for anyone in his life as he did for Nancy. He said: "Bess Combs, that's Billy's widow, is in the cabin where they lived when Billy was alive. I'm going to take you to her. Maybe Bess will help you get out of the state."

"I'll go with you to Missus Combs if you want me to," she said, "but I won't leave the state. I'm not sure what I will do. The only thing I'm sure of is that I'll never go back to Sherm. If he catches me, he may kill me, but I won't go back to him after watching what he did to Banjo."

"I'll take you to your folks, if that's what you want," he said. "I'll tell your pa about Rawls, and, before I'm done, he'll believe me."

"I guess you could make him believe you, Mister Devlin," she said. "I guess you're the kind of man who can do anything. Maybe that's what I will do. Lucky Fargo said Sherm would look for me at home. I don't know what he'll do to Pa, but, whatever he does, I think he'd do it whether I was home or not."

"What do you think he'll do first?" Dane asked. "When he gets home and finds you gone?"

"I don't know," she said. "When he's excited about something, like killing Banjo, he's awful sorry for a while and he prays a lot and asks forgiveness. Then he gets over it and does the same thing again."

She turned her back to him and began to cry. Dane got up and, going to her, put an arm around her. "You'll be all right. I'll see to it that you are."

She wiped her eyes and turned to him. "I'm not sorry about myself. It's Banjo. He was kind and decent and good. He hadn't done anything wrong. I tried to stop Sherm, but I couldn't do anything. I just couldn't."

"Of course you couldn't," Dane said. "The thing is, I'd like to know what to expect from Rawls. Will he get his crew and start looking for us, or will he come by himself?"

"He'll come alone," she said. "He never asks for help from anyone. The only reason

Ashton and Miles helped him hang Billy Combs was that they were with him when he caught Combs. I don't know whether he'll go to my folks' place first, or come this way looking for us, but I think he'll come this way, because he knows you're familiar with this part of the mesa."

He nodded. "That makes sense. We'll pull out about dawn. Now you go to bed. I'll keep the fire up."

"I'll sleep on the floor."

"No," he said sharply. "I'll take the floor and you'll take the bunk."

She was too tired to argue, and fell asleep the moment she stretched out on the bunk. Dane folded his coat for a pillow and lay down beside the stove. He thought about Rawls, convinced that the man would not try to dry-gulch him. There was no part of the coward about Sherman Rawls. But the possibility that Rawls might find them before he reached Bess's cabin worried Dane. He could not bring himself to think about what would happen to Nancy if Rawls killed him and got his hands on his wife. Dane had told her he'd take her home if that was what she wanted, but now that he considered it, he decided the only thing to do was to settle with Rawls before she went home. If Rawls found her there, he would go into one of his rages and kill her and her parents.

Dane slept at intervals during the night, his gun on the floor beside him. Several times he stoked up the fire, and twice he stepped outside to listen and to study the sky. The clouds were low and thick, blotting out the stars and moon. From the feel of the air, he was certain snow was coming. The best he could hope for was that the snow would hold off until he had delivered Nancy to Bess.

He woke Nancy before dawn. They drank coffee and finished the roast beef and bread. "I should have brought more," Nancy said. "I was in too big a hurry. I guess I wasn't thinking straight, anyhow."

"It's enough," he said, and went outside.

He circled the cabin, noticing the low clouds that were holding back the day. When he had made certain no one was hiding in the shed and in the aspens close to the cabin, he saddled the horses and brought them to the door.

If, by perverse luck, Rawls happened to stop and examine the cabin, he'd know they had been here and guess where they were going. But that was something Dane couldn't help. He fully realized that sheer luck would be a big factor in what happened from now on.

They mounted and rode south, dropping off the mesa into a narrow-walled cañon before they reached the easier route he had taken the time he had gone to Bess's cabin. If Rawls guessed they had gone this way, he might have left the Rocking R during the night and be close behind them now.

By leaving the mesa where they had, Dane felt sure he'd throw Rawls off the track, if he was close to them. The one thing he must avoid was meeting Rawls by accident. He wanted to pick his own time and place.

Dane rode down the steep mesa hill slowly, turning his head to watch Nancy. She wasn't a good rider, and she was frightened, but she hung on. When she pulled up beside him in the cañon, she gave him a small smile and said: "I'm still in the saddle, but for a while I wasn't sure I would be."

"You're doing fine," he said, and turned east.

They rode for an hour, the sky remaining gray and sullen and threatening, with no wind, then a flurry of snowflakes. Dane lifted his head often to study the slick rock rims on both sides of the cañon, but he saw no one.

The country was barren, with practically no grass even in the red soil of the bottom, just some sagebrush and a few stunted cedars. At least they were out of the bitter wind, and that made it easier on Nancy. Dane stopped once and helped her down. She rubbed her backside, smiling wryly.

"I'll be sore tomorrow," she said. "I used to ride quite a bit, but I haven't been on a horse for months. Sherm didn't have a side-saddle, and he said it wasn't decent for a woman to spread her legs around a horse."

He looked at the girl, wondering if she would ever be happy, if she could ever forget the nightmare these last two years had been. He said: "You'll be doing some riding again, now that you're rid of Rawls."

They went on, threading their way through a maze of red-walled cañons, Dane still watching the rim. They made a sharp turn to their left, and, without warning, came face to face with a rider. All three pulled up, shocked by surprise. Dane searched the face of the man, immediately sensing a familiarity about him but being unable to identify him.

Suddenly the other man wheeled his horse and, cracking steel, took off down the cañon the way he had come. Dane yelled — "Hold on!" — but the fellow kept going. Dane said — "Wait here, Nancy." — and started after the man, who turned and threw a shot at

Dane that went wide.

They rode hard, the distance between them remaining unchanged. The man must have panicked, for he cut sharply to his right into a narrow-sided cañon. Dane followed, and, glancing back just before he made the turn, saw that Nancy was behind him. He motioned for her to stay back, then he was in the side cañon.

It was short, a sheer wall rising ahead of him not more than one hundred yards away. The fellow was boxed. He had pulled in behind a nest of boulders at the far end and, jerking his rifle from the boot, threw another shot at Dane, who yanked Nero sideways behind a sandstone pillar that rose nearly as high as the walls and made effective cover.

Who was the white-bearded man, and why had he run? Why had he fired at Dane? The face was familiar, and the knowledge that he should have recognized the man kept nagging Dane. Now the man yelled: "Get back, Devlin! If you keep coming, I'll kill you!"

Then Dane knew. Perhaps it was the voice, or more likely it took this long to identify a face he had seen only a few times and certainly had not expected to see here. It was Doc Darby. That meant Keno King was around. But more than that, Dane was pinned here just as effectively as Darby was. He couldn't leave the box cañon without showing himself, and Darby would certainly shoot him in the back if he had a chance. Like Keno King, Doc Darby would not forget that Dane had killed Curly Heston in Layton City.

XIX

Sherman Rawls led the singing at the night service, trying to be as affable as ever. He hoped he was hiding the deadly fury that was in him, and keeping his face serene against the throbbing ache that was in his whole body, but he wasn't sure he was successful with either. The knowledge that his wife had actually held a shotgun against his back and threatened to kill him was a constant irritant to his temper. He didn't know what he would do or say to her when he saw her after church, but he was sure of one thing — she would never do it again.

Rawls sensed that the preacher and Fred Ashton and Joe Miles and everyone else wondered about the bruises on his face, but he gave no explanation. As soon as the service was over, he moved down the aisle toward the door, hoping to avoid the customary handshaking and small talk. But

Ashton, sitting near the back door, ducked out ahead of Rawls and was waiting beside the gray gelding when Rawls reached the horse. He asked: "What happened to you, Sherm?"

"None of your damned business," Rawls said, and untied his horse and stepped up.

"Maybe it is," Ashton said doggedly. "If Devlin is who I think he is, and you had a tussle with him. . . ."

Rawls whirled his horse and struck off across the mesa, leaving Ashton still talking. The storekeeper was smart, too smart. He'd guessed right about the tussle, although Rawls still didn't believe there was any connection between Devlin and Bess Combs. If there was, Devlin would be back. Or maybe he would remain on the Rocking R. In that case, Rawls would take care of him. If there wasn't any connection, he had seen the last of Devlin. Either way, Rawls wasn't concerned about Devlin, but he was worried about Nancy. What she had done was unthinkable. He'd fix her, he kept telling himself as he rode home. By glory, he'd fix her so she'd know from now on what a wife's duty to a husband was.

He put his gray into a gallop, and still it seemed an endless time before he reached the Rocking R. The first thing he noticed was that there was no light in the kitchen. Even when Nancy went to bed before he got home, she always left a lighted lamp for him in the kitchen. Well, she was just taking her mad out on him, he decided. He stripped gear from the gray and turned him into the corral. He stalked across the yard to the back door and went in, yelling: "Nancy!" No answer.

His anger rose until it was close to the killing rage he had experienced that afternoon. The pain in his head was worse, coming in hammering waves until it threatened to tear the top of his skull off. But he could stand pain. What he couldn't stand was being ignored by Nancy. She couldn't be sleeping so soundly she didn't hear him, he thought.

He stumbled over a chair before he found the matches in a box on the warming oven of the stove. He struck one and lighted the lamp on the table, then picked it up and went into the bedroom.

She wasn't there. The bed was empty, the covers in place just as she had left them that morning when she'd made the bed. He stood motionlessly, breathing hard, his hand raised to his forehead. For a moment he was unable to comprehend this. He had been sure he'd find her in bed.

He left the room and searched the rest of the house. When he failed to find her, he decided she must be hiding in one of the outbuildings. He lighted a lantern and made a complete search. In the bunkhouse he saw that Devlin had packed his war sack and was gone, which was exactly what Rawls had expected. If Devlin was Bess Combs's man, he'd have stayed around and dry-gulched him when he got home. So Ashton was wrong about Devlin, as Rawls had been sure he was. He put Devlin out of his mind. The important thing was still Nancy's whereabouts.

He blew out the lantern when he reached the kitchen and sat down at the table, an uncertainty in him that was a strange and disturbing feeling. Rawls didn't know what reason Devlin would have for taking Nancy, unless he had a fool notion he could collect a ransom. Then the thought occurred to Rawls that Nancy might have gone with Fargo to see her folks. He promptly discarded the possibility. She knew he wouldn't want her to do that. She never did anything he didn't want her to. He had taught her that the first week they were married.

He picked up the lamp, deciding he might as well go to bed, because there wasn't anything he could do until daylight. If Devlin had taken Nancy, he would probably have ridden south because he knew that part of the mesa. Probably he aimed to hide out in the broken red rock country, and would send word to Rawls that he could have his wife when he sent some money.

Rawls was halfway across the kitchen when a new thought hit him, hit him so hard that he almost dropped the lamp. Maybe Nancy had gone by herself and of her own free will! Maybe she wasn't with Devlin at all.

He set the lamp on the bureau, his hand shaking. She wouldn't do that, he told himself. She was his wife. Her place was here. He had treated her well. She certainly wouldn't go back home to her folks and starve with them on their hard-scrabble range. Here she had three meals a day, good clothes, and a comfortable house to live in. More than that, she was the wife of Sherman Rawls, the owner of the Rocking R. No, she wouldn't leave him.

He sat down on the bed, telling himself that the thought was preposterous, yet it would not die. He knew, now that he was thinking clearly, that Dane Devlin was not a man who would kidnap a woman. He tugged off his boots and blew out the lamp, forgetting his evening prayer. Nancy had gone of her own free will. It had to be that way. It was the only logical explanation of her absence.

Rawls slept very little that night. He would drop off and wake up again a few minutes later, an insistent question prodding his mind. *Why?* She couldn't have been serious about a kid like Banjo Quail. Rawls had no pangs of conscience over killing Banjo. He had clearly heard the boy ask Nancy to leave with him, so Rawls had done what he had to do to protect his home. Any man would have done the same.

He got up at dawn, feeling as if he hadn't slept at all, and built a fire. Putting on his coat, he went out into the hard, biting wind. In the barn he discovered that a small saddle was gone. Later he saw that Devlin's horse, Nero, and the bay were not in the pasture. He returned to the house and fixed breakfast.

Leaving his dishes on the table, he saddled his gray. He had recovered from the first numbing shock that accepting the truth had given him, but he still wasn't sure what he should do. No amount of thinking about it could tell him whether Nancy had left with Devlin or had gone home.

He decided to make sure first that she wasn't home. If she had gone with Devlin, it might take a long time to run them down. He rode west, the wind slapping him in the face, but he wasn't conscious of it. For the first time in the years he had lived on Red Rock Mesa he was facing disgrace. He couldn't go to the thin, drafty shack where her folks, the Minters, lived, and, holding his hat in his hand, bow and scrape and politely ask if his wife was there. They were trash, just trash. He wouldn't lower himself to do a humiliating thing like that. The greatest blow a man's pride could have was the knowledge that he could not hold his wife; the greatest disgrace a man could suffer was for that fact to become known.

He turned his gray and rode back the way he had come. He glanced up at the sky. It would be snowing by noon. He knew the country to the south as well as he knew the mesa. Now he decided she hadn't gone home, or she would have ridden in the wagon with Fargo.

So, because he could not face the public disgrace that would come to him if she had gone home, he convinced himself she was with Devlin. The storm that was coming would make them hole up somewhere. He knew every cabin where they could take refuge. He'd find them before night, he told himself. He'd kill Devlin and bring her home, and she'd never leave him again. She should have known better than to try it this time. No one else would even know what had happened.

When he finally made his decision, he was within sight of the house. He would have swung south at once if he hadn't seen two horses standing ground-hitched in the yard. He hesitated, angered by this, for it meant wasting time that he couldn't afford to waste. Still, he had to find out who his visitors were. If they were neighbors, he would have to give some explanation of Nancy's absence. If they were strangers, he wanted to know who they were.

When he reached the house, he dismounted, glancing at the horses. He had never seen them before. A man standing in the kitchen doorway called: "Are you Sherman Rawls?"

"Yeah, I'm Rawls," he answered, striding toward the man, who had backed up halfway across the kitchen. "Making yourself at home, ain't you?"

The man was a stranger. The second man, if there was another one, wasn't in sight. Rawls felt his quick temper rise, the thumping in his head increasing as his fury grew. "Answer me!" he shouted. "What are you doing here?"

"Don't get proddy," the man said.

Rawls was two steps inside the kitchen when he sensed the presence of a man behind him. He started to turn, but the warning that had stirred in him had come too late. A gun barrel smashing across his head drove him to his knees. He grabbed for his revolver, but another blow knocked him cold. He fell forward on his face, not stirring even when his assailant dug a toe into his ribs.

XX

Ed Trask holstered his gun and shook his head at Keno King. "His head must be solid bone. I hit him hard enough the first time to lay him out."

"Darby told us he was a tough one," King said. "Let's tie him up in bed. He might come around, and I don't want to wrestle with him. I'd as soon tackle a grizzly."

They carried him into the bedroom and dropped him on his back on the bed. They spread-eagled him, King tying his wrists to the metal posts at the head, Trask knotting his ankles to the ones at the foot.

King stepped back and looked at the unconscious man. "We turn the place upside down," he said, "and find a total of two hundred and three dollars and fifty cents. Maybe this wasn't smart. It's my guess he's the kind who won't talk. Look at that face of his. Ever see anything as ugly in your life?"

"I never did," Trask said. "Let's see if he's got any *dinero* on him."

King nodded, and Trask went through Rawls's pockets. He found an ancient silver watch, a knife, some odds and ends of leather, and a purse with a little over $50 in gold and silver. He tossed the purse to King and laid the rest of the stuff on the bureau.

"I don't like the smell of things around here," Trask said uneasily. "I figured Devlin would be gone, and it ain't surprising that the kid and the old man ain't around, but there's something damned queer about his wife's not being here. The storekeeper said his woman never went anywhere."

"I heard what he said," King snapped irritably, not liking the situation any better than Trask.

He left the bedroom and paced around the kitchen, as jumpy as Trask. He was more at home sitting at a poker table than he was in a ranch house kitchen trying to figure out where a man would hide his money. Too, he was in the habit of being backed up by seven or eight guns. Now he had only

Trask's, and he wasn't too sure of it.

The fire in the range had gone out and the room was getting cold. He jammed his hands into his pockets. He hadn't been in favor of this part of the operation in the first place, and now he liked it less than ever.

King had two reasons for coming to Red Rock Mesa. One was to hole up after the abortive train robbery until the heat cooled down; the second was to kill Dane Devlin. To him the latter had been the most important. His luck had turned sour from the minute Curly Heston had been killed. To the gambler, Dane Devlin was the symbol of that bad luck. King was superstitious enough to believe that he'd continue to have bad luck as long as Devlin was alive. King would have been satisfied to kill Devlin and then drift south to some hide-out along the Colorado-New Mexico line. The trouble was that they were almost broke. So, for the first time since he had organized the outfit, he had allowed himself to be outvoted by the others.

Trask wanted to get back to a poker table, but he needed a stake. Doc Darby had thought up some new schemes he was certain would work in the San Juan mining camps, but he needed a stake, too. So it was finally agreed they'd hit quickly and make a raise. They'd take Bess's money, steal some of Rawls's steers, and rob Rawls if they could find his money. The plan had been to come in the daytime and torture Rawls's wife until she told them where the money was hidden. But they hadn't been able to find the woman.

King talked about going after sure things, but actually he was influenced by hunches more than anything else. When he discovered that the Rawls's woman was gone, he was certain that his luck was still running bad and he was asking for trouble by pushing it. Since he'd had a look at Sherman Rawls, he was more certain than ever that his hunch was right. Now all he wanted was to get on his horse and ride out of here. But he had his tail in a crack. If he left without even making an effort to get Rawls to talk, Darby and Jeeter would raise hell. Trask wouldn't like it, either.

Trask came out of the bedroom. He said: "Keno, some of these cowmen are tough old birds, and I'm thinking that's what Rawls is. We could burn him alive but I don't figure he'll tell us anything. We might as well ride."

Surprised, King said: "I thought you were bound to stay here till we got something out of him."

Trask shifted uneasily. "There's something else. It's been my experience that gents like Rawls either trust a bank and leave their money in one, or they don't trust nobody and bury it, or maybe hide it. Well, when I was going through his desk, I found his bankbook. He's got better'n twenty thousand dollars deposited in a Montrose bank, so I'm betting he ain't got any more around here. That's why I'm willing to leave."

This suited King, but he knew what Darby and Jeeter would say — particularly Darby. He could lie and maybe make them believe they had roasted Rawls to a turn but he hadn't told them anything. The trouble was he doubted that Trask would stick to a lie without letting the truth slip.

King had taken a long time to recruit the outfit he'd had in Layton City. Devlin and the posse that had chased them after the attempted train robbery had cut his bunch to less than half. Whatever happened now, the last thing he wanted was for Darby to get sore and walk out on him.

"I'm willing to pull out," King said slowly, "but Rawls ought to be coming around. We'd better work on him just on the off chance you're wrong."

"He's conscious," Trask said glumly. "I asked him where the money was, but he won't talk."

King swore. "Why didn't you call me?"

He strode past Trask into the bedroom. Rawls had threshed around in bed, yanking at the ropes that bound his wrists until they were bleeding. Now he lay motionlessly, glaring at King with sheer hatred such as King had never seen in a man's eyes.

"Bess Combs told me you had buckets of money hidden in the yard," King said. "We want it. If you tell us where it is, we'll ride out of here and leave you the way you are. If you get stubborn, you're going to be hurt."

"I don't have any money hidden in the yard," Rawls said. "She's a lying bitch, like all women."

Trask took a cigar from his coat pocket, bit off the end, and lit it. When he had it going so the end was a bright red coal, he said: "All right, you had your chance to talk. Now you're going to get hurt."

He reached down and tore Rawls's shirt and undershirt away from his hairy chest. Then he jammed the end of the cigar against the rancher's flesh. Rawls gritted his teeth and glared at King, and said nothing.

King swore and threw the cigar across the room. "You're tough, Rawls, but you're not tough enough to hold out. I'm the gent that taught the Apaches all the tricks they know." He turned to the lamp on the bureau, lighted it, and held the blade of his knife over the flame. "I'll make the good side of your face look like the other side, if you don't talk and talk damned quick."

"Keno!" Trask called from the kitchen. "Come here."

"I'm just getting started," King snapped. "You can come here if you want to say anything."

"No, I'm not coming there," Trask said. "I'm leaving. You'd better pull out, too, unless you want to fight a dozen men."

King ran out of the bedroom and glanced through the west window of the kitchen. A band of riders was coming, eight or ten men at least. They were holding their horses to a walk. Looking at them, King had the weird feeling that this was a funeral procession approaching the Rocking R. Maybe it was his and Trask's funeral.

"The whole damned crew," he said. "Nobody but Bess and the storekeeper knew we were in the country."

"Wasn't Bess that fetched 'em," Trask said. "They're close enough for me."

He ran through the back door and across the yard to the horses, with King following a step behind. They swung up and left in a gallop, King drawing his gun and throwing a shot at the riders, who paid no attention to him. They held the same slow pace, obviously not interested in King and Trask, and this to King, who had expected immediate pursuit, was puzzling.

They pulled their horses down, King turning his head to watch the riders, who didn't change direction or speed. "I don't savvy," King said. "Maybe they didn't know anything about us. Maybe it was just an accident that they showed up today."

"All I know is that we were lucky," Trask said. "I sure ain't gonna argue with luck."

"Me neither," King said, relieved. "The old lady's going to side us for a change. Well, we've got Bess's *dinero* and we'll take as many steers as we can handle, so we won't ride out of here as broke as we came."

"What about Bess?" Trask said. "She'll have somebody on our tail because of Devlin."

King shrugged. "I don't think she'll bother us, and I'm not going to forget that she held a gun on me that time in Layton City. She'll show us a good time tonight, but after that she'll be in the way. We can't afford to have a woman in the way, now, can we, Ed?"

"No," Trask said, grinning. "We sure can't."

XXI

Jeter and Darby sat by the stove in Bess's cabin after King and Trask left, King ordering them to tie Bess in her bunk before they started after Devlin. She ignored them as she washed the breakfast dishes, but she was aware that both men were covertly watching her. Now and then she raised a hand to her blouse to touch the butcher knife she had hidden there the night before. She knew exactly where it was, yet her hand kept straying to it, the feel of the handle reassuring her.

Bess had never killed a man in her life, but from the moment King's bunch moved in, she had accepted the fact that she would kill the first man to lay a hand on her. The agreement King had made had been "for the time being." She had no illusions about what would happen to her once they had finished what they had come here to do. Now, seeing the way Jeeter and Darby glanced at her and quickly looked away, each obviously wondering if the other had seen where his gaze had strayed, she knew she wasn't safe at all. King had made a deal with her, but he wasn't here to make it stick.

Dawn light was filtering into the room when Jeeter yawned and said casually:

"Doc, you better get on your horse and take care of Devlin."

"The hell," Darby said, surprised. "You're coming with me."

"Not me," Jeeter said. "You think we could go off and leave this hellcat here by herself? She wouldn't stay here a minute, and you know it."

"Keno said we. . . ."

"Sure, I know what he said," Jeeter broke in, "but he wasn't using his noggin. Suppose she got loose? Even if we took her horse, she'd walk. She'd get help somewhere. We can't run no chances till we get them steers. No, I've got to stay here."

Darby scratched the back of his neck, not liking the idea of leaving Jeeter alone with Bess. But Jeeter was a stubborn man, and he didn't think he could change him. He said finally: "All right, but you keep your hands off her."

Jeeter laughed. "Sure, sure. I'll stay twenty feet away from her."

"You'd better, Jeeter." Bess turned and wiped her hands on her apron. "You try anything and I'll kill you. That's a promise."

Jeeter scowled. "By God, you're a tough-talking filly if I ever seen one. Before we're done, you won't be so tough."

"We're not done with her," Darby said.

"Until we are, you let her alone, or you'll settle with all of us. We may need her damned bad."

"Get moving," Jeeter said irritably. "You might as well quit worrying about her. You're too old to do her any good. I don't figure we've got any use for her. I never seen the day I needed a heifer like her to help me move a herd of steers."

"Moving a herd of steers ain't all we're fixing to do," Darby said as he got up and put on his coat.

"Think you can find Dane?" Bess asked.

"I'll find him," Darby said. "I had to hole up in this country once myself, and I know it pretty well. I ain't climbing to the mesa right here. I'll follow the cañon a piece and get to the top from there."

It was the smart way to play it. If Darby climbed to the top here and then rode west until he met Dane, he would be seen and Dane, being warned, would be a hard man to kill. On the other hand, by keeping in the cañon until he had reached a point close to where he would intercept Dane, probably somewhere along the southern leg of his daily route, he would run no risk of being seen except for the brief moment when he cleared the rim. He undoubtedly knew exactly where he could set his bushwhack trap, and, by starting now, he'd be over the rim and safely hidden when Dane reached the point where Darby expected to kill him.

Again Bess had the horrible feeling she could do nothing to help Dane. By staying here, Jeeter would keep her from leaving the cabin, depriving her of any chance she had to warn Dane. She cried in desperation: "Darby, you don't know the country. The only place you can get to the mesa from the cañon is right here."

He laughed at her. "Then you oughtta be happy."

He put on his coat and hat. Bess stood at the window watching until he saddled, mounted, and disappeared down the cañon. Then she whirled to face Jeeter. "Get out of here. Go outside. You stink up the cabin."

His face turned red. He started to get up out of his chair, then dropped back again. "If you're trying to start a fight, damned if you ain't gonna get what you're looking for."

Her feeling of frustration and utter helplessness to do anything in the face of Dane's danger added to the fury that had been in her from the moment King's bunch had moved in. To make it worse, she knew she was to blame for their being here. If Darby succeeded in killing Dane, she would be to blame, any way she looked at it.

"Sure I want to start a fight," she said. "I'm not like any other woman you ever ran into."

"You sure as hell ain't," he said thickly. "Now let me alone or I'll find out if you really are a woman."

She turned her back to him and walked to the other side of the room. But she was restless and couldn't remain still. She'd rather die than stay here, cooped up with Jeeter. If Dane was killed, she didn't much care whether she died or not. But dying wasn't the answer to anything. She had to live to get out of the cabin to warn Dane, and time was running out.

Jeeter turned so he could watch every move she made. She couldn't get close enough to him to use the knife. If he knew she had it, he'd take it away from her. Or use a gun to kill her. Whatever she did, she must not let him see the knife until she was in a position to use it.

She paced nervously around the cabin, racking her brain. If she could get Jeeter off his guard — find something to throw at him — make him think she could be persuaded to be friendly — insult him so he'd lose his head and do something foolish. . . . That was the only thing she could do, she decided. He wasn't overly bright; he could be goaded into making a fatal mistake.

"If I can't get rid of you," she said, "I suppose we might as well get along. How'd you like me to bake a cake for you?"

He glared at her, his slow mind reaching for some explanation of this change from hostility to friendliness. He said: "Sure, go ahead."

"I'll have to have some wood," she said. "Fetch some in."

He thought he had the answer then, and snorted in derision. "So you could hunt for a gun you've got hid out . . . or tackle me when I come through the door. If you need wood, you'll get it, and I'll be watching every move you make."

She sighed. "You're smart, aren't you, Jeeter? Didn't take you long to see through that."

He grinned, pleased. "You're damned right I'm smart."

"Well, I couldn't bake a cake anyhow. I don't have any eggs." She frowned, as if thinking. "I suppose King and Trask will be back pretty soon and I'll have to cook something for them."

"Doc will be back, too," Jeeter said. "I guess you forgot about him."

"No, I didn't forget. I don't think he'll be back. Devlin will kill him." She picked up her stub of a broom and began sweeping the floor, flicking up a storm of dust that filled the cabin and made Jeeter cough.

"Quit it!" he stormed. "Put that broom down. It's too cold to open the door and let the dust out. What do you think you're doing?"

"Cleaning up," she said blandly. "Ever see a woman who liked dirt?"

"I've seen some that could let it alone." When he saw that she wasn't going to stop, he drew his gun. "Put that broom down, damn it. Trying to choke me to death?"

She leaned the broom against the wall. "They wouldn't like it if you shot me, Jeeter. Put your gun away."

He grumbled something and slipped his gun back into the holster. "All right, all right," he said sullenly. "Go bake something. Or sit down. Just let the broom alone."

"We'll have to get some wood or we'll freeze to death," she said.

She put on her coat and tied a scarf around her head. Jeeter didn't want to go out into the cold, but he reluctantly slipped into his coat and followed her outside. A pile of dry cedar remained from the supply Billy had gathered the previous summer. She knelt and filled her arms with pieces that were small enough to go into the stove.

But they were mostly limbs, odd-shaped and twisted, and some kept dropping back to the ground.

Jeeter stood watching her, shivering, his coat collar up around his neck. He said irritably: "That's enough. Take it inside."

"If you're cold, you could get warmed up with this axe," she said.

"I said you've got enough!" he shouted. "Can't you get it through your thick head I'm giving the orders?"

She rose and walked to the cabin, calling back: "It seems to me you're not qualified. It's different with King."

He followed her into the cabin, slamming the door behind them. She dropped the wood beside the range and filled the firebox. She took off her coat and scarf, Jeeter standing motionlessly and glaring at her.

He asked: "What do you mean, I ain't qualified?"

She moved to her small worktable on the other side of the stove and, taking a dish off a shelf, set it on the table. "I'll make a dried apple pie," she said reflectively, as if finding it hard to make a decision. "I didn't expect the kind of company I got yesterday, but I happened to stew a pan of dried apples."

He took a step toward her and stopped,

fighting his temper. "I asked you a question."

"Pull off your coat, Jeeter," she said. "You'll get too hot wearing it in here."

He yanked off his coat and threw it on the bunk. He walked toward her and stopped again, the pulse pounding in his temples. "By God, you try a man. You sound like you think I ain't smart enough to give orders."

She wiped off the top of the table and, opening a flour sack, dipped a cup and spilled the flour on the table. She knew she had him. He'd lose his temper in a matter of seconds. She bent forward over the table, watching him while she stooped for another cup of flour. Her blouse had fallen away from her breasts, so that with one quick motion she could grip the handle of the butcher knife.

"No, you're not smart enough, Jeeter," she said. "You work harder'n Darby and Trask do, and a lot harder'n King, but you don't make any more money than they do. That makes you a fool, and shows that King's the one with the brains. You can't help it, Jeeter. It's just that you were standing behind the door when the brains were passed out."

He took another step toward her, goaded beyond endurance. She pretended she wasn't watching him. She lifted a can filled with salt from a shelf and, opening it, reached in and took a pinch, saying in disgust: "I told you before, Jeeter. You stink up the place. You're worse'n a billy goat. Go on back to the stove."

He let out a bellow like a wounded bull. He grabbed her by the shoulder and yanked her around to face him. His fingers slipped off her shoulder and, gripping her blouse, he tore it down the front.

"I'll show you who can give orders!" Jeeter yelled.

She hadn't been quite ready. She had a terrible moment, thinking he'd see the butcher knife in time to keep her from getting it, but he hadn't suspected her of having it. Apparently he saw the handle as the blouse ripped, but he was off balance as the cloth tore. He went back a step, one hand pawing at her in a futile effort to ward off the knife thrust he knew was coming.

She caught the knife by the handle as it fell forward. Jeeter cursed and reached for his gun, but she was too quick. She drove at him, the sharp blade in front of her. She saw sheer, stark terror on his ugly face as he whipped his gun from the holster, his left hand striking out again to thrust the knife aside. He still was too slow. The blade sank into his abdomen to the handle and he screamed in agony, the gun dropping to the floor as he gripped his belly with both hands.

He bent forward as the blade ripped up and out, and came away in Bess's hand, covered with blood. He stooped to retrieve his gun, his left hand still clutching his abdomen, his right hand reaching for the revolver. She kicked it away from his outstretched hand, sending it spinning across the hard-packed dirt floor.

"You . . . damned . . . sneaking . . . bitch," he whispered, and toppled forward.

She ran across the room, and picked up the gun, and jerked the door open. She stopped and stood motionlessly, sweat running down her body. Gunfire came clearly to her from down the cañon, and suddenly she had a feeling this was not the first shot that had been fired, that there had been shooting before this, but it hadn't registered on her consciousness because her attention had been riveted so closely on Jeeter.

She leaned against the wall, weak and sick. She had killed a man, but now it seemed unimportant. Dane was dead; Darby had killed him. The shooting stopped. Thinking about it, she decided she wasn't sure where it had come from. At first she'd thought it was down the cañon, but it might have been the wind that made it sound that way — or her distorted sense of direction.

She didn't know why she was so sure Dane was dead. She whirled back into the cabin, hid Jeeter's gun on a shelf, put on her coat, and tied the scarf around her head. She dragged his body outside, but it was too heavy to go far with it. She ran to the corral and saddled her horse. She tied her rope around Jeeter's body and, taking a dally around the horn, dragged him up the cañon.

Fifty yards or so from the cabin she found an overhanging bank. She removed the rope and rolled him close to the base of the bank. Returning to the corral, she turned his horse loose, giving him a clout with his bridle. She went back to the bank with his bridle and saddle, dropped them on his body, and, finding a broken cedar limb, dug at the bank until the overhang came loose and crashed down in a shower of dirt and gravel.

She threw the stick away and, mounting, rode back to the cabin. She was free. She could leave. She swung across the creek and started the climb to the top, then pulled up. If Dane was dead, she didn't care much what happened to her. She swung her horse around and rode back down the trail. Darby would return and she would kill him with Jeeter's gun.

Suddenly the tears began rolling down her cheeks as she thought about Dane. Now that it was too late, she discovered it didn't make much difference whether Sherman Rawls paid for the hanging of Billy Combs or not. What happened to the men who had helped him wasn't important at all. These weeks had changed her. She wondered if she could ever forget that she was responsible for bringing Keno King and his men here, and therefore was to blame for the death of Dane Devlin.

XXII

From where he stood behind the sandstone pillar, Dane could not see Doc Darby, and he knew Darby could not see him. Neither fact changed the situation as far as Dane was concerned. He couldn't stay here all day, any more than he could let Nancy remain where she was. He had to get the girl to Bess and he had to go back for Rawls. After that there would be time for thinking and planning. Nancy could safely do what she wanted to. Maybe Dane could persuade Bess to forget her passion for revenge on Ashton and Miles and leave the country with him. There was no longer any question about the identity of the men who had helped Rawls hang Billy Combs. Nancy had settled that. Dane could tell Bess he had the proof she wanted, but she might have changed her mind, particularly if she knew Rawls was dead.

Dane studied the rims. The wall to his right was sheer, about eighty feet high, without even a cedar of any kind or a bush to furnish a handhold. It had been polished by the restless wind until it looked as if it had been buffed by a giant hand. The opposite wall was different. It had a series of parallel ledges that angled upward toward the rim so that it had the appearance of a huge, distorted staircase.

Darby yelled: "Go back! Damn it, go back!"

Dane whirled as he heard a horse pound toward him. Darby fired a shot that kicked up dust from the cañon floor. Nancy, bending low over the horn, was whipping her horse into a run as she rode toward Dane.

He swore angrily, wondering if Darby would cut her out of the saddle. She would have no cover until she reached the pillar that gave Dane protection. Quickly he stepped into the open and threw two snap shots in Darby's direction. He briefly glimpsed Darby's bearded face above a boulder at the far end of the cañon. It disappeared as Darby dropped behind the boulder. Dane dived back to the cover of the pillar.

A moment later Nancy pulled in beside his horse, safe from Darby's gun as long as she remained behind the pillar. She looked down at Dane, the red dust whirling around her.

"You were safe out there," Dane said, angry at her for taking a risk that had been entirely unnecessary. "You had no business coming in here."

"Don't scold me, Mister Devlin," she said. "I've had too many scoldings the last two years."

He held up a hand and helped her down. "All right," he said. "You're here now. But you might tell me why you didn't stay where I told you to."

"I said once I thought you were a man who could do anything, Mister Devlin," she said, meeting his gaze squarely. "But there are times when even you could use some help. I thought this was such a time."

He turned away, scowling. She was right. He could follow one of the ledges on the left wall until he was above Darby, but he'd be in the open at least once, and Darby could pick him off if he didn't keep under cover.

Dane turned to the girl. "Can you use a rifle?"

She nodded. "I haven't fired a gun since I married Sherm, but before that I was a good shot."

"You're going to fire a gun now," he said. Taking his Winchester from the boot, he moved to the left, where a pile of rocks lay between the pillar and the cañon wall.

He searched until he found a slit between two rocks, through which he poked the barrel of his rifle. He squatted there for a moment, studying the end of the box cañon. He couldn't see Darby or his horse, but he could guess reasonably close where the man was hiding. He fired once, hitting the boulder just above where he judged Darby's head was.

The bullet screamed as it ricocheted off through space. When the sound died, Dane yelled: "Darby, come out with your hands up! If I have to come after you, I'll kill you."

Darby taunted him with a laugh. "You had me boogered there for a minute when I ran into you, but not any more. We've got a stand-off, Devlin, and you know it. I can wait it out as long as you can."

Dane stepped away from the rifle and

motioned for Nancy to come to him. He said: "Take a look through that peephole. You can't see him, but I figure he's just below the notch between the two tallest boulders."

She nodded and, squatting behind the rifle, looked through the peephole. "I can see it," she said. "What do you want me to do?"

"If he shows his head, shoot to kill him," Dane said. "If he doesn't show, fire about once a minute, just to make him keep his head down."

"Devlin, I'll make a deal with you!" Darby yelled. "You and the woman mount up and ride out of here, and I won't shoot! I've got myself boxed, but you're in the same boat if we don't make a deal!"

Dane didn't answer. He knew he couldn't trust Darby's word for anything. If he and Nancy started riding out of the cañon, their backs would be to Darby and he'd kill both of them.

Dane stepped back to the pillar and studied the pile of rocks. He could reach the first ledge by running across the rocks and making a long jump. From then on, it looked from here as if he could crawl along the ledge until he was directly over Darby's head. The trouble was he couldn't follow the ledge well enough with his eyes from this angle to be sure it was wide enough all the way for him to keep out of Darby's sight.

"I'm going to try it," he told Nancy. "If that ledge is as wide as it looks, it won't take long for me to get to where I can spot him. But I can't keep out of sight between here and the ledge. As soon as I start, you throw three quick shots. After that hold your fire for about a minute, then shoot again."

She looked at him worriedly. "Can't we wait him out, Mister Devlin? I don't know what I'd do if he killed you. I'm not afraid of Sherm as long as I'm with you."

So it was her fear of Rawls that had driven her to ride in here, fear that had made it impossible for her to stay in the main cañon where she would have been safe. She was afraid Rawls would find her there. He should have known that, Dane thought, but he had not fully realized how great her terror of Sherman Rawls was. Again he wondered if she would ever recover from the nightmare that her two years with Rawls had been.

"No, I've got to root him out," Dane said. "Ready?"

She nodded.

He hesitated, fully aware that for several seconds he would be in full view of Darby, that if the man was watching, he'd have time for two or three shots before Dane could reach the ledge. Darby was a good marksman, or he wouldn't have been a member of Keno King's bunch. The one chance Dane had was for Nancy to shoot so accurately she'd make Darby keep his head down.

Dane took a deep breath, backed up so he could get a running start, then raced across the rock pile in long strides, pausing briefly on the last rock before he made the jump to the ledge. He heard Nancy fire, and for a moment he thought she was succeeding in making Darby keep down. But just as his feet struck the ledge, Darby let go with a shot that hit the side of the cliff in front of Dane, stinging his face with rock splinters.

He dropped flat on his belly, as close to the cliff as he could get, breathing hard. Darby cut loose with two more shots, but they were well over Dane's head. For the time being he was safe. As long as he remained where he was, Darby couldn't see him. But that was small comfort. He couldn't settle anything by staying here.

As soon as he recovered his breath, he started crawling forward, keeping on his belly and having to move rocks out of his way as he wormed forward. Some went crashing down the cliff, raising a cloud of dust and starting small avalanches. This was wrong, he knew, for it showed Darby how much progress he was making.

He stopped after covering about forty feet. Nancy was firing at regular intervals. Now, considering his position, Dane wasn't sure he was as smart as he had thought. There was a good possibility that Darby had found a peephole similar to the one Nancy was using. If that were true, Darby would be able to pick him off sooner or later, without Nancy getting him in her sights.

Ahead of Dane the ledge widened so he was able to make the next thirty feet without moving any rocks. Now Darby had no way of knowing how close Dane was. From where he lay, Dane could make out the ears of Darby's horse and the crown of Darby's hat.

Dane paused again. Directly ahead of him the ledge narrowed so it would be impossible to crawl along it without being seen. If he got to his feet, he could take another long jump to the next wide spot in the ledge. But he was so close to Darby that the moment he stood up, Darby would drill him.

So Dane stayed belly-flat, cursing himself for getting into a tight squeeze like this. If he backed up, he was right where he started from. He wouldn't do that, but he couldn't go forward. While he hesitated, plagued by uncertainty, Darby squeezed off a shot that hit the cliff above Dane and brought down a small slide of dirt.

"Get on your feet and hook the moon, Devlin!" Darby yelled. "I've got you hipped! If I keep shooting, I'll bring that overhang above you down and you'll be buried under a ton of rocks! I'm going to count ten and then I'll start!"

This was a danger Dane hadn't considered. Darby could be bluffing. From where he lay belly-flat on the ledge, Dane couldn't see the overhang above him without exposing himself. But one thing was sure, he wasn't going to lie here and do nothing. He picked up a rock as big as his fist, carefully figured where Darby's horse stood, and lobbed the rock over the pile of boulders.

He must have hit the animal, for it snorted and plunged into Nancy's view. She fired immediately, either grazing the horse or frightening him. In any case, he lunged forward, striking Darby and spinning him into the open between the boulders and the base of the cliff. Dane fired twice, missing the first shot but knocking Darby to his knees with the second.

Dane rose and plunged forward, taking

the long jump to the wide shelf ahead of him. He ran forward until he was directly above Darby, who had been hit hard but was far from out of the fight. He saw Dane and tipped his gun barrel up, but he was slow. Before he could squeeze off a shot, Dane let go again, his bullet angling through Darby's head just above his right eye, killing him instantly.

For a moment Dane looked down at the dead man, feeling no regret, only relief. Darby had done his best to kill him. And he would have killed Nancy just as quickly if he'd had a chance.

Glancing up at the cliff above him, Dane saw that there was no overhang that could have been brought down by rifle fire. Darby apparently had been trying to scare him into showing himself. The bluff might have worked if Nancy's shot hadn't boogered the horse and made him catapult Darby into the open.

Wheeling, Dane holstered his gun and walked back along the ledge. He crawled down at the pile of rocks where he had started and took the Winchester from Nancy's hands.

He said: "We can ride now."

She nodded, apparently dazed from the violence of these last minutes.

He said: "I was wrong about your riding in here. I'm glad you did. You were a big help, right there at the last."

Again she nodded, and brushed at her eyes. Turning to her horse, she mounted and rode beside Dane out of the box cañon the way they had come. She'd had a part in killing a man, and it would be a while before she could forget it.

XXIII

The snow was coming down in fat, gently floating flakes by the time Dane and Nancy glimpsed Bess's cabin ahead of them in the cañon. Dane had considered the possibility of an ambush, knowing that King's bunch might have holed up inside the cabin. He had turned it over in his mind for the last half hour, and finally decided it was not a great risk, because King had no way of knowing he was coming here today.

When he reached the corral, he was reassured, for he saw that only Bess's saddle horse and pack animal were there. Bess stood in front of the cabin, a rifle in her hands. When he saw her, he called out.

"Dane?" Bess cried. "Is it you, Dane?"

"It's me, right enough," he said.

She started running toward him, tripped

and fell, then got up at once and came on. He stepped down and held out his arms. She flung herself against him and he held her hard. She kissed him, then put her face against his coat and cried, made weak by relief. He let her cry, finding satisfaction in the knowledge that she was feminine enough to give way to tears.

Presently she tipped her head back, shivering in the cold, as she brushed the back of a hand across her eyes. "I thought you were dead," she told him. "Darby knows the country, and he found out from Ashton where you rode. He aimed to dry-gulch you. When I heard the shooting, I thought he'd done it."

"It didn't work out the way he figured," Dane said. "We met up with him down the cañon a piece and we were both surprised some. He tucked his tail and ran, but he made the mistake of ending up in a box cañon, and I got him. Where's the rest of the bunch?"

"There were just four of them," she told him. "They tried to hold up a train in Wyoming and lost some of their outfit. King and Trask started for the Rocking R before daylight, to make Rawls tell them where he hid his money."

"He doesn't have any money hidden,"

Nancy said. "He keeps about two hundred dollars in his desk, but he won't send to Montrose for any more till the end of the month."

"This is Nancy," Dane said. "Rawls's wife."

Bess seemed to be aware of Nancy's presence for the first time. She glanced at the girl, instinctively disliking her. She turned back to Dane, asking: "What's she doing here?"

"Let's get out of the cold and I'll tell you," he said.

He gave Nancy a hand and they went into the cabin. Bess led the way, stiff-shouldered and suspicious. Dane shut the door and, taking off his coat, shook the snow from it. The fire had gone out in the range, but it was warmer in here than outside.

"You said four," Dane asked. "Who's the other one and where is he?"

"Jeeter," she said. "I killed him."

She told him what had happened and what she had done with the body. "I had to do it," she said, "and I would have killed Darby when he came back. I was sure he'd got you when I heard the shooting. Then I saw you and her coming, but I couldn't tell who it was, with the snow coming down."

"You're a lot of woman," he said. "Not

many women could have done what you did."

She was pleased by his praise, but still nervous and restless, her gaze constantly swinging from Dane's face to Nancy's, and back to Dane's. She said: "All right, now tell me what she's doing here."

Nancy sat down on the edge of the bed, shivering with the cold. She stared at the floor, sensing Bess's dislike for her. She said: "Mister Devlin brought me because my husband would have killed me if he'd found me."

Bess whirled to face Danc. "So you and her . . . ?"

"No," Dane said sharply. "Now get down off your high horse and I'll tell you what happened. You're too damned suspicious."

"I know about her and Billy," Bess said harshly. "She's just a tart. Maybe for once Rawls. . . ."

"You've got no right to say that!" Nancy flared. "I'm not a tart. I don't care what Billy told you. There wasn't anything for you to know about us. He was kind to me, just like Banjo was. That's all."

Dane took a step toward Bess, wanting to shake some sense into her. Then he got control of his temper and stopped, his hands fisted at his sides.

"I don't know what's the matter with you, Bess," he said, "except that you're a fool. Sit down and I'll tell you what happened, and why I'm going back to kill Rawls."

"No." Bess took his hands and looked at him for a long moment, her eyes searching his face. "I've been wrong, Dane. It goes against my grain to admit it, but I've got to. I don't really care about Rawls, not any more. All I want is to leave here with you. We can ride south, into New Mexico. I thought until a minute ago that I'd lost you. I thought you were dead. I can't go through that again, Dane."

"I've got to kill him," Dane said, "but not because of Billy Combs. I've been on the Rocking R long enough to know what Sherman Rawls is, Bess. He's an animal, and a crazy one at that. As long as he's alive, he'll abuse and bully and murder people."

"That's not your affair," Bess said. "It's the business of the people who live here."

"It's mine now," he said. "He tried to kill me. He did kill a boy who worked for him, a good, decent kid who didn't deserve it."

Bess turned from him and sat down. "All right, Dane. We'll go away from here after you kill Rawls. Maybe we'll get married and you'll go on killing men as long as you live, just like you killed Curly Heston."

"And Bosco and Doc Darby and the ones before them." He shook his head. "No, you're wrong, Bess. We'll leave here and get married because we love each other, but you're going to have to listen to me sometimes and try to understand that there are things a man has to do and a woman has no right to tell him he can't. You've got a hell of a mind of your own, Bess. Most of the time I reckon you'll have your way, but once in a while I'm going to have mine. Savvy?"

She stared down at her folded hands, knowing he was right and remembering how she had been afraid she had lost him when he hadn't come back to see her. She could not forget, either, how sick she had been with the fear that he was dead. She knew she had changed. She had been forced to come to grips with reality during the last week, admitting to herself for the first time that she had been both a wife and a mother to Billy Combs. That was the difference between him and Dane Devlin. Dane was a strong man who would resent the slightest hint of mothering. He wanted a wife who would be a wife, and that was all she wanted to be.

She lifted her head to look at Dane. "I'll listen now," she said.

He told her what had happened and why Nancy was with him. He finished with: "I had thought of asking you to take her across the line into New Mexico, but that wouldn't do any good. If Rawls is lucky and I'm not, he'll hunt her till he finds her, no matter where she is. Then I thought of leaving her with you till I got back, but, with King and Trask coming, we can't do that."

"Let her go home," Bess said. "She knows the way."

"No, she's got to be looked after," Dane said. "I've never met her parents, but from what I've heard about them, her pa wouldn't be any help."

Nancy got up and started toward the door, her face red. "I don't want you quarreling over me. I'll look out for myself."

Dane grabbed her by an arm and shoved her back on the bunk. "Bess isn't quarreling with me. She's stopping right now." He turned back to Bess. "And there's another thing. Nancy says it was Ashton and Miles who helped hang Billy. So now you're sure. You know how I feel about it. Even if they were there, they're not responsible for what happened. Rawls was. How about it?"

"I told you I don't even care about Rawls any more," she said. "I care less about Ashton and Miles. All I want is to leave this

313

country. I'm sorry I sent you here. I'm sorry I ever came back. Can't you understand that, Dane? You're all I want. All."

He smiled, a short, humorless smile that meant she had grown in stature in his opinion, that at last they understood each other, at least on everything except the killing of Sherman Rawls. He said: "Good. How would it be for you to take Nancy to Ashton's store, or to the preacher's house? I'd like to be sure she's safe for a few hours, some place where Rawls won't think of looking for her until I find him."

"All right," Bess said. "I'll go with her to Ashton's store and we'll wait for you there. I think we'd better get started. King and Trask will be back before long." She rose and turned to Nancy. "You love Dane, too, don't you?"

"Bess, for . . . ," Dane began.

"Keep out of this," Bess said. "A man never understands a thing like this, but a woman does. I'll do anything to keep you. I want Missus Rawls to know that."

Nancy stood up. "Yes, Missus Combs, I love him. He's the only man I ever met who makes me feel safe from all the things I'm afraid of. For two years I've known nothing but fear. I would take him from you if I could, but I won't even try, because I know how he feels about you." She paused, then added spitefully: "You'd know, too, if you had any sense."

"I guess I deserved that," Bess said, and walked to the door. "We'd better ride."

They went out into the cold, Dane feeling as if he'd been through a tug of war between two powerful forces. He had no idea how Nancy knew his feelings for Bess. He hadn't talked to her about it, but she knew just the same.

They mounted and, crossing the creek, started up the trail. Dane heard the rattle of falling rocks, the sound of hoofs above him, and looked up to glimpse King and Trask on the way down.

Behind him, Bess screamed: "Dane, it's them!"

Before the sound of her voice died, he saw the wink of gun flame through the falling snow, and heard the scream of a slug as it ricocheted across the cañon.

XXIV

Pulling his Winchester from the boot, Dane shouted to the women behind him — "Get to cover!" — and swung out of the saddle. He had no time to see if Bess and Nancy obeyed, but he didn't worry about them.

Bess could take care of herself, and he was sure she'd look out for Nancy.

He lunged toward the cliff side of the trail. Even now, in midday, the light was thin, and the snow was coming down so hard that King and Trask were shadowy figures above him on their horses. He held his fire, knowing he would be an indistinct target as long as he crouched against the rock wall to his right.

King and Trask kept coming on their horses, King shooting with his revolver. Dane waited, thinking that King was making two mistakes neither Jeeter nor Darby would have made. The distance was too great for a Colt, and he couldn't shoot accurately from the back of his horse.

Dane waited while the gamblers shortened the distance between him and them, King's bullets kicking up dust in the trail or striking the rock wall above him. When his revolver was empty, he threw it down, cursing, and reached for his Winchester. He was a deadly killer at a poker table, but this wasn't his kind of game and he was over his head.

Now Dane put his .30-30 to his shoulder, knowing he had waited long enough. Just as King's rifle swung into line, Dane fired. King's head and shoulders snapped back as if he had run full tilt into an invisible wire. His feet came free from the stirrups and he spilled out of the saddle, falling against the cliff, and rolling over to lie flat on his belly as his horse bucked down the trail.

Trask cried out and tried to wheel his horse and go back to the top. Dane fired and missed. Then Trask had his horse turned and was raking him with his spurs. He looked back and threw a shot that was wide by ten feet. Dane's second bullet drove through Trask's chest; the third raked the flank of the horse.

The animal started to buck, throwing Trask on the first jump. The gambler screamed as he went over the edge of the trail. He tried to grab at something to stop the fall, but his frantic hands found nothing more substantial than a small boulder in the dust at the edge of the trail. It went with him down the steep slope, in a thundering slide of dirt and small rocks.

Dane ran up the trail to where King lay. He was dead. Dane's bullet had caught him in the mouth, driving upward through the top of his head. It must have killed him instantly. Dane turned to the edge of the trail. The dust had drifted away, but Dane could not see Trask clearly through the snow. He might be alive.

Bess called from far down the trail: "Dane, are you all right?"

"Sure!" he shouted back. "King's dead! I'm going to see about Trask!"

Picking his way carefully down the slope, he took a zigzag course, making use of the gnarled cedars that were miraculously well-rooted in the side of the cañon. He found Trask alive, but buried by the slide up to his middle.

"I'll dig you out," Dane said. "I'll get you to the cabin."

"No use," Trask breathed. "I can cash in my chips as well right here as in the cabin. We thought old Lady Luck was on our side at last, but she sure as hell wasn't."

Trask was right. He didn't have long to live. He'd be dead before Dane could free his legs.

"Keno?" Trask asked.

"Dead."

"I thought you got him dead center, from the way he went out of the saddle." Trask stared at Dane, the snowflakes settling on his face. "Didn't figure on running into you. We thought Darby would take you."

"He's dead," Dane said. "So's Jeeter."

"Our luck's all bad. You started it, by shooting Curly Heston. Keno and me should have stayed a little longer at the

Rocking R, but Rawls's crew was . . . riding . . . in."

He tried to say something else, but life had bubbled out of him. The blood spread across his chest, dark against the coating of snow that had settled on him. Dane rose and worked his way to the bottom of the cañon, then strode upstream to the foot of the trail, where Bess and Nancy waited for him.

"That's the end of Keno King's outfit," he said.

Dane turned away and climbed to where he had left Nero. He rode to the top and across the mesa, with the women following. The wind was blowing hard, driving snowflakes before it and pelting him on the side of the face. It was much colder now, because of the wind. They would have to find shelter, he thought. The storm was getting worse.

He was tempted to turn back to Bess's cabin, but he remembered that Trask had said Rawls's crew had ridden in. Rawls, then, had brought his men in from the west rim to hunt for Nancy. Some of them would certainly show up at Bess's cabin. That meant more fighting, and the death of some good men like Lucky Fargo, when the only killing that could be justified was that of Sherman Rawls.

Joe Miles's ranch was the closest shelter, but Dane wasn't sure he could find it in the storm. Ashton's store was much farther. There were no lone cabins in this area. The only shelter of any kind was the cañon that held the hanging tree where Billy Combs had been lynched. At least they would be out of the wind there. They could find dry wood and build a fire. Perhaps the storm would die down later in the day.

Dane angled to the west, glancing back at the women. They had pulled their coat collars up around their ears and rode, hunched forward, making no effort to talk, content to follow him. Perhaps, with the snow falling like this, Bess would not recognize the cañon when they reached it. He hoped she wouldn't. Her life with Billy Combs was behind her; the bitterness of her memories would be softened by the passing of time. He did not want to do anything to bring those memories rushing back into her mind. But he could think of nothing he could do except take the women to the cañon and hope Bess would not know where she was.

Dane lost all track of time. For a short while he was afraid he had gone past the cañon, but presently he began dropping down a sharp slope. Not long after that they were in the cañon and out of the worst of the wind. He looked back at Bess. She said nothing and made no gesture of any kind, so he still did not know whether or not she realized where they were.

Before they reached the tree, a man appeared directly ahead of them, the sound of his horse's hoofs muffled by the snow. Dane's first thought was that he had stumbled onto Rawls as unexpectedly as he had met Doc Darby early that morning. He grabbed for his gun and had it clear of leather and swinging into line when the man called: "No, no! Don't shoot! Let me talk!"

Dane reined up, letting the .45 settle back into the holster. The man was Fred Ashton.

The women came on to stop beside Dane. Ashton approached slowly, apparently not recognizing Bess until he pulled up directly in front of her. He said: "Oh, it's you, Missus Combs. I was coming to see you. That sounds crazy, riding in this storm, and I guess it is, but I've been afraid too long. If a man lives with fear long enough, he becomes no man at all. I've lived with it almost that long." Ashton turned his gaze to Dane. "She sent you here, didn't she? You're looking for the men who were with Sherman Rawls when he hanged Billy Combs, aren't you?"

"I was," Dane said. "But I'm not any more. We didn't know for sure who they were until Nancy told us."

"Then you know now." Ashton stared at the ground. "It ill becomes a man to beg for his life, but when he has a wife and as many children as I have. . . ."

"No need to beg," Dane said curtly. "We're not looking for you, just for Rawls."

Ashton straightened and then leaned forward, his eyes searching Dane's face. "You don't know, do you? Of course you don't. You wouldn't have any way of knowing." He turned his horse, motioning for them to follow.

Dane glanced at Bess, uncertainty tugging at him. This could be some kind of trap. But, no, that was impossible, with neither Rawls nor Ashton knowing he and Bess would be here. He rode after the storekeeper, with Bess beside him and Nancy a few feet behind them.

Presently the hanging tree appeared ahead of them, at first vague and indistinct in the swirling snow, and then, as Dane rode closer, the outline becoming clear. He reined up, staring at it, unable to believe what he saw. A chill traveled down his backbone. He wiped a hand across his eyes and looked again, and saw the same thing.

A body swayed from a limb, probably the same limb from which Rawls had hanged

Billy Combs. This time it was Rawls himself, looking like a suspended snowman. Behind Dane, Nancy cried out. Reining her horse up, she sat staring at the body of her husband.

For a time, no one spoke, the three of them shocked into silence. He had indeed met Rawls unexpectedly, Dane thought, and for the last time. It was a strange twist of fate that Sherman Rawls's life would come to an end on the same tree from which he had meted out death to so many others.

Dane asked in a low voice: "Who did it?"

"Fiddleback Quail and Missus Rawls's father and their neighbors," Ashton said. "Fargo took Banjo's body home. They kept Fargo there while they got the neighbors together. Then they came after Rawls, fetching Fargo with them. They found Rawls tied to his bed. Looked like he'd been tortured some. They saw a couple of men leave the house as they was riding up, but didn't think much about it. They locked Fargo in a storeroom, telling him what they were going to do. Then they brought Rawls here and did it."

So it was Banjo Quail's father and his neighbors that Trask and King had seen coming, not the Rocking R crew. If the two outlaws had not gotten the drop on Rawls in some way and tied him to his bed, Rawls would have whipped Fiddleback Quail's bunch and sent them hightailing back the way they had come. Dane was as sure of that as he could be sure of anything.

"We can't leave the body . . . ," Dane began.

"Fargo's coming with the wagon." Ashton wiped his face with his hand and looked at Bess. "I started to see you to tell you it was me and Joe Miles who were with Sherm that day. I couldn't go on living like I was, thinking that every minute you or Devlin would find out I was one of 'em and come and shoot me. I got so I was jumping at every little sound, and snapping at my wife and kids. I just couldn't stand it any longer." He motioned to Rawls's body. "I went to the Rocking R to tell him I couldn't stand living this way. I found Fargo in the storeroom where they'd locked him up, and he told me about Banjo, and about Missus Rawls leaving with you. That was when I decided to talk to Missus Combs. I thought if there was any mercy in her. . . ."

"There wasn't, the day I stopped at your store," Bess broke in. "It's different now. I don't care what happens to you. Dane, let's get off the mesa and never come back. The storm isn't so bad we can't ride in it."

"Wait!" Nancy cried. "Mister Devlin, stay and work for me. You can have the big house. Run Rocking R, make it mean something different than it has all this time when Sherm was running it."

Dane looked at her, mightily tempted to say yes, for he was remembering the first day he saw the mesa and had told himself that here was a country where a man could live in peace and sink his roots into the fertile soil. Then he had learned there was no peace on Red Rock Mesa, that there could be none as long as Sherman Rawls was alive. Dane glanced at the dead man, thinking this was indeed justice. As long as he lived, he could never blot the picture of Banjo Quail's battered face from his mind.

He turned his horse so his back was to Rawls's body. He said: "I wish I could stay, Nancy, but it wouldn't work out. You'll find somebody. So long."

She put out a hand toward him, then dropped it. She said: "So long, Mister Devlin. And thank you."

He touched the brim of his hat to her, then said to Ashton: "You can be your own man now."

"I will," Ashton said. "I will."

Dane rode out of the cañon, with Bess beside him, and they turned east. Bess said:

"If it hadn't been for me, you would have stayed, wouldn't you?"

"Yes," he said. "But there is you, and I'm taking you a long way from here, some place where you'll forget about Billy Combs and never be reminded of him again. I won't share you with him. I've got to have all of you."

"You have all of me now," she said. "It's queer how you think you want something so much you risk your life and give your time and all your thoughts to scheming how you're going to get it done, but in the end there's no satisfaction in it." She smiled at him. "It's a long time ago, but, when I was a girl, I used to think I'd like to do something big and fine so people would remember me. But something went wrong, and the dreams died. You've got to bring them back, Dane."

"We'll bring them back," he said. "I've had a few of my own."

She put a hand above her head and caught a snowflake. Then she laughed. "Isn't it a fine day, Dane?"

He looked at her, puzzled. The first bad storm of the year, and she called it a good day. Then he understood. It was a good day because the burdens of the past were rolled off her shoulders and she was free at last.

"A fine day," he said, and smiled at her. "It takes good eyes to see the sun on a day like this. I'm glad you can."

ABOUT THE AUTHOR

Wayne D. Overholser won three Spur Awards from the Western Writers of America and has a long list of fine Western titles to his credit. He was born in Pomeroy, Washington, and attended the University of Montana, University of Oregon, and the University of Southern California before becoming a public schoolteacher and principal in various Oregon communities. He began writing for Western pulp magazines in 1936 and within a couple of years was a regular contributor to Street & Smith's *Western Story Magazine* and Fiction House's *Lariat Story Magazine. Buckaroo's Code* (1947) was his first Western novel and remains one of his best. In the 1950s and 1960s, having retired from academic work to concentrate on writing, he would publish as many as four books a year under his own name or a pseudonym, most prominently as Joseph Wayne. *The Violent Land* (1954), *The*

Lone Deputy (1957), *The Bitter Night* (1961), and *Riders of the Sundowns* (1997) are among the finest of the Overholser titles. *The Sweet and Bitter Land* (1950), *Bunch Grass* (1955), and *Land of Promises* (1962) are among the best Joseph Wayne titles, and *Law Man* (1953) is a most rewarding novel under the Lee Leighton pseudonym. Overholser's Western novels, whatever the byline, are based on a solid knowledge of the history and customs of the 19th-Century West, particularly when set in his two favorite Western states, Oregon and Colorado. Many of his novels are first-person narratives, a technique that tends to bring an added dimension of vividness to the frontier experiences of his narrators and frequently, as in *Cast a Long Shadow* (1957), the female characters one encounters are among the most memorable. He wrote his numerous novels with a consistent skill and an uncommon sensitivity to the depths of human character. Almost invariably, his stories weave a spell of their own with their scenes and images of social and economic forces often in conflict and the diverse ways of life and personalities that made the American Western frontier so unique a time and place in human history.

The employees of Thorndike Press hope you have enjoyed this Large Print book. All our Thorndike, Wheeler, and Kennebec Large Print titles are designed for easy reading, and all our books are made to last. Other Thorndike Press Large Print books are available at your library, through selected bookstores, or directly from us.

For information about titles, please call:
  (800) 223-1244

or visit our Web site at:
  http://gale.cengage.com/thorndike

To share your comments, please write:
  Publisher
  Thorndike Press
  10 Water St., Suite 310
  Waterville, ME 04901